The Secrets of Peaches

The Secrets of Peaches

a novel by

jodi lynn anderson

HarperTempest
An Imprint of HarperCollins*Publishers*

HarperTempest is an imprint of HarperCollins Publishers.

The Secrets of Peaches

ALLOY ENTERTAINMENT   Produced by Alloy Entertainment
151 West 26th Street, New York, NY 10001

Library of Congress Cataloging-in-Publication Data is available.
ISBN-10: 0-06-073308-X (trade bdg.) — ISBN-13: 978-0-06-073308-7 (trade bdg.)
ISBN-10: 0-06-073309-8 (lib. bdg.) — ISBN-13: 978-0-06-073309-4 (lib. bdg.)

Typography by Christopher Grassi
1 2 3 4 5 6 7 8 9 10
❖
First Edition

For Jill

Before

Summer was one thing. Summer was skinny-dipping in the lake. It was lying on the grass with sopping-wet hair. It was carving their initials—L.C.S., B.D., M.M.—into the magnolia tree. It was summer when the Darlington Peach Orchard—green as a jewel, soft as a piece of velvet—had shrugged itself around them as if it would last.

But on September fifth, a breeze wafted through the rows of trees and settled like a fog. It didn't smell like peaches at all. It smelled, strangely, like cinnamon and cayenne pepper. It smelled like far away. It smelled like the dark.

That night three friends, Leeda Cawley-Smith, Birdie Darlington, and Murphy McGowen, turned over in their beds, halfway between sleeping and awake, uneasy. Many miles away, in a small suburb in Mexico, a statue of the Virgin of Guadalupe stood on the outskirts of town, waiting for a new arrival . . . or an old friend. A knot of bats in the caves at the Buck's Creek Nature Preserve felt an ancient breeze waft across their wings. A green urn sat at the Bridgewater Funeral Home on Main Street, waiting for its first and only occupant.

There were spaces waiting to be filled. There would be spaces left empty.

Before another summer, Leeda Cawley-Smith would disappear into black water. Murphy McGowen would run naked for the last time. And Birdie Darlington would find something ancient and new, borrowed and blue in the cider shed.

Now, on the first night of fall, the orchard shivered. Methuselah, the oldest pecan tree on its property, began to slowly draw in her roots. And the last peach of the year—ripe, sweet, and unnoticed—hung suspended for another moment and fell.

One

If there was one thing Murphy McGowen had always known, it was that she would someday make it out of Bridgewater, Georgia. Among her scattered musical taste, her scattered curly hair, and her scattered past (which included clothes scattered at the edge of the lake and parts of Bob's Big Boy scattered over Route 1), planning her exit had been the one constant. That, and her long-held desire to streak across Mayor Wise's front lawn. She just hadn't gotten to it yet.

If Murphy hadn't had a tattoo of Ringo Starr on her back already, she would have had these words from Bruce Springsteen's "Thunder Road" tattooed there: *Two lanes can take us anywhere.*

Songs of escape were written through Murphy's DNA like eye color (hers were cat-green), and she had the words down exactly. The song went like this: going to NYU and spending the rest of her life feeling like she'd finally landed in the right place. As fickle as Murphy could be about many things, there was never a variation on this refrain.

"Murphy, can we go?" Leeda asked. "The dogs look hungry."

She nodded at Birdie's papillons, Honey Babe and Majestic, who sat on the wet bus-stop sidewalk staring at the three of them, their butterfly ears cocked expectantly. The tiny dogs appeared to be smiling—they always did when Birdie was around and when they were together. They were so attached to each other Murphy called them John and Yoko, even though they looked more like a cross between Bambi and the Muppets.

"I just fed them before we left." Birdie looked over her shoulder at Leeda, who was tugging Birdie's auburn hair into a braid. Leeda yanked it. "Oh, I mean, um, no, I didn't. They're starving." She rolled her eyes at the dogs, who smiled back.

"You're the worst liar, Birdie." Leeda dropped Birdie's braid and threw her head back despondently. She stared up through the plastic ceiling of the shelter area where they sat. The rain sent splat patterns across its surface. "I have so much studying to do."

"A week into school and you're already obsessing," Murphy observed.

"I guess." Leeda shrugged. She was on what Murphy considered a perfectionist recovery program. Leeda went for first place by default, always.

"Five more minutes. One will come. Pretty please?" Murphy looked at Leeda, who was still staring at the rain-splattered ceiling. Next she turned to Birdie and poked her in the arm, which was lying across her own warmly. Birdie was a furnace. "Please?"

"She just wants to see one more," Birdie said, fluttering her eyelashes at Leeda. "Then we can go." The thing about Birdie was she was a born ambassador. It was probably from all the time she'd spent hovering in the no-fly zone between her recently separated parents.

Murphy studied them both. Leeda looked straight out of Martha's Vineyard—all perfect cheekbones and alabaster skin with a smattering of sun-induced freckles and clothes that were totally season-appropriate. Even loose and sloppy like she was today, she looked like the kind of loose and sloppy you saw in *People* magazine when they caught a celebrity all tired and mussed up at the airport. Birdie, on the other hand, was curved and rosy and Renoir soft. She looked like the milk-fed farm girl that she was.

The two were second cousins but nothing alike. Leeda was straight up and down, and Birdie was as gentle and easy as the rain. Leeda had grown up wearing mostly white and exceeding everyone as the glossiest, the smilingest, and the most southern of the southern belles in Bridgewater. Birdie had grown up with dirt under her fingernails, homeschooled on the orchard, her feet planted in the earth.

Before Judge Miller Abbott sentenced Murphy to time on the orchard picking peaches that summer, Murphy had pegged Leeda for uptight and Birdie for weak. But their time together—picking peaches, sweating in the dorms at night, cooling off in the lake—had been like living the fable of her life. The lesson being that when you think you know more than you do, you end up looking like an idiot.

Murphy, mind restless, tapped her feet on the sidewalk and stared at the initials carved into the Plexiglas walls. She poked at the pack of cigarettes in her pocket, although she'd given up smoking because her boyfriend, Rex, kept telling her it was a stupid habit. She wore faded jeans that clung to her curves and a vine-green T-shirt that matched her eyes. Murphy didn't have to dress sexy to look sexy. She could wear a nun's habit and still look like she needed to cover up. Murphy and Birdie let their heads rest back against the wall like Leeda's.

"It feels like somebody pushed the pause button," Birdie said. She was right. It seemed like the gray Georgia fall would never end—it would be just one long rainy afternoon after another, on into the apocalypse.

They sat in silence. "What day's graduation?" Murphy asked, her voice skating across the crackling of the raindrops. "May fifteenth? I wonder if it's too early to book my bus ticket."

"Don't say that!" Birdie said.

Murphy felt the restlessness bubble up the way it always did when she thought of all the days that stood in her way. "Do you think once I leave, if I look back, I'll turn into a pillar of salt?"

Leeda rolled her eyes. "The drama." Murphy grinned at her.

She knew the reference was backward. In the story, Saul's wife turned into a pillar of salt because she looked back over her shoulder at the reckless and rotten city behind her. But Murphy was the one who'd always been too loud, too reckless, too rotten for Bridgewater. The number of times she'd been whispered about, caught, and raked across the coals (usually because she asked for it) were too many to count. Because she couldn't keep quiet, because she couldn't contain herself, because she couldn't say no to boys, Murphy had always had the distinct feeling of being a splotch of tarnish on an otherwise silver southern town. Bridgewater would be a whole lot more wholesome without her.

A thunderstorm groaned in the distance. Murphy glanced over at the newspaper vending machine at the front page of the *Bridgewater Herald*, dated September 10. In the bottom-left corner, the weekly updates read *Carrie Ann Acherton rescues wounded hawk at Winkie Doodle Point, Judge and Mrs. Miller Abbott expect first grandchild.* She longed for a home where wounded hawks didn't make the front page. A home where nothing was called Winkie Doodle. Then she heard it. Murphy's pulse quickened at the distant wheeze as the bus pulled off the exit ramp of Route 75. She could trace its route like a favorite song: hitting the one stop sign and turning right around the bend, it appeared in little speckles through the trees lining the edge of the parking lot.

"Ha!" Murphy said as it pulled toward them and she read the destination above the windshield. *New York.*

"Hallelujah." Leeda sat up and smoothed her hair.

Murphy reached into her pocket and wrapped her fingers around the rock she'd picked up from the parking lot outside her trailer. She stood and waited as the bus wheezed to a stop. It let out another sigh as its door hissed open, revealing the beautiful black rubbery stairs.

She watched in bewilderment as two people got off. Who voluntarily got off a New York City–bound bus?

"Hey," she said to the bus driver. "New York, right?"

"Yeah."

Murphy had been doing this, from time to time, since she was twelve. She estimated that all in all, she had probably sent about forty rocks from the Anthill Acres Trailer Park to New York City. She figured that if she sent enough of her life piece by piece, eventually it would all end up there.

Murphy took her rock and leaned forward, tucking it into

the bottom corner of the top stair, where a bunch of shoe debris had gathered. She stood back and grinned at the bus driver. "Have a nice trip."

He just stared back at her, shook his head, and pulled the handle to close the doors.

She watched the bus pull away into the gray afternoon. This moment always gave her a restless kind of hope. There were no guarantees, and there was so much time in her way. But there was also less waiting ahead each time. Murphy stuck her thumbnail in her mouth and chewed on it, grinning. Her feet began to bounce like a sprinter's gearing up to run.

It couldn't keep raining forever.

Two

In the photo of Leeda Cawley-Smith's eighth birthday party that sat on the parlor banquette, Leeda was invisible. It wasn't easy to see—she *looked* visible. There she stood in her white Ralph Lauren Kids dress. Her white Ralph Lauren Kids boots. Her white-blond hair and her white barrettes. Against the green and blue of the summer background, ready to blow out her candles, she looked like Alice in Wonderland. But if you looked closer, you could see how invisible she was. It was the way her mom's back was turned at the crucial moment. Not that it was just that moment. It was a permanent state of being.

As a kid, Leeda had often wondered if she were at least part ghost. It was the way she was always trailing behind her mom like she was on some kind of invisible leash. Lucretia would drift from school function to social event to the beautifully appointed dinner table, and it always seemed Leeda could never quite catch her attention. The photo was like hard evidence. It showed a perfect kid. A kid surrounded by other kids who always wanted to get on her good side. A kid who was allergic to dust, to dirt, to second best. A kid whose invisibility was perfectly invisible.

Leeda stepped outside her family's house onto the emerald-green yard of Breezy Buds Plantation. Standing with her arms crossed, dressed in daffodil yellow, anyone looking on would have said Leeda Cawley-Smith was hard to miss. She had the kind of fine looks that weren't just admired but were held in a sort of awe. Her first couple years of high school, she was always looking in the mirror, checking if it was still there—the thing that made people want to be next to her without her having to lift a finger or flex a mental muscle. Now, her face glowing in the soft September sunlight, she looked more beautiful than ever. What had changed was that Leeda didn't care anymore.

Above her, a magnolia arched crookedly, its big waxy leaves rustling, rubbing against one another like paper. Some of the leaves had turned yellowish around the edges. It was one of those days—light and shady and breezy and cool—that made Leeda feel inexplicably, utterly free.

Two weeks ago, for a first-day-of-school present, Murphy had presented Leeda with a notebook titled (in black marker) *Notes for a Truly Leeda Leeda*. It was full of all sorts of stuff Murphy had compiled. Thoughts on life. Thoughts about Leeda. Bits of advice. Doodles of peaches. The book had said nothing about climbing trees. This was Leeda's idea.

Looking behind her to see that no one was watching, she began to climb. From a distance, she must have looked like a wet rag being thrown up into the limbs, hurling herself from branch to branch, her long legs dangling limply. A breeze blew the branches, which groaned and swayed, but she kept climbing. Finally she looked down. Her heart pounded. A breathless smile crept onto her lips.

"Ha," she said to herself, or maybe to the tree. Leeda had been afraid of trees since she'd gotten stuck in one at that birthday party in the picture.

Leeda smiled at the scrapes on her knees. Carefully, slowly, she scooted herself next to the crotch of the limb and sat, holding on to either side of the branch for balance. She was just level with her bedroom. She swung her legs, giddy. A thrill shot through her stomach every time she looked down.

Leeda peered into her room, feeling like a voyeur. Big white bed, white desk, bare white walls. She momentarily wondered what it would look like to a stranger looking in. She leaned in closer, looking for clues. But there was very little to go on. She wondered if *that* was a clue.

That's when a face appeared in the window and Leeda went fumbling backward with a start, clutching the branch and scraping her arms. There was a click of the latch and a creak as the window slid upward, and Lucretia Cawley-Smith leaned her face out.

According to the "Lucretia Cawley-Smith Survival Guide," on pages seven, eight, and nine of *Notes for a Truly Leeda Leeda*, one was supposed to avoid verbal communication with Leeda's mom as much as possible and sing *meow meow meow* silently to oneself when spoken to. One was also supposed to hint that Lucretia's mustache was growing back whenever she started to dissect one's appearance. And one was never, ever supposed to give Lucretia what she wanted. Because she was the kind of person who made a mile out of every inch you gave.

"Leeda! What on earth are you doing out there? Look at your clothes." Leeda looked down at her pale yellow sweater, caked with cracked bark and dirt.

"Leeda, honey." Grandmom Eugenie appeared beside Lucretia. "I can see your underwear."

Leeda's grandmom wore a plum tweed suit, the puckers of the skirt matching the puckers around her mauve-painted mouth, making her a purple stripe in Leeda's white room. Her face was as dry and silky as a cornhusk.

Today Eugenie was hatless, her thin white hair clinging in well-coiffed waves to her head. On Sundays for church, she wore a hat twice the size of her head. At Steeplechase, once a year, her hat dwarfed any comparison or relation to the actual size of her head. At last year's race, she wove around with a souvenir stirrup cup like a trophy-wielding munchkin, drinking straight bourbon out of it.

Leeda had heard once that little dogs lived longer lives. Eugenie seemed to prove the rule because she was four foot four, ninety-four, and showing no signs of breaking. Leeda sometimes feared that Grandmom Eugenie would live on eternally and be passed on down the line to her like a set of china.

"I have news for you." Lucretia smiled, sticking her head farther out Leeda's window. The sunlight caught her blond hair. Her blue eyes sparkled. She was beautiful. "The Magnolia Garden Guild has offered you the honor of being . . ." Long pause, bigger smile. "Pecan Queen."

Leeda didn't say anything. She studied her nails and swung her legs, glancing down at the ground and holding tighter to the limb. Her grandmother and mother had been Bridgewater's Pecan Queens when they were in high school. And her sister, Danay—who was in Florida this year with her new husband, taking off school for an extended honeymoon and a job as

Snow White at Disney World—had been the Pecan Queen an unprecedented two years in a row. (Danay had made a natural progression from complete princess to official queen.) It was a sort of family legacy. Leeda guessed she'd just mentally blocked out that her turn was coming. "I'm really busy with school."

Lucretia looked surprised for a moment, then gave Leeda her biggest Magnolia Garden Guild smile, the kind that made you feel like you were standing in southern sunshine. Lucretia could sell a raffle ticket to anyone. "It would mean a lot to me."

Leeda considered this, but only for a minute. Being Pecan Queen meant putting Vaseline on your teeth and tape over your nipples for the whole year, appearing at the Elks Club ziti dinners, cutting ribbons with oversized scissors at all sorts of openings, smiling fakely and looking pretty all the time, and throwing the pecan goodies from the royal float at the Pecan Festival Parade on Thanksgiving. But most of all, it meant dancing with the she-devil that was her mom, who would hover over her 24/7, the way she had with Queen Danay. It was the opposite of what she wanted for herself this year, which was smiling for real, leaving her bra off from time to time, and spending as much time as possible with Birdie and Murphy.

"Aren't you flattered?" Eugenie squawked, wedging herself through the window opening next to Lucretia. She looked like one of those parrots that sit on a pirate's shoulder. That was what Murphy would have said. A tiny smile crossed Leeda's mouth.

"Yes, Grandmom." Leeda knew she was supposed to love being a Bridgewater beauty. People kissed up to her all the time. It was kind of tiring.

"Oh, Leeda, your mother gave birth to you, and just look at

those narrow hips," Grandmom Eugenie added.

Leeda wanted to laugh. It was ironic, actually. There was a time she could have tasted being queen because Danay had gotten so much attention from her mom that way, attention Leeda had always wanted. But now Leeda was wise enough to know the great secret—that no matter how hard you tried to be perfect, your mom could be missing love for you that was supposed to be there. Leeda could never do enough to make the love appear. And she was over it. There were other places to find love. She had found it at the peach orchard that summer with Birdie—who she'd known forever but had never *really* known—and with Murphy. She'd found it while working under the hot Georgia sun, not being perfect at all.

"Sit up straight, Leeda," Grandmom Eugenie barked. Leeda straightened. It was a reflex. Despite her small stature, Grandmom Eugenie had always been huge and intimidating to Leeda.

"Leeda." Her mom's voice turned solemn, and Leeda looked up. For an almost imperceptible moment, something real and genuine flashed across Lucretia's face. It made lines on either side of her mouth and snuffed out her smile altogether. "Leeda, I didn't want to tell you this now, but I think you should know."

"What?" Leeda said, suddenly anxious.

Lucretia looked over at Grandmom Eugenie, then at Leeda again. "I went to the doctor the other day and . . . they found something."

Leeda went stiff inside. Stiff and uncomfortable. She wanted to ask what. But she was scared to. The breeze wafted her hair up and away from her face. She stared down at her dangling legs.

"It's called hyperhidrosis. It's very rare."

Leeda swallowed, feeling ill. In her family, you didn't ask questions about deep, unpleasant stuff. She wasn't even sure she was allowed to ask anything now. But she warbled, "What is it?"

Lucretia stuck her chin in the air and waved a hand dismissively. "Don't you worry about that, honey. Just . . ." She turned serious, ran her fingers along the windowsill thoughtfully. "I'd like . . . to see you do this for me."

"I brought my tiara," Grandmom Eugenie added, producing a tiny tinsel crown from out of nowhere. Leeda could see the tiny shake of her grandmother's hands as she clasped its thin edges.

Lucretia tugged on her small platinum hoop earrings to straighten them out. "Being Pecan Queen was one of the most fulfilling experiences of my life."

Leeda knew this was true. The Cawley-Smiths still had an eight-by-ten glossy of Lucretia-as-queen in a silver frame, signed, on the table by the front door. Murphy said it was a perfect summary of Leeda's mother's personality that one of her most prized possessions was a picture autographed by herself.

"Please?" Lucretia asked.

Leeda examined the tree's bark, unsure what to say. The Murphy on her left shoulder told her to run like hell. The Birdie on her right shoulder welled up with sentimental tears. Finally she looked back up. She could see where her mom had missed a button on her shirt. For some reason, Leeda wanted to reach out and fix it.

"Okay," Leeda said. "Yeah, of course." Her heart fluttered.

"Good," Lucretia said flatly. Then the window closed as abruptly as it had opened.

Leeda stared at the green leaves rustling in the breeze and then at the limb underneath her. "Damn," she muttered. Then she slowly, carefully shimmied her way out of the tree.

It was harder going down.

Three

*B*irdie lay on her stomach in her white T-shirt bra, her bare belly against the soft fabric of her quilt, her toes working a loose thread at the foot end of the bed. Now and then she let out an angsty sigh. She held a crumpled piece of paper in her hands.

The thing about Enrico's letters was that she could feel them. He stuck things in them like leaves, scraps of notes from his classes with the frilly bits where the paper had been ripped out of a spiral notebook, little folded-up poems from the grade school kids he tutored. He also sent things like pencils, matchbooks from cafés, wrapped mints. Birdie turned them over in her hands as she read his words, usually several times, pulling out the best parts and letting her eyes leap along them like skipping stones. She loved his handwriting, open-looped and crooked—honest and unassuming.

She focused on one bit of the letter over and over again. *If you come to Mexico at New Year's . . .*

Honey Babe and Majestic watched her from their doggie bed. They were wearing a pair of matching red-and-green-striped sweaters that Birdie had knitted. Across Honey Babe's back she'd embroidered the word *Hola*. Across Majestic's, *Amigo*. Birdie pulled a sock off her foot, rolled it up like a doughnut, and threw it to them. Honey Babe chewed on the sock while Majestic tilted her head at Birdie questioningly. "He wants me to come to Mexico," Birdie whispered.

She had known the orchard Enrico and the Texas Enrico. But now that they wrote to each other, his letters were full of Mexico—his little house at the foot of the mountains outside Mexico City, his mom who drove a bus, his dad who worked at the Zócalo as a security guard, his brother who was still in grade school. He had gotten a scholarship to transfer to the National Autonomous University of Mexico in Mexico City next year. In Birdie's head, Enrico's life took on the shape of a cartoon. It was all so exotic and breathlessly foreign to her. Birdie lived in the smallest corner of the world—or at least it felt like it.

She laid the paper down and rolled onto her back, running her feet up and down the wallpaper, throwing her arms back over her head, restless and bursting at the seams. *If you come to Mexico at New Year's* . . . It was out of the question, of course. There were several layers of reasons why: Out of the question asking her parents. Out of the question finding the money. Out of the question staying with Enrico's cartoon family in cartoon Mexico. But she wanted to, so badly she could taste it.

She stood and stepped over the pile of textbooks on the floor and surveyed herself in the mirror on the back of her bedroom door. It was hot, and glancing in her mirror, she saw her cheeks were flushed. Birdie's jeans hung loosely off her hips, the ankles slinking over her red Crocs. Her auburn ponytail was swept back with sweaty little curls clinging along where her ears met her head. She felt pretty. No, sexy. She wondered what she would look like to Enrico with bigger lips. She stuck her tongue over her upper lip, flattening it out so that it looked like a big lip.

Behind her, Birdie's room had become a testament to all things *español*. Murphy called it Casa del Infatuatión. Her desk was strewn with Spanish language CDs from the Bridgewater library, a Mexican flag hung from her closet, and Spanish lesson books lay open and half finished beside her bed.

A handful of dried peach leaves sat on her nightstand, a last remnant of the summer. Looking at them made Birdie long for June. She had the urge to escape her room and walk the orchard. Instead she padded down the hall to Poopie's room.

Poopie was watching *Beaches* on TBS and writing on a slip of paper. Birdie plopped beside her and made big lips at the ceiling. "What are you writing?"

"A letter," Poopie said.

"To who?"

Birdie looked over her shoulder and Poopie snatched it away quickly, then flashed a smile. "My sister."

Birdie studied Poopie like she didn't already know every line of her face. She was small and taut and tan, like a peanut. Her black hair was always pulled back into a messy bun and her eyebrows were straight over her open, almost-black eyes. Poopie Pedraza had arrived years ago—from the same suburb of Mexico City as Enrico and several of the other workers—to work as a cook. Since then, she'd become the linchpin that held the Darlington house together. And sometimes Birdie too.

"Why do you look like that?" Poopie asked.

"What?"

Poopie made a face like Birdie's, all full of consternation.

Birdie groaned. Even with Murphy and Leeda, she was embarrassed talking about Enrico. But she needed to spill a little. "Enrico wants me to come to Mexico for New Year's," she offered.

Poopie's eyes lit up with interest. "Oh yeah?"

"Yeah."

"You want to go?"

Birdie shrugged. She'd been homeschooled and on Friday nights she usually helped Poopie clean all the linens. On Saturdays, she caught up on invoices and office work and studied the tomes she'd ordered online on fruit pests and parasites, crop diseases, and fertilizing. A weekend at the beach was out of the picture, much less a trip to Mexico. "Does it matter?"

Poopie made a sympathetic murmur and folded up her letter. "Our town is beautiful," Poopie told her wistfully. Like most of the orchard workers, Poopie and Enrico were from a place outside Mexico City. "I wish you could see it. . . ." She motioned Birdie in front of her so she could braid her hair. It was a ritual they did.

Birdie sighed as Poopie tugged gently at her hair. "I wish it was still summer."

"We're already on our way to next summer."

"I guess. Murphy says next summer, she'll plant another nectarine tree in her garden," Birdie breathed. Poopie tied a knot at the bottom of Birdie's hair to keep the braid in place.

"She won't have time before she leaves," Poopie said lightly.

Birdie groaned. "Don't rush it."

Poopie shrugged. "Seventeen is a good year, Avelita." *Little bird.* "But there are better ones." Birdie leaned back and let

Poopie wrap her in a hug. Poopie pecked her on the cheek. "Not everyone is so *still* inside like you."

Birdie didn't get why not. Why did people have to go off for college and bigger things? It seemed backwards to her that people left their families and their homes behind. It seemed like a betrayal.

She stayed beside Poopie and they watched the rest of *Beaches*. They both cried. Poopie clutched Birdie's hands, saying, "No, no," at the part when Bette Midler says, "We haven't *grown* apart, you've fallen apart," and then again when Barbara Hershey's daughter finds her passed out on the ground. They had probably seen *Beaches* three thousand times.

When it was over, Birdie shuffled back to her room, the house creaking around her as she walked. She sat on her bed and looked at the knickknacks on her shelves, coated in a fine layer of dust. She gazed at the old paintings of the house—from two different angles—that had hung side by side on the far wall since before she was born.

Finally she couldn't resist anymore.

The minute she let them out, Honey Babe and Majestic went racing off into the orchard. Birdie stepped out onto the grass and turned right, walking between two rows of peach trees whose leaves were just on the verge of turning.

The unmown grass poked through the holes in her Crocs. It was just warm enough outside to be pleasant, with just the slightest cool breeze rustling the trees. The monotony of autumn gray had given way to a few clear days.

Birdie breathed in the fresh air. As she walked, she took it all in: the dips in the ground, how each tree grew slightly differently depending on its altitude, the bugs floating around, what they were, which ones could be harmful to the crop. Birdie couldn't help her watchful eye even when she was relaxing.

A crunch of gravel announced a gold Chevrolet pulling into the Darlingtons' long driveway. Father Michael from the Divine Grace of the Redeemer church stepped out and Birdie waved at him. She always felt a little sheepish around Father Michael because she suspected that priests could read minds. Particularly when you had gone to the same priest for confession since second grade.

"How's your mother, Birdie?" Father Michael called. He was one of the few people in town with a foreign accent. He was Italian. He was a good friend of Poopie's and came over at least once a week to hear her confession and get a palm reading, which Poopie dabbled in.

"Good, Father."

Father Michael nodded, smiled, and glided up the stairs onto the porch. Birdie watched him disappear into the house. She wondered if he thought her mom and dad were sinners for getting divorced.

Turning, Birdie wound around the side of the house toward Murphy's garden. The nectarine tree had been picked over by people and animals, but some of the late flowers were still blooming. You could see everything Murphy had taken back from the kudzu, marking the territory that belonged to the humans and not the woods.

She turned left and hooked back behind the empty dorms, sunk into the ground. They blinked at her with empty eyes now that the workers were gone and wouldn't return until April. She could almost see Enrico relaxing on the porch stairs after a long day, his smooth tan skin coated with white dirt. Birdie's dad had told her, just last week, that both dorms would have to be torn down and rebuilt. They had gotten so old. You could tell just by the exhausted way they sagged.

She trailed through the northwest corner of the farm, turning left at the line between her family's property and the Balmeade Country Club. She checked the fence for holes as she came down along the brushy, wild-grown edge of the orchard to the pecan grove. Once, near the ninth hole with Murphy and Leeda, she'd nailed Horatio Balmeade in the head with a half-eaten peach. Thinking about it brought a smile to her face.

Up ahead, the rows of pecans—eighteen trees altogether—stood across from one another in perfectly straight lines. The pecan trees were enormous and unwieldy, full of knots and peeling bark, thrusting their heavy limbs in every direction. Poopie always said the trees were spooky. If she'd been walking through the grove and you asked her where she'd been, she'd twist her arms and claw up her fingers to imitate a tree.

The trees were uniform height except for Methuselah, which hung above the others like an old witch. She was the most ancient by at least two hundred years. No one knew how old pecans could get or who had named Methuselah. She appeared in the oldest plans for the orchard, which dated back to the 1800s.

Now that Birdie was outside on her family's property, which would one day be hers, she felt centered again—shifted off Mexico and Enrico and all the fluttering. Looking around, she always knew exactly where she stood. She turned to watch the sun, which was sinking beyond the house. It made her feel peaceful that at least the orchard sunsets would always be around—all her life, she would be on this spot.

Some things really did last.

Four

Outside Bridgewater High School, which still had a confederate flag hanging next to the American flag outside the principal's office, Rex Taggart's truck was parked and idling. Murphy paused as she pushed through the front door, her backpack slung low over one shoulder. Then she stepped back once, nervous. Then hopeful. As with all things she really wanted, she tried to lower her excitement level by thinking about stuff that bored her, like Impressionism and Raisinettes. Just that morning she had decided to ask him. And Murphy liked to move fast. Why waste time?

Murphy swayed her hips as she approached the truck. She was small—short—but she walked big. Murphy opened the passenger door and stared inside at him. He sat with one hand on the wheel, the other resting on a small pumpkin in the passenger seat. He smelled like a combination of oil, the outside, and just . . . *Rex*. His eyes were a deep bottle-green that looked brown if you didn't really look. His hair was messy. His style was no style—jeans and a dark green T-shirt.

"Boo," Rex said, holding up the little pumpkin.

"Scary." Murphy set it on her lap as she got in. "It's not even October yet, goofy." October was still two days away, unfortunately. Murphy was counting days like the Count of Monte Cristo stuck in the dungeon.

Rex shrugged. "You can never start carving too early."

Murphy gazed at the tiny uncarvable pumpkin and then looked over at Rex and pinched him. "You couldn't stay away from me, huh, stalker? That's okay. You don't have to use pumpkin excuses."

"How was your day, Shorts?" he asked, an easy smile creeping sideways across his mouth. He seemed to be taking her in—her loose low-cut button-down shirt the color of a tea stain, green cords she'd bought for $3.50 at a garage sale, her curly hair wild around her face like a lion's mane. Murphy knew she was being admired and stretched like a cat.

"I saw my guidance counselor," she answered him.

"And?"

"He said I need to pick safety schools. Did you know that when they say, 'This will go down on your permanent record,' they really mean it?"

Rex feigned the appropriate level of surprise, reaching for her fingers and studying them like they were diamonds. "No way."

Murphy nodded. "Yep." So when she'd climbed the Orange Street electrical tower and had to have the fire department come get her down, that had gone on her permanent record. Same for stealing underwear from Wal-Mart. And getting caught naked with Elliott Howe under the stage during *The Crucible*. Apparently.

"But they'll love me. They'll say I'm just sassy. Anyway, I've seen the stats." Murphy had looked up NYU's admitted fresh-man profile statistics every year for the past three years, and despite her aversion to schoolwork, she was always way ahead of the curve. SATs, no problem. GPA, no problem. Class rank, no problem. For all she knew, she'd be valedictorian. Not that she'd stick around long enough to give a speech.

She ran her free hand over her backpack, which contained two packs of gum, notebooks mutilated with blue pen drawings, and her crumpled application to NYU. It was wrinkled and torn because she'd loved it to death ever since she'd gotten it. Clutched it like it was a hot air balloon.

"Of course they will," he agreed.

She eyed him. "What are you doing here anyway?"

"Well, Shorts, I thought we could crash out." He was trying to get a rise out of her by calling her Shorts. Murphy hated nick-names. She made a big deal of not caring and looked behind her. He had a backpack, a thermos of what was almost definitely sweet tea, and a tiny radio.

"Are you trying to seduce me?" She sighed, as if it could be a bad thing.

Rex shrugged mysteriously and steered them out of the parking lot. Murphy picked at the lint on her cords, giddy. She should wait to ask. But Murphy McGowen was not built to wait for anything. She glanced at him sideways.

It made her want to vomit, how happy she was. She went out of her way to hide from both of them how much she liked him. But whenever she was with him, she felt like she was stretching out instead of shrinking. She'd always had to resist the urge to trip girls like that, girls walking down the hall talking about their boyfriends incessantly. She'd settled for the satisfaction that their boyfriends were secretly checking her out.

"By the way." Rex dropped her hand to shift the gear. "Pops wants you to come to dinner."

"I can't that night."

"Which night is that?" Rex asked.

"I'm really busy." Murphy couldn't imagine anything she wanted to do less than meet Rex's dad.

"Saturday it is."

Murphy threw up her hands. "I have a lot of studying to do." Murphy had a bad record with parents. They usually eyed her like she was a black widow spider come to poison their boy. Which usually, she sort of did—with the way she moved her hips when she walked, with the way she wore her shirts buttoned two buttons too low. In Bridgewater, everyone knew everyone. And there was no way Mr. Taggart hadn't heard about Murphy. She'd been in the newspaper three times last year alone—for filling the school fountain with dry ice, for indecent exposure at the Easter Revival, and for mooning the governor of Georgia when he'd come through town on a goodwill tour.

But the difference between those parents and Rex's dad was that Murphy actually cared what Rex's dad thought. Because it was Rex.

"Fine." Rex guided the truck onto an old dirt road, powerful and easy at once. Sometimes Murphy compared herself to him. She just felt powerful. Never easy.

"Fine?"

He lifted one shoulder. "Yeah."

Murphy sucked in her bottom lip and stared at him. She

loved and hated that he could let something go and let her know how wrong she was at the same time. He glanced over and smiled at her. She involuntarily smiled back. *Vomity.* Her question danced on her mouth. She opened her lips a few times, but it didn't come out.

He drove her to the orchard and parked in the grass by the side of the road, just near the south end of the pecan grove, and they climbed out. A set of train tracks ran their way straight across this southern edge of the property. Rex took Murphy's hand and she trailed behind him, pausing as she crossed the tracks. She looked down them, to where they disappeared. Tracks were one of her other favorite views. They seemed to lead to so many amazing things just out of sight.

"Do you think in your last life you might have been a hobo?" Rex asked. "Because you look hungry for a train."

They strolled toward Smoaky Lake, balancing their picnic goodies awkwardly. The water was a muddy warm brown, rippling in the breeze against the rocks and dirt that made up its small shore.

After checking the ground for fire ants, they plopped on the grass. Murphy leaned back on her elbows, breathing the dry, earthy smell in the air and tapping the tips of her Pumas together. She felt stretched out to every inch of her skin, waiting for Rex to kiss her. The moments before were always delicious.

Thump.

Rex had pulled her AP Art textbook out of her bag and dropped it between them. Murphy frowned.

"What's that for?"

"You'll figure it out." He slid it toward her and then stretched his lean body out on the grass, his bangs dangling over his eyes. Murphy watched him for a moment covetously. Coveting his body and his superhuman resistance to her. Rex was unlike any guy she'd ever known. He didn't try to get her clothes off every time he saw her. He didn't blink at Murphy like a pigeon when she said something halfway intelligent. She sighed, rolled onto her stomach, and opened the book.

As she read, Rex kept his distance. He left space between them for Murphy to cross.

"You wanna see something great?" she asked after about half an hour of silence. Rex rolled on his side and tucked his hand under his head. Murphy slid her book toward him. It was opened to Piet Mondrian's *Ocean 5*, a painting that was all black lines, all perpendicular, on a flesh-colored background.

Rex studied it. "What's good about it?"

Murphy moved a curl hanging in her face. "Well, it's like . . . you know how some things look really good from far away, but you get close and they sort of come apart?"

Rex nodded. Murphy smiled, more curls flopping over her face. "It's the opposite. It only makes sense when you get really close to it."

Rex brushed her curls to the side with his hands and kissed her just on the apple of her cheek. "Like you." Murphy breathed in how good he smelled until he pulled away.

"The orchard feels empty," Rex said, lying back, longing stretching between them like an elastic cord. She peered around. Behind them, obscured by the trees, was Orchard Road, the one-lane street that saw about three cars a day. It ran along the property's south line and eventually looped up around its eastern edge. To their far right was the gravelly drive that cut the orchard, gently and lopsidedly, in two. Then there were the peach rows themselves—the hundred acres of trees that stretched over a vague roll in the land in low, crisscrossing lines.

"My mom and I used to have picnics here." Murphy pointed toward the southeast end of the property, far beyond the peach rows. "For Easter. We used to sneak in."

Rex looked at her, grinned. "Let's plant a flag here," he said.

Murphy smiled up at the clouds drifting overhead. She knew Poopie had seen signs in the clouds. Murphy saw nothing but cauliflowers now. She turned to Rex. He was building an intricate little twig flag. He did everything intricately. Sickening as it was, part of Murphy wanted him to be serious—she wanted them to have a house and a flag. Part of her wanted to pin him to her.

"C'mon." Murphy pulled Rex to his feet and convinced him to go in the water with her. They stripped out of their shirts and pants. They paddled around the cold lake in their underwear and pressed their goose bumps against each other and spit water in each other's faces. When they got out, covered in flecks of old leaves, Rex got a tarp from his truck. They curled up in it like caterpillars even though it smelled like cars.

Shivering but warm, Murphy had the feeling she got when she dove deep underwater. Like she was a treasure chest half buried in the sand ten thousand feet down. Like she was Eve lying in a cluster of reeds in the oldest garden before being nude was naked.

"Tell me something about you," Murphy asked.

"Like what?"

Murphy settled into his side, her curves pressed against his lean, long lines. She drew him in like she was spinning a web. He looked at her and swallowed, sliding his hand around her waist. He stared at her without his usual confidence.

"Something juicy. Something nobody knows," she told him. It would be easy. Rex was doggedly private.

He thought, pulling his body away slightly and clearing his throat. "My dad knows everything about me. But I can tell you something nobody knows but him."

"Okay."

"Uhhh . . ." Rex thought. "I wet the bed until I was nine."

Murphy laughed. "That's horrible. You must have been a jacked-up little kid."

Rex shrugged. "I was going to a shrink after my mom left, and he said it was probably separation anxiety." Murphy pressed into him further, wanting to squeeze into any places he was missing. She didn't know anything about Rex's mom except that she wasn't around. She wondered if everywhere families were as crooked as the ones she knew. All the families she knew—even the ones with two parents—were missing parts.

"Don't ever tell anyone, okay?"

"Of course. Dummy," she added.

She twirled a waxy tarp string around her finger, cutting off the circulation and turning her finger red. "I had an idea." She tried to sound as casual as possible, as if she hadn't been waiting to ask this. Her heart beat a little faster. Her stomach turned. She couldn't believe how hard it was to say.

She pursed her lips a few times, and Rex watched them, then touched them. "What is it?" he whispered.

"When summer comes, why don't you move to New York with me?"

"Ha," Rex laughed. But when she stayed quiet, he tried to catch her eye. She was staring at her red fingertip. Finally she looked at him.

He lowered his chin to his chest and eyed her sideways. He seemed to be considering. "What's it like for us in New York, Shorts?"

"Well." Murphy swallowed. "We go to the Met and the Rose Room at the library and Saint John the Divine." As she said them, it occurred to her these weren't really Rex things. Seeing Rex indoors anywhere was like seeing him in a zoo.

"It's nothing like here," she finally told him. In Murphy's mind, New York was, in essence, the polar opposite of Bridgewater, Georgia. She wouldn't be Jodee McGowen's daughter, and Rex wouldn't be the guy who dropped out of high school to do odd jobs. Their rough edges wouldn't be in anybody's way.

Rex took it in, nodding. "It sounds great. But I wouldn't go for New York. Or to get out of here. I'd be going for the girl."

Murphy said nothing. She tried to let her face go blank.

He brushed his bangs out of his eyes so he could look into hers. "Oh, don't look so horrified. I *love* you, Murphy." He smiled and tugged on a curl of her hair. "Live with it."

Murphy stayed as still as the spider she was, catching Rex's words and spinning them around. He said *love* so matter-of-factly. Like he'd already said it to her a million times, even though he never had. The grass held them like a soft web.

"Then you'll come with me?"

He looked at her intently, then sighed. "I'll think about it," he finally said.

"Till when?" Murphy pressed.

"Till I'm ready."

Murphy grinned and looked up at the sky. "Like when?"

"You want a date?" he asked, smirking.

Murphy nodded.

"How about a date at my house, with my dad, for dinner?"

Murphy heaved a sigh.

Rex smiled gamely. "And I'll tell you by Thanksgiving—how's that?"

"By the time the tofurkey lands on my table," Murphy said solemnly.

"Before a bite even touches those pretty lips." Rex nestled into her, tightening his arms around her as if he were a kid, and kissed her neck. She felt how bare he was in front of her and how much she needed him too, even though she had no interest in needing him.

In the cool night air, wrapped in only the tarp and their wet underwear, she wondered if maybe they *could* have a house, and a flag, and a way to hold on to each other. For the first time, Murphy began to wonder if maybe they could be the rare ones that didn't end.

Five

*P*lunk *plunk plunk.* Birdie woke with a start and looked toward the window.

Plunk. Plunk plunk. Slow on the draw as usual, Majestic and Honey Babe leapt up and raced to the window seat, sticking their noses against the glass, fogging it up with nose prints. Birdie shuffled behind them and looked outside. Murphy and Leeda stood on the grass, in a triangular patch of pure sunlight, staring up at her. Birdie opened the window and grinned. They launched into a pathetic rendition of *"Feliz Cumpleaños,"* still holding handfuls of old peach pits.

"You sing worse than Poopie," Birdie called down.

"We gotta go to school," Murphy yelled up. "But we left your presents by the door." They raced off across the light-striped grass, looking chilly and underdressed. Birdie could see them through the other window, hopping in Leeda's car at the head of the long white gravel drive. They left dust hanging in clouds behind them.

Birdie slipped her feet into her pink bunny slippers and shuffled downstairs. Somebody—most likely Poopie—had turned on the heat for the first time all season. It smelled like last year's pecan bread.

She scooted past the kitchen to the front door, Honey Babe and Majestic bumping into her heels and gnawing at the cotton-tails of the slippers whenever they caught up. She opened the front door, cool air greeting her. The presents lay on the dusty porch—one newspaper-wrapped bundle, one sparkly purple with a flounce of silver ribbon. Birdie scooped them up and looked over at the peach rows. The leaves had a new orange tint to their tips, like a woman who'd dyed the ends of her hair red. Birdie closed the door and opened the newspaper bundle—a sweater from Murphy that said *Hola* across the front, clearly scavenged from some secondhand bin. Birdie laughed. Next she opened Leeda's—an iPod with a peach engraved on the back.

"Happy birthday, honey," her dad greeted her when she got to the kitchen door.

"Thanks." Birdie smiled, sliding into the chair next to the empty one where her mom used to sit before she and the family dog, Toonsis, had left them. Poopie was standing at the stove, and her dad was sitting in his usual spot. The Darlington kitchen had had the same color scheme Birdie's entire life. Yellowing counters, rust-colored linoleum, off-white cabinets that had gone yellow too. A big window above the sink overlooking the orchard saved it from being drab.

Birdie looked around the table for her traditional blue birthday eggs. Every year, Poopie put blue food coloring in her eggs because that's what Birdie had liked for her birthday when she was little. But this year, all Birdie saw was the regular old yellow kind. She then took another look around for presents. Her dad always spoiled her for her birthday. But all she saw was one colorfully wrapped bundle in Poopie's arms.

"*Feliz cumpleaños*." Poopie handed her the gift.

"Thanks, Poops." Birdie half stood and gave Poopie a kiss on the cheek. She already knew what the package contained. She glanced up at the window, where a tiny wooden statue of Saint Francis, the patron saint of animals, watched over the driveway leading up to the orchard, his back turned to them. Next to him was a jagged crystal Poopie had picked up at some hippie store in Savannah and a dried four-leaf clover taped to the windowsill. A tiny gilt-edged holy calendar marked with the date, October 10, and a painting of the Virgin Mary were tacked to the yellow wall.

Birdie had grown up steeped in Poopie's superstitions, and she had her own collection of little wooden santos hidden upstairs in her closet—her mom had hated them. Birdie always forgot what they meant, but Poopie had probably given her a dozen over the years, one for every birthday. She was pretty sure she had the patron saint of lightning, the patron saint of spirituality, and the patron saint of first periods already. Poopie had carried the infant Birdie on one hip while twirling crystals and crucifixes and clovers in her free hand. So Birdie, a southern farm girl, had grown up sleeping with quartz under her pillows to help her with tests and looking to the clouds for signs.

Birdie opened the bundle. It was a man saint, staring at her solemnly.

"Saint Anthony," Poopie told her. "The patron saint of roads and going places." She gave Birdie a wink. Birdie stared at the little guy, curious. He looked very serious and sad, like the weight of the world was on his shoulders. She had always wondered why God's favorite people had to look that way.

"That's a nice one," Walter said, so enthusiastically that Birdie gave him a second glance. For a while after her mom left, her dad had been so broken, Birdie had thought he would never be whole again. Today he was Humpty Dumpty put back together. All smiles and rattling newspaper. "How's school?" he asked.

"Fine." Birdie sat, bewildered, wondering where her present was. Because she was homeschooled, school was always fine. No lunchroom gossip. No horrible teachers, or great teachers, or any teachers. No nothing new. With the exception of some occasional help from Poopie, school ran on autopilot. So did Birdie. It was like she had been born responsible.

"You on top of everything enough to take on a little project?"

By *project*, Walter Darlington always meant *farm work*. Sitting still all day behind a desk didn't quite compute to Walter Darlington, mostly because it was the opposite of what being a farmer was all about. Birdie had known forever she would go to Laurens Community College, half an hour away, to major in agriculture. When school was over, she'd inherit the farm. It was all wrapped up for her like a package.

"Yeah," Birdie muttered through a mouthful of potatoes. Truthfully, she had plenty to do already: laying out green manure for the new plantings, inspecting the trees for bugs and nests, walking the property to make sure nothing was out of place. Not to mention carving out family time into separate slices—some for afternoons with her dad, going over their work for the coming months. Some for her mom, who had moved into Howl Mill, a new condo complex just outside town.

"I want you to clear off the cave. The one under the eaves behind the barn. Try to draw some bats."

The bat cave had been covered over forever. It had always been something they talked about doing. Bats could be very good at insect control, an alternative to pesticides.

"Sure, Dad." Birdie sank back in her chair.

Snuff. Honey Babe was dancing on her hind legs by Birdie's chair, begging for scraps. Birdie absentmindedly reached out to scratch her ears.

"Great." Walter shrugged lightly, almost *flip.*

Birdie stared down at her non-blue eggs. She looked over at Poopie, then at her dad, who apparently had no present for her. She sighed wistfully.

"Poopie says you want to go to Mexico over the break," her dad said, his face still in his newspaper.

"That's not . . ." Birdie could feel her face going red. She shot a betrayed glance at Poopie, trying to think of a way to say yes and no at the same time. "Um. Yeah, well, you know, his parents invited me." She put heavy emphasis on the word *parents.* Nothing shady about it. Definitely nothing sexy.

"So they'll be there?" Walter asked, taking a sip of orange juice.

Birdie studied him. She felt like she was being lured into a trap. "Yeah." He wasn't actually considering it. Was he?

Walter shrugged. "I don't see why you shouldn't go. I thought that could be your present—"

"Really?" she squawked. Her hands grabbed each other to keep from flying into the air. She leapt up from her seat and wrapped her arms around her dad, tight. As she pulled back, she wondered if she should hightail it upstairs before he changed his mind. But Birdie was hungry. Famished, in fact.

She flopped back down onto her chair and they went back to eating, the picture of an all-American family: father, daughter, empty chair for Cynthia, Poopie the New Age Mexican cook, and Saint Anthony, the patron saint of going places.

In the fall of 1520, a flock of bats ventured out of their cave for their nightly hunt. When they returned, a tree had fallen over the entrance hole, and the enraged bats terrorized everything in their path—foxes, eagles, wild boar. By sun break, approximately 127 animals were chased out of what would one day be known as Kings County, Georgia.

Six

"She's a vampire. You know that, don't you?"

"Murphy..."

"Do you know the thing about vampire bats?" Murphy chewed on a cigarette she hadn't lit. It was part of her quitting technique. "They prey on the same victim night after night. They have this stuff in their saliva that keeps the wound open so they can come back the next day and feast again, right where they left off. That's your mom. Subtle." Murphy pulled out the cigarette and sighed as if she were actually blowing smoke out the passenger-side window of Leeda's BMW.

"You're a metaphorical genius, Murphy. Truly."

"I've got lots more metaphors for dear Lulu," Murphy said, tilting her head in a knowing way, grinning. "Leech. No," she thought out loud. "Mosquito." And then her grin disappeared. "But seriously, you can't do it, Lee. I don't care what kind of a disease she's got."

"God," Leeda said, squeezing the steering wheel, a lump in her throat. Sometimes it was shocking how insensitive Murphy could be. Sometimes Leeda wanted to throw her out the car window. "Murphy, she's *sick*."

"How sick? What's hyperpsychosis anyway?"

Honestly, Leeda didn't know. She didn't like to look at anything scary too directly. There was only a faint uneasiness in her stomach. Deep down, like at the bottom of a pit. She tried not to think about it during the day. But at night, in the dark, in her bed, she would feel it flutter inside her.

"You know, Lee," Murphy said, philosophical, "when I met you, I thought you were this really selfish, uptight person. All looking like this . . ." Murphy made a tight, tense face, pursing her lips. "But you know what? You're worse than Birdie. Seriously. You're a pushover."

Leeda wondered if that was true. "I just hate letting people down," she said. Anyone. Didn't matter who.

The orchard rushed around the car as Leeda steered into the drive. She breathed in the smell of the grass and the musty smell of the white dirt as she parked, leaving the windows down. They got out and trekked over to the barn and around the back. A big cloud of dust was flying out through the huge, sagging doors. They stepped to the threshold, a little shocked to see the piles of ancient tools, farm gear, dusty saddles, and old furniture scattered everywhere. Birdie stood in the middle of all of it.

"Dang, Birdie," Leeda said. "If we get all this stuff cleaned out, are we going to find the earth's molten core?"

Birdie brushed her long bangs out of her eyes, her hands covered in dust and rotted hay. She grinned sheepishly. "I told you it was a big job."

Birdie had enlisted Leeda and Murphy to help clean out the

entrance to the mouth of the cave, which lay beneath the eaves at the back of the barn. It had been buried over the years under almost every piece of junk the Darlingtons owned. Now the junk was all covered in webs and dust and rotted, unidentifiable debris.

"There are caves all over the place under the orchard," Birdie told them, heaving an old hacksaw aside. She said it mostly for Murphy's benefit because Leeda had known about the caves forever. They had always seemed so mysterious and exciting to Birdie when she was little. "That's why the dorms are sinking," she went on.

"Those dorms are death traps," Murphy said, running her finger through a layer of dust on an old windowpane, nonchalant. "I bet they're fire hazards too, all that rotten wood."

"Totally. Dad wants to tear them down and rebuild now that we have the money. But I don't think either of us has the heart to do it."

Leeda looked around. The same pieces of machinery had been sitting in the same places for years, covered in a thick, pungent layer of damp hay. "Who was the last person to use any of this stuff?" she asked.

"Probably . . . who was that guy? . . . Nebuchadnezzar," Murphy answered dryly, heaving a heavy metal rake off a cracked wooden chest of drawers. Birdie snorted.

There was a pay phone outside the front doors of the barn that the workers used during the summer. It began to ring. They all looked at it.

"It's Rex. I'm not here," Murphy said. They listened to it ringing. Leeda's heart gave a little thud. Just a little one. She and

Murphy hadn't talked about Rex much since Leeda had given him up. Or since Murphy had won him away. Or whatever had happened. Leeda wasn't in love with him. But it still hurt for the moment that that phone used to ring for her, all summer long, and now it was ringing for Murphy.

"Why aren't you here?" Birdie asked.

"I stood him up for dinner with his dad and he's calling to yell at me." Murphy leaned sideways, hands on rounded hips. Hay hung from her curly pigtails. She looked like a sassy farmer's daughter from a rock video.

"Why'd you stand them up?" Birdie asked.

"I don't know." Murphy shrugged carelessly. "Dad, dinner, boring."

Leeda looked at Birdie, who looked back at her. They both knew it was Murphy-speak for being intimidated.

"Tons of spiders in here," Leeda said, curling her arms around herself. She had noticed a big orange fuzzy one scuttling across the hay. Murphy made what was supposed to be a spider face, sticking out her bottom teeth, and clawed up her fingers.

"That looks like Poopie's pecan tree face." Birdie shot a reassuring smile at Leeda, the kind she'd been shooting her since Leeda had told her about her mom. Birdie, who was always careful, was being extra careful around her today. It only exaggerated how *un*careful Murphy was.

They dug in again, hauling salvageable equipment like sawhorses and rakes onto the grass outside to uncover other, useless stuff like old rusted scythes and pecan shakers. Dust clouds ascended into the air and bits of debris settled in their hair.

"Don't bats eat fruit?"

"Mega-bats do. But micro-bats eat insects. We want the micros. But the megas actually would be okay too. They only eat overripe fruit, and they pollinate."

Leeda got a shiver. How mega was mega?

Hard as she tried, Leeda couldn't work nearly as fast as Murphy and Birdie. Her arms were twice as thin. Two Leedas put together would make a Murphy. But she did her best.

"I bet you could sell a lot of this stuff on the Internet," Murphy observed. "Like this." She pulled an oval frame out of a heap of junk and turned it around, revealing an old, cracked mirror. "People love broken stuff. It's shabby chic."

Leeda's reflection bounced back at her. Her forehead looked long and wide, and her lips stretched out to either side of her face. "One day all this will be yours, Bird."

"You'll both be Pecan Queens," Murphy said darkly. Leeda rolled her eyes at Birdie for help.

Birdie's face lit up. "You're gonna be Pecan Queen?" She clapped. God bless Birdie.

"Yup," Leeda answered. "And Murphy's going to help me with my queen duties."

Murphy snorted. "Help you what? Get your tiara—"

"Look!" Birdie interrupted, pulling the last of the debris away. They peered down into the hole. Cool air came up, blowing on their faces.

"Spooky," Murphy breathed.

They stepped back from the cave entrance and flopped down. The cool grass felt good on their sweaty backs.

"Are you gonna help me with the queen stuff or not?" Leeda asked Murphy. "Like come with me to the appearances. I have to cut ribbons and do photo ops and give little speeches."

"You've got to be kidding," Murphy said flatly, twirling her hair.

"Can you get them to put it in the newspaper if we get bats?" Birdie asked. "People don't understand them," she said plaintively.

Leeda turned, taking in her friends' profiles. Lying back on the grass, Murphy looked seductive, like she was flirting with the branches above their heads. She always did. Leeda knew she couldn't help it.

"Lee, you know what it's like with your mom," Murphy started, still staring straight up. "She's like an abusive boyfriend. Did you ever see *Sleeping with the Enemy?*" Only Birdie shook her head. Leeda was trying to tune Murphy out. "What about *Enough*, with Jennifer Lopez?" Birdie shook her head again. Murphy looked at Leeda, seeing she wasn't biting, and sighed. "I just don't think it's a good idea."

"She's still my mom. She won't be around forever, you know." Leeda clenched her jaw unconsciously. She shouldn't have to say that. She didn't even want to say it. She felt like she would jinx her mom somehow. "I need you to be my cheerleader, Murphy."

"Birdie can."

Leeda's eyes met with Birdie's, who smiled obligingly. "Birdie has to run a farm, for God's sake, Murphs."

"Why is everyone giving me nicknames all of a sudden?"

"I always wanted to call you Smurphy," Birdie offered. Murphy shot her a death look. Birdie tried to hide how disappointed she was. "I *like* Smurphy. It's witty."

"Who else gave you a nickname?"

"Rex calls me Shorts." Silence. Leeda had nothing to say to that, and Birdie was clearly daydreaming about the bats. "I asked him to come with me to New York after graduation." More silence.

"That's good, right?" Leeda finally asked.

"Well, if by *good* you mean taking your heart out of your chest and leaving it on the road for him to stomp on, then yes."

"What'd he say?" Leeda asked. A tiny, petty part of her wanted Rex to have said no. She didn't know why.

Murphy shrugged. She swallowed and held up her fingers to look at them. "He'll tell me by Thanksgiving."

Birdie looked thoughtful. "Why do you have to know so long before you leave?"

Murphy sighed. "I just . . . do."

Leeda worried for Murphy in a lot of ways. She was more skilled than anyone Leeda knew at protecting herself. Which meant she hid all the good stuff from strangers. Leeda worried that in a new place, people wouldn't take the time to figure that out. Anyone looking at them would have thought Murphy was the stronger of the two—bolder, brasher, tougher—but Leeda felt fierce protectiveness when she thought of Murphy being alone in New York.

"Murphy, you know what?" Leeda asked, an idea suddenly forming in her head. "Whether he comes or not, I can come with you."

"Yeah?" Murphy turned on her side, looking at Leeda straight on.

"Yeah . . ." Leeda nodded, making the decision as the words came out. "Yeah. There's no reason why not. I don't really care where I go to school." Leeda knew she could get in almost anywhere she wanted, and her parents were dying for her to go to Columbia anyway because her dad had gone there.

Murphy smiled huge, which made Leeda feel better. Birdie sighed wistfully. Leeda tugged her long auburn ponytail. "And Birdie will hold down the fort at good old Darlington Peach Orchard. If she doesn't run off to Mexico and become a señora."

Birdie's forehead wrinkled thoughtfully. "Do you think Enrico will . . . *expect* something? You know, since I'm staying with him?"

"I don't think he's that kind of guy, Bird," Murphy said.

"I can't believe Mom and Dad are letting me go. I can't even believe *Poopie's* letting me go."

"Bird, it's really not that big of a deal to visit your boyfriend," Murphy told her.

"To Poopie it is. You know how holy she is. Sin and all that."

"I've never even heard the word *sin* come out of Poopie's mouth." Murphy rolled her shoulders against the grass. "I mean, I don't think it'll rain frogs or anything if you crash on his couch."

"You never know." Birdie sighed. A pecan fell out of a tree above and hit her on the forehead. "Ow. *See?* I get hit with a pecan just for thinking about him on the couch."

"Ha," Murphy said. They were quiet for a while, the dust motes still spinning around them in the afternoon sunlight. They could hear birds moving around in the peach branches. Leeda's mind floated to her mom again. Now that the sweat had cooled on her, she was chilly.

"This tree looks ancient," Leeda said, looking up.

"It is. It's Methuselah."

"It looks kind of droopy and sickly to me," Murphy mumbled.

"They're all droopy," Birdie told her.

Murphy sat up on her elbows to survey the grove. "This one looks ill, though."

"If you were that old, you'd be droopy too." A root was poking Leeda in the back. "Gravity."

"Okay, yeah, I *get* gravity. But whatever. I'm no tree expert."

"This tree is going to outlive us all," Birdie replied.

Leeda smiled. "Bury your heart under Methuselah."

After splitting up with Murphy and Birdie, Leeda strolled down around the south side of the orchard, listening to the crickets waking up and enjoying the perfect breeze. She had goose bumps on her arms.

Her feet took her to Smoaky Lake. A large boulder curved up from the south side of the lake, touching the still water. Leeda climbed onto it, her shoes scratching and slipping as she made her way to the flat top. It was the perfect place to sit—like a table decorated with rocks and dirt. Murphy called it the butt rock because of the crevice down its center.

Leeda took a handful of pebbles in her left hand, tossing the stones one by one into the lake with her right. It was addictive. Whenever her mind started to drift to her mom, she threw another rock, and it went sort of blank as she watched the ripples fan out over the water. Eventually she'd thrown everything she could find. She dug into the crevice, wrinkling her nose at what kind of bugs might be hiding inside. When she couldn't dig anything out, she peered down into the small dark crack and saw not a rock, but a tan ... something.

Curious, Leeda reached for a stick lying nearby and chipped away at whatever it was, sending tiny chunks of caked dirt and decayed leaf bits scattering onto the rock. After a few minutes, she could make out a very tiny ... plastic ... foot.

A few more jabs and two legs were clearly exposed. It looked like a miniature scene from *CSI*. Leeda leveraged the plastic leg just enough with the twig so she could reach it with the tips of her fingers and pull it out.

It was an old, ratty Barbie. She had long black hair and wore black clam diggers and a tank top. Her eyes were caked in mud and her hair was stringy and matted, but her outfit had a retro, urban flair, and she wore a devil-may-care Barbie smile.

Leeda smiled too. Poopie was always finding good omens. If there was such a thing, this certainly seemed like an excellent candidate. Maybe it was saying not to worry. After all, there was no one better equipped to look out for herself than her mother. Leeda knew it was a long shot, but she made a big fake smile back at the Barbie anyway and chose to believe it.

Then, in an un-Leeda-like move—considering the Barbie was dirty, muddy, and ancient—Leeda took it with her.

Seven

"*Excuse me, what time is it?*"

"*¿Perdón, a qué hora es?*" Birdie repeated in Spanish. She was listening to her Spanish lesson while loading most of the debris they'd cleared from the cave into the pickup truck, her iPod clipped to the waist of her baggy jeans. There had been no sign of bats, and she thought it was possible that the clutter was scaring them off. She craned her neck toward the house, hidden beyond the peach rows, looking for Poopie. She had done this several times, sure that she'd see her in her green rubber boots, stomping out of the peach rows toward her like the determined peanut she was, plunging in to help like she had promised she would about two hours ago.

Birdie sighed and looked over at her dogs. Honey Babe lay like Cleopatra against the wall of the barn, exposing her belly insouciantly. Majestic did the same thing, imitating her. Both papillons had their sweaters on. Birdie grinned at them and grabbed a rusted, heavy old rake, hauling it up into the truck bed with a grunt.

"*My clothes are dirty.*"

"*Mi ropa esta sucia,*" Birdie chimed, wiping an itch on her forehead with the inside of her elbow. Honey Babe looked over at her quizzically.

"*I have to wash my clothes.*"

"*Tengo que lavar mi ropa.*"

"*Your shirt is very pretty.*"

"Uhhh, *tu camisa es muy bonita.*"

"*How much do those pants cost?*"

Birdie thought, then blurted, "*¿Cuántos dólares son los pantalones?*"

The sky was getting dimmer, and Birdie couldn't see the sun. It was almost six.

"*This ends lesson six. Lesson seven . . .*"

Birdie pushed the pause button, letting her mind drift. She tried telling Enrico, in her mind, that his shirt was nice. She pictured him in his hallway in Mexico.

"*Tengo que lavar su ropa,*" the imaginary Birdie said. *I have to wash your clothes.*

Enrico looked slightly embarrassed and pulled off his shirt.

"*¿Puedo llevar tus pantalones también?*" Birdie pressed. *Can I take your pants also?*

Birdie felt her face flame up. Her eyes shot toward the house to check for Poopie.

Birdie grabbed the last rotted old wood scraps and an old tire and leveraged them on top of the other junk, then closed the truck bed door. She got in and drove back up the drive, parking just by the dorms. The dump would be closed now—she'd take everything tomorrow.

Sliding out, she decided to walk down to the pecan rows and

see how the leaves were changing there. Late October was one of Birdie's favorite times for the trees. As she walked, her thoughts drifted back to Enrico. A smile crept onto her face as she worked out the words for asking him to lie in her bed while he waited for his clothes to dry.

Suddenly Birdie's eyes lit on Methuselah. Murphy was right. There *was* something a little wrong with her. Her branches definitely sagged. And some of the roots, poking above the ground, looked shriveled and shrunken. She'd have to look in the books in her dad's office to find out what it was and how to treat it.

Birdie patted the tree affectionately as she moved past, then headed back to the house, her sweat cooling and making her shiver.

Inside, Birdie could hear Poopie's voice upstairs. Birdie's stomach growled.

She pulled off her jacket and kicked off her shoes and padded up the stairs to ask Poopie what was for dinner. Peering in, Birdie saw piles of photos strewn across the bed and a box, half packed full of letters and knickknacks. Birdie gazed at the items curiously, feeling like a voyeur. Poopie sat with her back turned, looking out the window, the phone cradled in one hand, the other hand resting on a little figure on her windowsill. It took Birdie a moment to recognize it as Saint Anthony. Poopie had him turned toward her as if he were being included in a conference call.

". . . seventeen years . . ." she was saying. Birdie stood next to the doorjamb, catching bits and pieces of Poopie's Spanish. She sounded serious, and Birdie hadn't meant to eavesdrop. She backed up, but just as she did, she heard the phone being laid in the cradle. So she came back, floating in the doorway for a moment.

"You okay, Poopie?"

Poopie jumped, then smiled at her over her shoulder. "Yes." She looked at the Saint Anthony in recognition, then looked embarrassed. "Oh, oh, sorry. I was just borrowing him." She handed him to Birdie.

"Thanks," Birdie said, confused. She was halfway down the hall when she remembered what she'd wanted to ask Poopie in the first place. She backtracked, and at the doorway, she froze.

This time, Poopie sat facing the window, her back shaking with silent tears. She sniffled and leaned over her lap, her hands on her forehead.

Birdie stood, unsure what to do. She had learned a thing or two growing up with her mom and dad. Sometimes pretending you didn't notice things made everyone's lives smoother—especially the people who were hurting. If anybody deserved a smooth life, it was Poopie. Birdie quietly crept to her room and closed the door. She put Saint Anthony on her dresser. She stared at him, the patron saint of going places, as if he could clue her in.

Where was Poopie going?

The next day Enrico and Birdie sat in silence on the phone. Birdie felt like she could listen to him breathe for hours. She could hear him doodling on his notebook—magnolia flowers, stars, peaches—drawings he would send to her in his next letter.

She picked at the stray threads on her *Hola* sweater. Since she'd told him she was coming, there was anticipation stretching across the line too. The idea of seeing him in Mexico had turned from something funny to talk about to something big and scary to get ready for. What if it wasn't like it had been this summer? What if there were spaces between them where their lives didn't meet up? What if Birdie didn't like it in such a strange place?

"She wouldn't look at me today," Birdie finally said, sitting in her bedroom's front window and staring out at the peach trees across the lawn. Poopie, with "so much to do," was standing in the grass, drinking a beer with a hand on her waist. The peach trees had fully changed color now—the leaves were as orange as tangerines with tiny specks of green clinging on. The crisscrossing rows looked like flames leaping up from the grass.

"Ask her, Birdie, what's wrong." Enrico had said it three times already.

"She'll tell me when she's ready. She tells me everything."

"Well, maybe with this you have to ask."

Birdie rubbed Honey Babe's ears distractedly.

"She said something about seventeen years," she offered, thinking out loud because she'd already told him this. "In Spanish." She thought of Saint Anthony. "Do you think she's going on some top secret trip?"

Enrico was quiet for a long while. Birdie wanted to curl up in the easy sound of his breath. She felt like she could almost reach out and touch him.

"Birdie, when do you think Poopie will retire?"

Birdie looked down at the phone cord, pinching it, a nervous prick in her stomach. *"Retire?"*

Enrico laughed gently. "She will want to retire sometime. She will want to go home sometime."

Home. Birdie swallowed. "This *is* home." Birdie realized how it sounded as soon as she said it. It sounded . . . egocentric. *Anglo*-centric. As if Poopie's whole life revolved around the Darlingtons. Enrico didn't call her on it, though. Of course, *home* was the town he and Poopie shared in Mexico. He didn't have to say.

"How long has she worked for you?" he asked softly.

"Since the year I was born," Birdie answered, picking at some fuzz on the *o* on her sweater.

"Seventeen years," Enrico said slowly, apologetically.

For a moment, Birdie stopped breathing. She stared out the window at Poopie, down on the grass, oblivious to being watched. Her mind spun with thoughts of what it meant if that were true, what it meant about the way Poopie saw things.

"We're not just . . . people she works for," Birdie said, suddenly on fire. Poopie had been there to pick her up, to give her advice, to tell her when she was off the mark, to set her straight. She'd been there to do that Birdie's whole life.

"She loves you. Of course she does."

Poopie wasn't a second mother. She was something else. If Birdie's life revolved around someone, it was Poopie. "She does," Birdie asserted. She felt sick. Poopie loved her. She was sure she did.

But maybe not like home. Maybe not like Birdie loved Poopie.

"Maybe it's not that, Birdie. It could be many other things," Enrico told her tenderly.

"Maybe," Birdie said softly, once again listening to the comforting silence of Enrico's breath.

When they finally said good-bye, Birdie stayed by her window.

The sun was setting earlier now, and the house's wide yard had an orange tint leading to the peach trees. Poopie had put down her beer and walked with a slow, aimless gait into the orchard. Like she was walking for the pure pleasure of walking, not like she was going to get something from the cider shed, or pick tomatoes for the salad, or get in her truck and drive to town. She wove back and forth between the peach trees, floating softly along the pale dirt that rolled out like red carpets between them. She reminded Birdie of some kind of blissed-out hippie.

Why hadn't she noticed before? Of course, Poopie was leaving. She had the look of someone who was already gone.

On Halloween morning, when Birdie Darlington was five years old, she decided to draw a portrait of Poopie on the pantry wall. Using a red crayon, she outlined Poopie's long skirt, her long black hair, her busy hands reaching out. It seemed like the perfect tribute, but when Birdie stood back to admire her work, she was shocked to see that what she had drawn wasn't Poopie at all, but the Virgin Mary. Terrified that she was witnessing a miracle, Birdie ran away and later blocked it from her mind completely.

Eight

"**Y**ou have to put it on thick for something like this," Lucretia said. "You're not just going to Homecoming. You're the Queen."

Leeda remembered this already. She remembered all the advice her mom gave her. Smile no matter what. Don't slump. Put the makeup on thick.

Birdie lay across Lucretia's bed like a dead fish, her head hanging over the edge as she studied the carpet and picked it apart with her fingers. Leeda's parents' bedroom had come straight off an Ethan Allen catalog page—headboard, side tables, bureau—all smooth, clean, matching, the whole bed so fluffed it nearly swallowed Birdie up. On her mom's side was a Patricia Cornwell novel. On her dad's was a biography of John Adams. Leeda wondered vaguely if her parents ever talked when they were sitting here, fluffed up on all their pillows. She could feel her mom's gentle breathing on her face as Lucretia worked and her own breath falling in line with her mother's. The gentle, synchronized rhythm made her sleepy, like a kitten.

"I'll call her," Leeda said. "Just give me the phone and I'll call her."

Birdie continued to pick at the floor. "Maybe she's not ready to tell me."

"But you already know," Leeda told her. All day, Birdie had been wilted like a dying flower. She'd come to help Leeda get ready for the homecoming Halloween football game since Murphy was supposedly finishing her NYU application.

"Well, even if Poopie goes, you can still keep in touch. You can still call her." Leeda tried to sound even, unconcerned. Only because she hoped the evenness might rub off on Birdie. The truth was, she wasn't sure Birdie could survive without Poopie. Leeda couldn't imagine Birdie in that big farmhouse with just her dad.

"And then you guys will leave too." Birdie patted her hands on the carpet, frustrated. "And then I'm only gonna have peaches to talk to."

"You won't only have peaches to talk to," Leeda said evenly. A prick in her eyebrow pulled her attention back to her mom, who was holding a pair of tweezers and wrapped up in concentration. Leeda sighed, content. She couldn't help basking in the intimacy of having her makeup done. Leeda toyed with the idea of asking her mom how she was feeling but decided against it. She *looked* okay. These days, it always made Leeda feel a little better just to *see* her.

"There," Lucretia said, turning her toward the mirror. Leeda studied herself. She hadn't changed into her gown yet, and the makeup looked funny with her jeans and sweater. But her mom was beaming. So she guessed she looked good. She guessed if her mom looked that happy, the whole thing was worth it.

"Have you practiced your wave?" Birdie asked, pulling

herself up on the bed and brightening a little or at least making an effort. Leeda waved at her, mock graceful.

Birdie laughed valiantly. She climbed off the bed and gave her a big hug. "Ah, Lee. I love you. I gotta pee."

She left Leeda standing with her mom, and Leeda felt sort of awkward about the love. She wondered how long it had been since her mom had told her she loved her or vice versa. Some people made it look so easy.

Halloween night was unseasonably cold. There was a harvest moon, huge and orange, rising behind the football field. The green grass rose stiffly under Leeda's high-heeled shoes, which dug into the mud. The whole ceremony was slightly pagan: Leeda stood in the middle and her royal court—her friend Dina Marie and another girl—flanked her sides in varicolored dresses, like demigoddesses. Leeda fiddled with her swan pendant, watching the bleachers warily, worried about Murphy and her mom being alone together. Murphy had saved Leeda and her mom seats on the bleachers. She found them side by side in the fourth row up, looking like they were ignoring each other. Leeda breathed a sigh of relief, but then she saw an odd sight—Murphy handing her mom a thermos. It was probably poisoned.

The ceremony went on and on. Leeda smiled and waved and received some flowers. The Pecan Queen always doubled as the Homecoming Queen.

Finally, after half an hour of standing in the cold, Leeda was released and made her way into the bleachers, where different people touched and congratulated her. She moved between

Murphy and her mom, shivering. Murphy handed her a warm blue thermos and snuggled up to her.

Leeda took a sip from the thermos. It was hot apple cider. Her mom was drinking out of a red one. She hadn't keeled over yet.

The Bridgewater High School football team was dismal, but Lucretia insisted it would be bad manners to show up for the game and then leave. She knew everyone in the stands and waved and winked and smiled to people like an actress at the Oscars. She had bustled around the bandstand beforehand, making sure the band was going to play the right music. She'd replaced the tiara they were using with Grandmom Eugenie's. She'd managed to bend everyone to her will easily, wearing a genteel smile all the while.

Leeda scanned the bleachers. Judge Miller Abbott and his son sat nearby with a group of guys from school behind them. Dina Marie scooted to the end of their row to sit next to the guys. Every time Dina laughed her flirty laugh, Leeda could see Murphy wince and roll her eyes. The boys shot glances over at them repeatedly. Boys always stared at Leeda, but they stared at Murphy harder because Leeda looked fine like china, but Murphy looked like the world's most decadent banana split. Boys were scared of both of them. Scared of Leeda because she looked too cool to touch and scared of Murphy because they were afraid she might bite them.

Rex was sitting in the bleachers way up behind them next to some guys from work.

"Why isn't Rex sitting with us?" Leeda asked.

Murphy looked over her shoulder. "I don't know. I told

him I'd catch up with him after the game." She didn't look Leeda in the eye as she said it.

"Oh, Murphy, you're so cold," Leeda told her.

Murphy looked at her like she was an idiot. "Why?"

"Because you want him to miss you." Murphy always surprised Leeda with how cruel she could be.

"Well, Thanksgiving is less than a month away, and I just think maybe he needs a little reminder. . . ." Murphy balled up her fists and then released them. "So he can remember why he has to come with me."

Leeda looked back at Rex. The way he kept glancing over at them made Leeda's chest ache a little. "Murphy, take it easy on him."

Murphy twirled her hair like she hadn't heard her. Leeda looked back again, pinchy. He had never looked like that for Leeda. She ran her hands up and down her goose-bumpy arms.

"So Bird's moping, huh?" Murphy asked.

Leeda nodded. Earlier that evening, while she zipped Leeda into her strapless dress, Birdie asked for the ten-thousandth time if it was really okay if she didn't go to the football game. She'd headed home instead, dragging her red Crocs along the hall carpet as she shuffled out of the house.

"Here, darlin'." Lucretia pulled off her heavy cashmere coat and wrapped it around Leeda. "You have such thin little arms," she said, taking Leeda's wrist and waggling it, then tucking it back under the coat. "Small people get cold faster. I'm the same way." Lucretia wrapped her arms across her black cashmere turtleneck and shivered. Leeda gave her a mystified glance. Normally Lucretia wouldn't throw a life preserver to a drowning man.

Bridgewater scored a touchdown. Everyone cheered and the band launched into an off-key rendition of "We Will Rock You."

Judge Abbott leaned forward over Murphy's shoulder. He had hair going white at the temples, an ample stomach, big glasses, and a square jaw. "How's your mom, Murphy?"

"Fine." Murphy cracked her gum.

"Where you headed after graduation?"

Murphy rested her chin on her hand, looking bored. "Anywhere but here."

Judge Abbott laughed. "Well, don't sugarcoat it," he said, patting her on the back. He was one of the few authority figures in town—maybe the only one—who actually liked Murphy. He always seemed amused by her and a little protective. "What about you, Leeda?"

Lucretia answered for her, twisting the top onto her thermos. "Leeda applied early decision to Columbia last week. Her aunt invited her to spend the summer in San Francisco. She has a lot of decisions to make."

Leeda knew she was expected to add something but didn't. She'd sent her application in without much fanfare, but spending the summer in San Francisco was not an option. Now that she'd spent a summer on the orchard, it was out of the question that she'd miss a summer there. She just hadn't bothered telling her mom that. It would just stress her out, and maybe she didn't need stress. Her mom hated the orchard. It was too unruly.

"But she could do anything. Go anywhere," Murphy said, then cracked her gum again.

Leeda looked at her mom, hoping she wouldn't take Murphy's

bait. But Lucretia was on to another topic—the hotel the Cawley-Smiths owned.

"You know, Miller, I haven't seen your wife in our spa in quite a while. Tell her to come in for her next treatment on us." She looked at Murphy, whose crazy brown hair leapt out of her cheap wool hat like snakes in a trick can of nuts. Then she winked at Judge Abbott as if they were in on some private joke. "Murphy, you should come in for a cut before your interviews start."

Murphy squinted at Lucretia with exaggerated concern. "Do they do waxing? It looks like your mustache is growing back." Lucretia's face went icy, and she looked at Leeda. Leeda gave Murphy a look to lay off. Then her mom turned around and took another sip of her hot cider.

A few minutes later, the crowd did the wave. When it got to them, Murphy reached over Leeda, took Lucretia's hand, and lifted it. Leeda shot her a look, but she shrugged innocently. The next time the wave came around, Murphy did the same thing. Lucretia actually went along happily. The next wave, when Lucretia started waggling her arms in the air on her own, Leeda began to get uneasy.

"You spiked her cider, didn't you?" Leeda muttered.

Murphy just nodded and kept her eyes on the game.

As the game crept into the third quarter, Leeda had to admit that her mom became a lot more fun. Murphy had convinced Lucretia that every time the ball went into the end zone, she should yell, "Poot!" Lucretia complied happily. She waggled her long, thin arms in the air and wiggled her hips, yelling, "Poot!" and then looked around like the class clown, hoping she'd gotten a rise out of someone.

"Lucretia," Murphy said, like she was talking to a patient at a mental hospital. "At the end of the game, everybody's gonna rush the field. Are you in?"

"Murphy, she's not a puppet," Leeda hissed, trying not to laugh.

"She's having fun."

"I'm having fun," Lucretia purred, pulling Leeda's arm out from under the coat again and holding it softly, friend-like. Leeda didn't hold back, didn't move her arm an inch. She let it rest there.

"That's because Murphy spiked your cider, Mom," she finally said.

"Oh, I know." Lucretia opened her eyes for emphasis, then laughed, leaning in and across Leeda's lap to look at Murphy. "Do I look like I was born yeeserday?"

"Oh God, she's slurring," Leeda said.

"I'm not an *alien*." Lucretia held up one finger toward the sky to indicate outer space. "I'm not *all* boring." Her perfect chignon had gone slightly akimbo. A few tendrils snaked around her ears.

"I thought you were," Murphy said. "But you're pretty funny."

Leeda, half amused, half nervous, tried to make more room between her mom and Murphy. Lucretia kept turning around to tell the people behind them that her daughter was the Pecan Queen and wasn't she pretty. She said Leeda was going to Columbia next fall and a whole bunch of things she'd just made up, like that Leeda had been Little Miss Kings County and that she had been approached to be a model.

At the end of the game, Lucretia linked her arm through Leeda's as they walked to the car. To her left, Leeda heard a squeal and turned to see Murphy being swept up over Rex's shoulder.

"I'm taking this peanut with me," he said to Leeda casually, his arm hooked gently around Murphy's thighs, her upper half disappearing over his shoulder. "That okay? You need help getting your mom home?"

"No thanks." As they walked away, Leeda gave Murphy the thumbs-up. Murphy rolled her eyes.

They didn't make it as far as Lucretia's room. Lucretia grabbed the frame of Leeda's bedroom door as they walked past and flopped inside onto Leeda's bed. "I'm fine here," she said.

"But it's only eight thirty, and I need my room. . . ." Leeda stood for a moment, looking at Lucretia stretched out on top of her white comforter. *Fine.* She sat on the very edge of the bed and patted her mom's shoe awkwardly. "You want some water or anything, Mom?" It hadn't occurred to her until that moment that maybe it wasn't good for her mom to drink.

"No thanks, honey." Lucretia flopped her head over to look at Leeda, who was about to go. "I guess I'll never understand how you pick your friends," Lucretia mumbled, sounding more like the mom she knew. "By the time you get to be my age, you'll understand better about girlfriends."

"Murphy's good for me." Leeda sighed, unsurprised. "Maybe you never had the right friends."

"What about Rex?"

Leeda felt the words like a nasty pinch. She believed Rex and Murphy belonged together. She did. But it still hurt sometimes.

And she hated that her mom could use it against her and that Murphy and Rex had given her the ammunition.

"I'm sorry." Lucretia exhaled, shocking Leeda. The phrase wasn't in her mom's vocabulary. It *had* to be the cider talking. "Maybe I just don't think anyone's good enough to deserve you." Leeda couldn't tell if it was her mom's pitch-perfect flattery or if she really meant it.

Then her eyes widened. "What's *that*?" Lucretia asked, thrusting a finger toward Leeda's desk, where the Barbie she'd found sat, washed and clean.

"The Barbie? I found it."

"Where?"

Leeda shrugged. "At the orchard. Near the lake."

"Did you find it in a rock?"

Leeda did a double take, from her mom to the Barbie and back. "Yeah?"

Lucretia laughed. "That's *my* Barbie!"

"What do you mean?"

Lucretia only shook her head. "I can't believe it. I lost it a million years ago. That is just amazing."

Leeda looked at the Barbie again. Now it didn't look like a good omen. It looked . . . eerie.

"Can I have it?"

Leeda felt hurt. *She'd* found it. "Um, maybe?"

Lucretia, surprisingly, seemed okay with that.

"Well, good night, Mom."

But her mom didn't reply. She was looking at the mirror on the back of the door, reflecting both of them—Lucretia in the bed and Leeda in her long ice-blue homecoming dress.

"Do you know you and I have exactly the same shoulders? That's why I wanted you to wear this dress. It shows them off."

Leeda looked behind her at the mirror. She'd never noticed—she did have her mom's shoulders—straight as a ledge across, with the tiny bird-like clavicle bone protruding softly and perfectly on each side.

"They broke the mold when they made our shoulders."

Just in case, Leeda got a glass of water from the kitchen. She saw some trick-or-treaters from the window, a fairy and a ghoul grabbing handfuls of candy from the basket on the porch.

When she went back upstairs, she watched her mom for a moment, sleeping, her pale arm thrown over her forehead, looking so human. For the first time in a long time, Leeda saw her mom the way she had when she was a kid—like the most beautiful, elusive creature on earth.

Leeda put the glass on the nightstand. She took the Barbie off the dresser and laid it beside Lucretia on the bed.

Nine

Outside Kuntry Kitchen, the trick-or-treaters were popping into every door like gophers. Murphy slid out of the passenger side of Rex's truck and eyed a witch and a spider scurrying past her.

Rex's arms came around her, wrapping her up tight. He pressed against her back and kissed her on the neck, walking her forward a few steps.

"You take me to all the nice places," she said, seeing where they were moving. Sometimes when Rex hugged her, she felt the need to squirm away just so he'd know he didn't have her so much. But she let him walk her up to the door and open it for her. When Murphy saw who was sitting in the first booth on the left, she instinctively stepped back. Rex's dad stood up and smiled. Rex nudged her from behind, and she practically tripped forward again.

"Great to finally meet you, Murphy." Mr. Taggart reached out for Murphy's hand. Murphy glanced down at her tight, low-cut sweater self-consciously. She shot a death glare at Rex. He smiled back at her. His look said, *Rex 1, Murphy 0.*

"Hi, uh, Mr. Taggart," she said, taking the hand he offered.

Just across the aisle, the cooks bustled behind the counter to the sounds of sizzling grease. Kuntry Kitchen was a hole-in-the-wall with five booths back to back, a six-item fried food menu, and a little alcove where a bluegrass band played on Friday nights. They had the worst dinner in Bridgewater, but the banjo picker was the third-best in Georgia, and the place was packed to hear him every week. She hated to admit it, but Murphy actually loved the whole scene.

They all slid into the booth, awkwardly quiet, Mr. Taggart wearing a tentative smile. They watched as a couple of people squeezed by them and made their way to the booths in the back. The band launched into their first number.

"So, Murphy, Rex talks blue streaks about you," Mr. Taggart finally said.

Murphy threw a glance at Rex, intent on looking careless as the band kicked along a rolling rendition of a number called "Butter Beans." Some of the patrons sang along. "I didn't know Rex talked blue streaks about anything."

"Your mom's Jodee, right?"

Murphy nodded.

"She came in last week looking for a garden hose. She's a nice woman."

"Thanks." Murphy melted slightly. Usually if people were trying to be polite, they didn't mention Murphy's mom at all. She kept her eyes on the banjo picker, his fingers moving up and down the frets like wildfire.

They ordered: fries for Murphy, a grilled cheese for Rex, a burger for his dad. Mr. Taggart had an almost feminine way of looking at his son. Glowing and affectionate. He had the humble, open look of someone who liked people, who always let others go first in line, and who had very little to hide. People with nothing to hide always made Murphy nervous. She always felt like her own ribs hid a glistening and secret black heart. But Mr. Taggart looked so awkward and kind that Murphy felt she should say something. She knew Mr. Taggart worked at Ace Hardware. "Do you know a lot about tools?" she finally asked. She could have kicked herself for sounding like such an idiot.

"I'm a little handy," Mr. Taggart replied in the totally gracious way that made Murphy suspect he was more than a little handy. "But I know more about cooking. I keep telling Rex he needs to bring you home for dinner." The smile Mr. Taggart gave her was direct and hopeful. "Has Rex told you he's a bit of a cook too?"

Murphy shook her head. "He hasn't mentioned that."

Mr. Taggart swallowed. He looked slightly afraid of her, like he wanted her to like him or something. It took Murphy by surprise.

"Don't be fooled—he's not modest," Mr. Taggart told her, scratching his chin. "He just lets other people do the bragging for him. Looks better that way."

Murphy glanced at Rex, who leaned back, relaxed.

"Girls eat it up," Rex said with a crooked smile.

Two booths beyond them, Murphy noticed Maribeth McMurtry, a lunatic-fringe evangelical woman of hulking proportions, sitting with a couple of friends eating country-fried steak. On Sundays after church, Maribeth stood downtown giving out freaky flyers on how the unsaved could survive

Armageddon by chopping off their own heads. Birdie had taken one of the flyers once when she and Murphy were getting slushees. She had looked like she might pass out when she saw the illustrations. Even gentle Father Michael at Divine Grace of the Redeemer had tried to talk Maribeth into toning it down a bit. Now Maribeth's godly brown eyes drifted up to Murphy's and narrowed. Murphy's gut did a little thud.

The thing about Maribeth McMurtry was that Murphy had made out with her much-younger husband last year after streaking the Easter Revival, when she didn't know he was anybody's husband. She had simply thought it would be a funny story to French-kiss a guy named Patsy. Afterward Patsy had told her she would make a great clerk at the Outreach Center after she graduated from high school. The whole thing had been a mistake. But one she'd assumed only she and Patsy knew about.

But now Maribeth kept looking in her direction and then muttering to her friends, who turned around to look too. Murphy tried not to be nervous.

"I hear Kuntry Kitchen's hiring," Murphy quipped, turning her attention back to Rex. "You could meet all the girls you wanted."

"Ha," Mr. Taggart laughed. "I bet you keep him on his toes, Murphy." He gave her a Southern-gentlemanly wink.

Rex put his hand on Murphy's back and scratched gently. Mr. Taggart sank back in his booth, turning to the band and tapping his feet to the music, obviously content.

It hit Murphy like a hammer. Rex's dad didn't hate her. And she didn't hate him. In fact, it startled her how much she liked him.

Once their meals came, Murphy and Rex occupied themselves kicking each other's feet under the table and laughing at his dad's jokes. Every time he got to a funny bit, his eyes swept Murphy, making sure to include her. Murphy sat against the wall, inches from Rex, letting him hold her hand and feeling squirmy.

"I hope you'll come down to Destin with us sometime," Mr. Taggart said. "We go every summer."

Murphy thought about how she'd be gone by summer, but she didn't want to say so. "That sounds great," she answered, because it did.

The music went on for a little over an hour, every minute of which Murphy enjoyed thoroughly. She felt the weight of the intimidation she'd been feeling lifting off her shoulders. Finally the waitress placed their check on the linoleum table. Murphy fished in her pockets.

"Don't be crazy, now," Mr. Taggart said, grabbing the check. Murphy grinned sheepishly and sat back, noticing Maribeth and her friends walking up the aisle. Murphy looked in the other direction, pretending not to see them.

"Hussy," Maribeth hissed as she walked by, loud enough for everyone near them to hear.

Rex looked at Murphy. Murphy looked at the fry counter, her shoulders going tight. If he and his dad hadn't been there, she would have danced around yelling, "I'll swallow your soul." She would have said something about what a saliva-y kisser Patsy was. She would have done *something*. But instead she looked down at her lap, trying to keep her hands from shaking.

Mr. Taggart sipped at his water as if nothing had happened and valiantly took a bite of his last remaining fry.

After Rex's dad had left, they stood on the sidewalk outside. She felt like she should say something.

"You okay, Shorts?" Rex asked, gently tilting her face up to look at him.

She looked at him, looked away, looked at him again. "I wasn't thinking. I used to not think." There had been a lot of things Murphy used to do and not do. She wanted to be born again, but not in a Christian way. It wasn't that she thought she had done anything wrong. She just didn't think all the things she'd done said anything about who she really was. Even if everyone else in Bridgewater disagreed with that. "I'm innocent," she said, hoping to sum it all up and feeling like she never could.

Rex pulled her to him by the belt loops of her baggy jeans. "I know who you are, Murphy." He kissed her lips and tugged at her curly hair. He gave her the naked look again, the in-love-with-her look.

Murphy wanted to tell him she loved him for that. And Rex seemed to be waiting for it. For some sign of love. For her to say the words. But saying she loved him would be like throwing in a good hand. No more pairs, no flush, no full house.

"I couldn't take anyone who uses the word *hussy* seriously anyway."

Murphy pasted her mouth into an amused grin and looked away.

"I mean, unless I lived in the 1890s," he added. "I mean, maybe *trollop*, but not *hussy*."

"*Trollop*'s a much better outdated word," Murphy agreed.

He stared at her, turning serious. "My dad likes you."

Murphy gave a hardened, one-note laugh, as if she didn't believe it. But she did, and it scared her somehow. A kid in a ghoul mask bumped into her and kept walking. Rex stuck his hands in his pockets.

"When I leave Bridgewater . . ." Murphy stumbled over the words. "I won't be this . . . me . . . anymore. I'll be something bigger."

"Like when a hermit crab moves into a new shell." He kissed her cheek. "I get it, Murphy. You don't have to say."

Anthill Acres Trailer Park looked especially underwhelming as Murphy shuffled up the dirt walkway toward her house. It was nearly ten o'clock, but only the kitchen light was on inside. Outside the trailer, the remains of Yellowbaby, Murphy's dead car, sat cold and unused. The parking lot, and the trailer in general, were an accumulation of too many things that no one had taken the time to throw away. That was how Murphy felt about life in Bridgewater. It was an accumulation of junk she couldn't wait to leave behind. She grabbed the mail out of the black box on her way inside.

"Hey, Mom." She nodded to Jodee, sitting at the table, and Jodee, mouth full, waved back.

Murphy sorted through the mail and tossed all the junk stuff in the recycling bag. Mail at the McGowens' was usually even steven between junk ads and bills. Once every two weeks, there was a paycheck for Jodee. It always seemed unfair that her mom got so many more bills than checks.

Spread out on the table, where they'd been for weeks, were the various brochures for colleges they'd received in the mail over the course of the summer and early fall. Jodee had organized them there, in the middle of the kitchen, in an obvious attempt to hypnotize Murphy into applying to schools closer to home. All the in-state schools were on top like a silent accusation—there were so many perfectly good schools in Georgia.

Jodee hadn't bothered to change out of her work clothes: a knee-length skirt she'd gotten at Village Thrift and a white polyester blouse. Murphy watched her mom and compared her to Leeda's. Jodee had lines in her face and glossy lipstick and long, wild, pretty hair. Outside of work, she dressed too sexy for anyone's comfort except maybe lechy guys. She'd never told Murphy not to drink, or set a curfew for her, or warned her to work hard at school. And she had always tried to look about ten years younger than she was. She had said, more than once, that Murphy's dad had left her—when Murphy was a baby—because she was getting too old. But as Murphy had grown up, she'd decided that was probably something her mom said to sound like she knew how they'd ended up just the two of them. Sometimes she had wondered if her mom even knew who Murphy's dad was.

"How was work?" Murphy mumbled.

Jodee smiled. "It was good, honey. I got in trouble for yapping too much with the women from accounts payable. But . . ." Jodee shrugged. "My boss is a nice guy."

Murphy's mom, no matter how bone tired she looked, always had something nice to say about her job at Ganax Heating. She loved the other women who worked there. She loved that after she sorted the mail, she had lots of downtime. She was always trying to get Murphy to apply for a part-time job there. The thought had crossed Murphy's mind, more than once, that she'd rather have her eyeballs punctured than work at Ganax.

"You got your applications finished?"

"Applica*tion*, for NYU." Murphy sat down on the plasticky bench seat behind the table. "Singular. I have to send it tomorrow." She felt like she couldn't state her intentions to her mom enough.

Jodee's face expressed concern. "You're only applying to one school?"

Murphy nodded and leaned forward to turn on the kitchen TV.

"Murphy, that's just foolish."

"It's only early applications, Mom," she explained. "Anyway, I'll get in."

Jodee looked at her like she wanted to say more. Murphy didn't see that there was anything more to say. She had a deep, primal aversion to applying anywhere except exactly where she wanted to be. To go to New York without going to NYU would be like doing things halfway. No other school was part of the picture she'd been holding on to forever. "Do you know Leeda's mom has this glass egg that Leeda said cost four thousand dollars?" Murphy had always been good at changing the subject.

"Hmm." Jodee nodded.

In her mind, Murphy calculated that her mom would have to work at Ganax for over five hundred hours to buy the Cawley-Smiths' glass egg.

"How's Rex?" Jodee asked.

"He's Rex." It rankled Murphy sometimes that Jodee was so enthused about her boyfriend. It amounted to some kind of pressure. And she was sure Jodee would like nothing better than for her to stay in Bridgewater and settle down. She felt the question always circling the back of her mom's mind: *Isn't love enough?*

After watching TV for a while, Jodee leaned her head back in her seat and dozed off, and Murphy shuffled into her room to go over her application one last time. On the far wall that came within an inch of butting against the foot of her bed—her room was more of a cubby than a room—hung a bunch of pages she'd ripped out of a magazine once. They were all black-and-white pictures of New York. One aerial photo of the whole city. One of a puddle on a New York sidewalk with a building's reflection in it. Another of a man sitting outside a shop in Chinatown. Murphy took a deep breath and looked at her application.

Murphy Jane McGowen.

Age?

17.

She read the two lines over to make sure there were no typos. Nervous excitement coursed through her.

She hadn't said it right to Rex. To her, New York wasn't just leaving behind what she didn't want to be. It was the chance to have everything that she could never have.

It was her glass egg.

Ten

"**Y**ou ready?"

"Yes, Bird."

"You sure?"

"Yes, Birdie."

The morning after homecoming, Birdie stood next to the blue post office box on the wide, empty street outside the Bridgewater post office, her brown eyes twinkling, her soft cheeks flushed. She held Murphy's large white NYU application envelope an inch into the slot.

Thwuff. Birdie pushed the envelope all the way in and let it go, listening intently as it landed with a muffled rustle. Then she shimmied around the box, kicking her legs out like an elf. She circled it not once but three times.

"What are you doing, Birdie?" Rex had his arm slung around Murphy's neck.

Birdie paused, giving them a "duh" face. "Good luck dance. This is for early admittance. . . ." She did a knee-toe kick all around the box. "And this one's for getting the moolah . . ." she said, doing the shimmy.

"Wow, I didn't know you were the financial aid fairy too."

"Money, money, money," Birdie sang, rocking back and forth.

"You're lucky community college is cheap," Murphy said.

Birdie stopped dancing, looking slightly deflated.

"What do you want to do now?" Rex asked.

"Vomit." To have her application out of her hands was both a relief and a new stress. Now, over the next several weeks, she'd have to wonder where it was, who was reading it, what they thought. She envied Leeda, who'd turned in her early application to Columbia a week ago. Which was typical.

Birdie turned worried. "Are you okay, Smurphy?"

"Murphy Jane does not enjoy handing the controls to someone else," Rex said, yanking Murphy's hand to kiss her on the knuckle. He'd seen her middle name on her application this morning. She could kick herself for leaving it lying around.

"All the name-calling is killing me," Murphy said flatly.

"Are you gonna take good care of her in the big city, Rex?" Birdie asked innocently. Murphy rolled her eyes, but then she looked at Rex, a little breathless.

He smiled at her, easy. "If she's lucky and she prays real hard."

Murphy grinned at him dryly, but inside, she bucked. More and more, she wanted to hear he was coming with her. "Luck's my middle name," she said cavalierly.

Rex laughed. "Okay, M.J."

Murphy heaved a dramatic growl, ignoring him. "Let's go get Leeda and celebrate."

Murphy summoned her inner frigid diva, pretended to be Lucretia, and called Leeda out of school, which she herself was already skipping. Leeda appeared in the school parking lot in pink, her blond hair wild and soft, reminding her friends all over again she was, without a doubt, the most beautiful girl in Bridgewater.

Minutes later, they were stacked in Birdie's truck heading down Route 75. Birdie crept along in the right lane, staying at exactly the speed limit. From the passenger seat, Murphy watched car after car pass them. "Bird, if you drive any slower Miss Daisy is going to catch up with us."

The trees at Mertie Creek drooped over the bar in smooth arches of orange leaves. Rex went in and got them a pitcher of beer. Behind the bar the girls pulled the rough-hewn benches around the fire pit. They *cheers*'ed Murphy and her application. The trees had started to lose their leaves, and the creek was visible now, snaking behind the bar. Murphy and Leeda flung old bottle caps they dug out of the gravel at each other, trying to make it between the other's hands. Birdie curled over her civics textbook, which she'd had behind her seat in the truck.

"Hey, Bird, is Laurens Community College really that rigorous?" Murphy prodded her.

Birdie looked wounded for a moment. "I've just been really busy with work at home."

Murphy squinted at Leeda's fingers, gauging the distance. Leeda wiggled her thumbs mockingly. "Poopie jobs?"

Birdie shrugged.

Every time Murphy called Birdie, she was washing the curtains or scrubbing the windows or waxing the floor: all stuff Poopie would have normally done. She'd spread green manure among the new peach plantings and laid out new fruit for the bats.

"Maybe Poopie thinks now that you're all grown, you don't need her anymore," Leeda offered. "Just tell her you still need her."

Birdie had her chin in her hands. "The bats still haven't come to roost. I even thought I'd put Poopie's Saint Jude out by the hole, but I can't find him. I've tried everything else."

"Maybe you should dress up like Count Chocula," Murphy said.

"I'm supposed to do a ribbon cutting at the nature preserve where all those bats are," Leeda said.

Birdie looked distraught.

"Good one, Lee." Murphy leaned back. "That's like pouring lemon juice in her wounds."

"I kind of like cutting the ribbons." Leeda scowled at Murphy's disgusted look. "*What.* I'm having ... a good time."

"Blah."

"I'm telling you." Leeda fiddled with her nails, smoothed out the pleats in her knee-length Burberry skirt. "My mom's ... into me or something. Maybe now that I'm leaving. Or that she's sick. Or something. She calls me, like, three times a day. She's not so bad right now."

"Not bad relative to Satan?" Murphy quipped. Birdie snorted, covering her mouth. And then she stopped laughing immediately and looked around as if lightning might strike her. She always got a little wigged at the word *Satan.*

Leeda went stick straight and closed her lips tight. But Murphy couldn't help it. She had seen the million ways Lucretia had broken Leeda's heart. It showed in little things Leeda did, like how she spent so much time on her hair or how she went all stiff when everyone around her was relaxing. In Murphy's opinion, it showed in all the ways Leeda didn't know how to just *be*.

Murphy looked over at Birdie, who was staring up at the sky with her mouth half open, blinking like an idiot. "Counting peaches, Bird?"

Birdie blushed. "No." She leaned in, elbows on the table, and held her hair in bunches on top of her head, like mouse ears. Then she flung herself forward dramatically, turning to look up at Rex sheepishly from where she lay. "I'm dying," she murmured.

"Here we go," Leeda said.

"He's just so . . . just . . . a . . ."

"He's a *café con leche* love biscuit," Murphy said. They all knew Birdie was talking about Enrico by the stupid goofy look on her face. Rex let out a short choppy laugh.

But Birdie just sank deeper against the table. "You know what? I even like the letter E better now," she said despondently. "I always thought it was a boring letter. You know, not like X or Q. I can't believe I'm going to see him in fifty-four days."

Murphy slumped against Rex, pretending to be passing out. Birdie let her arms flail forward in obvious capitulation to patheticness.

At four, music started playing from the speakers under the eaves. Rex pulled Leeda up to dance, singing the words to some cheesy song to make her laugh. Murphy lay back and watched them, content. Rex kept stealing glances at her over Leeda's shoulder.

And then she felt it. An ache. It was like it fell out of the sky and landed square on top of her. She wanted to know so badly what was going to happen. It hurt how much she needed him. She swallowed and touched the hollow of her throat.

Birdie sat up and rubbed her eyes.

"If Enrico wants to go to second base, do you think I should?"

"Second base?" Murphy laughed. "Birdie, what are you, from the fifties?"

Birdie bit her lip thoughtfully and shrugged, doe-eyed as usual, her hair in silky tangles from where she'd been pulling on it. Murphy shook her head wonderingly. "Second base," she muttered, and took another sip of beer.

"I told Poopie I'd cook Thanksgiving dinner."

"That's frightening," Murphy replied. Birdie was a notoriously bad cook. Her mind drifted off too much. She forgot things until they started smoking.

"I think I'm going to name my first child Myrtle so I can call her Mertie for short," Birdie said.

Leeda plopped down beside her. "Drat, you beat me to it." Rex sat down beside Murphy and pulled her close to him.

"I'm sure Stepford Mom already has names picked out for *all* your kids," Murphy joked.

Birdie snorted. Leeda just ignored her.

The day felt like heaven on earth. The sun kept peeping at them through the passing clouds, and to Murphy it felt like kisses from angels, though she would never have admitted it.

"Birdie, your heer, it ees so scruffy, but I loooove it," Leeda said in a thick Enrico accent, brushing her fingers through Birdie's hair to smooth it out. She began to braid it and Birdie leaned back against her.

There was a long easy silence, and Murphy tried to think of something fun to talk about. "Thunderstorms, cool or scary?"

"Cool," Birdie answered.

"Cool," Leeda agreed.

"Cool because they're scary," Rex said.

Murphy picked wood splinters off the table, nodding. "Favorite three things about yourself." Everyone was silent. "I'll start." Murphy chewed on a thumbnail glibly. "My curvylicious-ness, my taste in music, and how dang funny I am. Bird?"

Bird rubbed her lips, thinking. "The orchard. Me as a kid. Mmm, my hair."

Leeda kept braiding. "I'll take a skip," she said.

"There's no skipping. Except for boys because they're not so interesting." She pinched Rex. Leeda stared over Birdie's shoulder blankly. She seemed to really be thinking.

When several seconds went by without a response, Rex took over, asking if Birdie really wanted to know what all the bases meant. Then he explained them in the gentlest terms imagina-ble. She listened with half her head tucked into the collar of her shirt, squinting in embarrassment, the visible tops of her cheeks red. Murphy kept her eyes on Leeda, who seemed to be some-where else.

The afternoon wore on into dusk, and the temperature started to drop. Leeda wrapped half her cardigan around her and the other half around Birdie as they sipped cold beers. Rex kept his hand on Murphy's knee under the table. She could feel the warmth of his palm through her jeans. Murphy set her hand on top of his.

By the time they dragged themselves away, the parking lot

was draped in dusk. Wind blew leaves across the back road. On the highway, Leeda fell asleep against Murphy's shoulder, and Birdie turned the heat on full blast, though most of it escaped through the cracks in the old truck's dried-out window seals.

At Anthill Acres, Murphy waved to the girls as Birdie pulled out, and she and Rex crunched up the gravel to the stairs of her trailer.

She crossed her arms and looked back at her door.

"Look." Rex blew into the air. "First mist."

Murphy watched the mist rise up and disappear. "Nice," she said, rolling forward and backward on her feet and rubbing her arms. He stood looking up at her from under his eyebrows for a while.

Every time they were alone together, the same question came to Murphy's lips. She rocked back and forth on her feet, fighting with herself about whether or not to ask if he'd reached any decisions yet.

"I think you should say it," he said, taking her by surprise.

"Say what?" Murphy asked. She immediately knew. And it made her go hot and cold inside. She gave him her best innocent, ignorant look.

Rex shrugged. "You tell me."

"Tell you what?" Murphy grinned, nervous, palms sweaty. She tried to think it to him through telepathy. That should be enough.

He swallowed. Looked embarrassed. "I need to hear it, Murphy."

Murphy's eyes sank away from his face toward the gravel.

"Good night?" she asked, turning it into a joke. "Don't let the bedbugs bite?"

Rex looked at her a minute longer, straight, the way she could never really look at him. He kissed her at the corner of her lips. Then, before she could think of anything halfway decent to mumble to stop him, he got into his truck and pulled out. Murphy watched him as he disappeared behind the trees. The ease with which he left made her breathless.

Maybe he didn't understand, but *that* was why she couldn't say it. Because she loved him, but also because she couldn't pin him to her. Because he was too big and true to be sure of.

Georgia winter always teased its way in. On November fifteenth Judge Miller Abbott played his last eighteen holes of the season at the Balmeade Country Club in summer-like weather. He was shooting well until, on a putt at the ninth hole, his ball was knocked off course when it ran into—of all things—a peach pit. The nearest peach tree was three hundred yards away.

That night, a cold breeze swept into Bridgewater. The leaves went fluttering like butterflies, and Judge Abbott began to have what he later called "the orchard dreams."

Every night far into the following year, he dreamed of Jodee McGowen reclining nude by Smoaky Lake, like she was Eve lying in a cluster of reeds in the oldest garden in the world.

Eleven

Three-quarters into November, Cynthia Darlington steered her car out of the parking lot of Liddie's Tea Room. "You sure you won't spend the night?"

"Yeah, thanks anyway." Birdie stared out the window as they zipped past the loblolly pines butting up against one another alongside Orchard Road. Already Birdie felt like she was starting the afternoon late. Summer days always lasted longer than she expected them to, but November days snapped past as clean and crisp as sweet peas. Birdie had forgotten that.

She glanced over at her mom, whose hands were wrapped tight around the steering wheel, her nails a gleaming pink. Birdie glanced at her own fingernails—they were short and had little specks of dirt under them. She watched the peach trees, bald in most places, as Cynthia pulled toward the house.

"See you Thursday, honey," Cynthia called behind her as she climbed out of the car.

"Okay." Birdie leaned over to wave in at her mom, wondering how she was going to have a whole Thanksgiving dinner on the table by then.

Running through a mental list of chores, she crunched up the driveway toward the house. And then, remembering Methuselah, she turned in that direction. Checking on the tree was one of the items on her list. She walked between the dorms, sunk crookedly on either side of her, and then turned left. As she absently watched her feet on the grass, her mind drifted to Poopie. Birdie had wanted to ask her a hundred times a day if she was leaving, but the words always got caught inside her. If she asked, she'd know the answer. There would be no five percent maybe it wasn't true. But the ninety-five percent true was killing her anyway, so why was she waiting? When she looked up, a figure startled her, and she stopped short.

Her dad turned to look at her over his shoulder. He was standing in front of Methuselah, hands stuffed in his overall pockets.

"Hey."

"Hey, did you see this tree's dying?" he said lightly, rubbing his chin and then apparently gauging the distance between the tree and the edge of the property.

Birdie looked at Methuselah. "I'm gonna do some research on how to treat it."

Walter shook his head, shrugging. "It's just old age. She's gonna come down."

Birdie felt a tiny lump in her throat. "I've been reading up on it," she shot back defensively. "It could be scab, or crown gall, or a zinc deficiency." She'd Googled it.

"I don't think so, honey. We need to call and have someone come chop it."

"No!" Birdie blurted, horrified. Walter looked at her, surprised.

"Birdie, this tree's too close to the road to let it fall on its own." Birdie glanced over at where the knotty grass met the black tar of the single lane of Orchard Drive. She swallowed.

"Let me take care of it," she said. "Please?"

Walter studied her, then shrugged his broad shoulders. "Okay. You're a big girl."

Birdie heaved a sigh of relief. There was no doubt in her mind she could save the tree.

Walter turned back toward the drive, waving once over his shoulder. "I'm headed to town."

"What for?" But her dad hadn't heard her. As she walked up to the house, she heard the sound of his truck pulling away.

Inside, the house was deeply, unsettlingly quiet. Birdie let the dogs jump on her and lick her hands. "Poopie?" Nobody answered. She pulled off her scarf and rubbed her cheeks and glanced at the chalkboard. No messages. Honey Babe and Majestic followed Birdie from room to room, tip-tapping along. Birdie could feel the wind leaving her sails. She reached for the mail and found a letter from LCC on the table with a bunch of forms to fill out. It surprised her because she hadn't sent anything to them yet. Her dad had sent in her materials, she guessed. She marveled at how her future was taking shape with her hardly lifting a finger.

She sank onto the kitchen chair and stared around. She knew there were a million chores she could do. But she couldn't think where to start.

Finally she picked up the phone and dialed Enrico.

"Hello?"

"Enrico." She scratched the back of her neck, which immediately prickled. "Hey."

"Birdie," he said, sounding out of breath. Birdie could hear loud voices behind him, talking and laughing.

"Hey. Sorry I haven't called in a while. Things are so crazy here."

"That's fine," Enrico said lightly, unconcerned. Birdie tightened her fingers around the bottom edge of the phone. She felt like Enrico was getting fuzzy so far away. Were they growing fuzzy to each other?

"You okay, Birdie?"

"Yeah." Birdie pushed a toe into the linoleum. "I guess."

Enrico laughed. "You sound quiet." *He* sounded happy. Excited. Lively.

"I . . ." There was a loud shuffling on Enrico's end of the phone and then a couple of girls' voices in the background.

"Birdie, I have to go. I'll call you tonight."

"Okay."

"I'm sorry. I'll call you."

"Okay."

Birdie listened to the phone click. She tried to quell the jealousy in her gut. She circled the downstairs rooms one more time, looking for Poopie. The dogs circled behind her. Finally she went out the back door and dragged the crates of peach preserves up from the musty cellar. She'd haul them down to the Pecan Festival on Thanksgiving morning and sell them at the Darlington Orchard booth. Next she tackled the back porch with a big scrub brush and bleach, something she'd always seen Poopie do. She wasn't sure what time of the year she was supposed to do it, but it couldn't hurt.

Then she trudged down to the bat cave to check for any signs of life and, seeing none, grabbed the bucket-like container she'd bought and began scattering its stinky contents all around the opening, wrinkling her nose. It was a mixture of bat droppings and secret ingredients that the label guaranteed to work. Upon more thought, she went into the house and got two bowls of orange juice and placed them by the opening too. If they got mega-bats, well, that was better than nothing.

Afterward she did laundry, leaning on the dryer with her chemistry textbook vibrating under her hands, the warmth of it heating the drafty old room. She heard her dad come back from town and head upstairs.

Around eleven she heard the front door open and padded out to the hall to see Poopie coming in.

"Hey," Birdie greeted her.

"Hiya, honey." Poopie unwrapped her scarf and warmed her hands next to the radiator. This was the way it was now. Like everything was the way it *had* been, on the surface.

How could Birdie begin? How did you tell someone you were still a kid? That you still needed them? That if they left you, you'd crumble? Did you just blurt it out? "You want some tea?" Birdie asked, turning on the stove.

"No thanks," Poopie answered. She looked ready to go. She backed up.

"Poopie," Birdie blurted. "Can I talk to you about something?"

Poopie got a cagey look on her face and busied herself straightening the napkin holder on the table. "Maybe tomorrow, honey, I'm tired."

Before Birdie could even register surprise, Poopie pecked her on the forehead and hurried up the stairs. No, she didn't hurry; she *ran*.

Long after midnight, when her clothes were dry, Birdie climbed to the dark upstairs hallway and into her room, setting her alarm for six. She pulled Honey Babe and Majestic under the covers with her and curled around them, snuggling their warmth tightly. She had the kind of thoughts in the dark that grew bigger the longer she lay there. Murphy, Leeda, her mom, Enrico, Poopie . . . everyone seemed to be speeding away, and Birdie was a road sign in the rearview mirror. The dogs, at least, were stuck with her.

She didn't remember that Enrico hadn't called back until she woke up in the middle of the night, shooting out of a dream. She squinted in the dark, trying to recall where she'd been—and then it came back to her. She'd been standing on the cartoon ground in Mexico, rocky and dry and flat, watching a single peach blossom blow across its surface.

Birdie chased it, but it was too fast. It blew away from her.

Twelve

"*H*e was *terrified* of me," Lucretia told Leeda, pulling into an empty parking spot at Buck's Creek Nature Preserve the day before Thanksgiving. Leeda watched her, listening raptly. Her mother's face was flushed and animated. She'd been telling Leeda how her dad had proposed. All her life, Leeda had never heard the story.

"Of course he was." Leeda's stomach hurt from laughing. Everyone was terrified of her mother. She couldn't imagine how scary it would be to also be in love with her.

"I mean, honey." Lucretia reached out and took Leeda's fingers. "His hands were shaking. I'm telling you, they were *quaking*." She shook Leeda's hands to demonstrate. Leeda noticed the moistness of her mom's palm and studied her face, which was covered in a fine layer of dew. It worried her. But she forced herself to laugh.

They climbed out of the car and brushed themselves off. Leeda wore a thick green wool cardigan and jeans. She was supposed to dedicate the new nature trail at five and then head home to get her things ready for the Pecan Festival tomorrow morning. Leeda couldn't believe tomorrow was her Pecan Queen finale already. She looked at her mom's dewy complexion again and wondered if things between them would change back after pecan season was over.

It was brilliantly cold and bright as they made their way toward the small gaggle of people already standing at the head of the trail. They listened as the park rep—Mindy, by her name tag—explained the many benefits of the new trail, including a convenient view of the wild turkey dam and the bat flight that took place at dusk.

Lucretia shot Leeda a bored look and Leeda looked bored back, as if they were in on some private joke. But the truth was, Leeda wasn't bored. She liked hearing about the bats. She wanted to memorize as much as she could to tell Birdie later.

When the talk was over, Leeda smiled and cut the ribbon. Photos were taken and the small crowd dispersed. Mindy stood by the large wooden trail map at the edge of the parking lot, waving.

"Are we allowed to go see the bat cave?" Leeda asked. She felt like Birdie's spy, casing the joint.

Mindy shrugged. "If you want. Just follow the trail. Straight down, about two hundred yards."

Leeda looked at her mom hopefully. Lucretia scrunched up her face. "Come on, it'll be good." The minute the words left her lips, Leeda felt the pressure. She didn't know if it would be good or not.

They walked gingerly through the dried leaves, Lucretia keeping a careful eye on her clothes as Leeda pushed the branches aside. She felt like any moment her mom would call the whole thing off and head back to the car. She hoped they didn't hit any spiderwebs.

The cave, when they came to it, was a black jagged slice, encrusted like a black jewel into the wooded slope. To the left, the land swept downward into a low valley. Leeda crept up to the cave and peered into the dark curiously, then peered back at her mom. "Want to see?"

Lucretia shook her head, looking stiff and uncomfortable. "It's quiet out here."

To Leeda, it felt like they were the only two people for miles. She couldn't remember ever having her mom so wholly and completely to herself.

"Birdie says if you catch it at the right time, you see the babies too. But I think that's spring."

The air got darker around them. They both fidgeted, nervous. Leeda thought she could hear something. But no. And then it got louder—a *thrum thrum thrum*.

Leeda stepped back, suddenly afraid. And then the bats burst out of the cave. Leeda stumbled backward into her mom, who grabbed her by the shoulders and pulled her close. She could feel the air of hundreds of wings flapping and hear the soft, tiny *thwaps* and the tiny chirps and squeaks. Her heart was in her feet as they flew past.

As they watched, the flock looked like it was swimming through the sky, up above the low trees. Leeda turned to follow the bats' progress over the woods and into the valley. They moved off like a spot of ink, diluting as they got farther away. Lucretia let go of her shoulders and she sank forward.

And then Leeda started to laugh.

It wasn't a laugh at it being funny. It was a laugh from fear, relief, and the tickle of the wind of the bats. Behind her, her mother laughed too.

They were quiet in the car on the way home. Leeda watched the occasional house zip by, set back from the street, obscured by trees or tall grass, on the long country road that ran between Buck's Creek and Bridgewater. The heater was blowing directly on her knees, and she held up a hand to warm her fingers. The car smelled like heat.

Occasionally Leeda glanced over at her mom. She opened her mouth, then looked out the window. Finally she got up the nerve to break the silence.

"Mom?" They were coming into Bridgewater city limits.

"Hmm?"

"Can I ask you something?"

"Okay."

"Did I do something? Sometime? Did I do something wrong?"

Lucretia kept her eyes on the road. Her forehead wrinkled slightly. "What do you mean?"

Leeda kept her hands firmly on her lap and looked out the window. "We've always had this . . . thing. You know . . . it's different with Danay. When you look at her, you look different than when you look at me. I just want to know if I did something to make you feel that way."

The warmth seemed to seep right out of the car. Lucretia sat up straighter. Leeda felt immediately that she had said the wrong thing.

"I don't know what you're talking about."

They drove on, Leeda fiddling with her fingernails and looking out of the window. When her mom turned into the driveway, she cleared her throat and let out a deep breath. She had the door open before she'd even pulled the key out of the ignition. The cold air burst in and made Leeda zip up her coat as they climbed out.

Leeda followed her mom up the long walkway that led to the front door, winding its way through shrubs shaped in squares. She couldn't walk fast enough to keep up with her. "Mom, please, I just want you to be honest with me. I can take it. Mom? *Mom.*"

Lucretia was fumbling for her keys, than stopped at the door and turned toward Leeda, looking disappointed, annoyed. It was a look Leeda was used to. But it was too late for her to go back. She wouldn't let herself.

Leeda swallowed, hard. "Mom, do you *like* me?"

"That's a ridiculous question." Lucretia turned and pushed her key into the door.

"Mom. Please stop. I'm talking to you."

"No, you're not. This conversation is over."

"But ..."

Crack.

The front door opened. Danay stood in the doorway, with her long brown hair in a thick red headband like Snow White herself. She smiled a big white smile and reached out to hug their mom like it was the easiest thing in the world.

"Gobble gobble," she said.

Thirteen

"**S**he's not coming?" Murphy cocked her head dramatically, following Leeda down Main Street on Thanksgiving morning. She sipped her Pumpkin Spice coffee from Dunkin' Donuts.

"Of course she's coming. She's just behind me. I think she's having breakfast."

Murphy's stomach growled at the word *breakfast*. She looked behind her, as if Lucretia might materialize in the crowd.

As happened in Georgia, the cold had gone warm just when you thought winter was setting in. It was light-jacket weather. Sometimes it did Murphy's head in. She longed for real *winter* winter. She always had.

People had started rolling in to the festival at dawn, so now, at eight thirty, the booths were already set up on either side of Main Street, loaded with baked goods made by the teachers at Bridgewater Middle School, wreaths and handmade soaps and jelly candles from the Curious Cottage Gift Shop, a quilt being raffled by the Divine Grace of the Holy Redeemer. Murphy glanced longingly at the junk food stalls. "Do you think the fried Mars bar truck will be here?"

"You're such a guy." Leeda readjusted the garment bag she was carrying, trying to keep it steady over one shoulder.

"I like my guy-like qualities," Murphy said, trying not to scan the crowd for Rex. As usual, she'd been avoiding him. Over the past three weeks, she'd seen him a handful of times, letting him come over to play Ping-Pong in the cold parking lot one time, letting him watch late-night TV with her and her mom for a few nights, fooling around with him in his room twice when his dad was out. She wanted to make sure she kept him unsure of the next time he'd see her. Like Leeda had said, she wanted to make sure he knew what it was like not to have her. But today—today was the day he'd promised her an answer about New York.

The pecan booths were at the end of the line. There were several from different pecan growers around the county. They saw Birdie's booth with a banner that read DARLINGTON ORCHARD, but no Birdie.

"Did you bring the pecan goodies?" Murphy asked. The pecan goodies were the Pecan Queen's signature duty. Macy's had Santa at the end of their parade to launch the Christmas season and keep the universe moving along on time. In Bridgewater, the Christmas season didn't begin until an airborne pecan goodie socked you in the eye.

"Mom's bringing them."

"You know if she doesn't show up and you don't have pecan goodies to throw, the kids are going to riot."

Leeda rolled her eyes.

They ran into Leeda's grandmom, who was with her chauffeur. She was wearing her old tiara and making him help her find the drink cart. "Don't forget to sit erect," she said, patting Leeda's hip and disappearing into the crowd.

All the parade exhibits and participants were cloistered, like every year, in the parking lot behind the middle school. Leeda and Murphy made their way to the back of the crowd—past a rolling petting zoo, the Elks Club, the Freemasons, the Duck Carvers club, the Young Riders, Little Miss Kings County, and the Bridgewater High School band. Leeda would be on the last float with the famous pecan goodies in tow.

Rex was standing at the float with the rest of Leeda's court, Dina Marie and Melissa Gentian, a gorgeous little junior. Dina Marie laughed loud and donkey-like at something Rex had said, but Murphy was above being jealous. They both seemed to dote on her boyfriend, who sensed her watching and looked behind him. Before Dina Marie could see, Murphy made a bucktooth face at her back, and Rex shook his head but smiled. Of *course* he was waiting for her. Murphy's heart leapt with triumph.

Leeda disappeared into the bathroom to dress, and Murphy sauntered up to Rex. Would he tell her now? Later? *When?*

"Hey." He put his hand at the side of her neck, kissing her. "I've been calling you."

"Been so busy with Miss Queenie." Murphy rolled her eyes in exaggerated exhaustion toward the bathroom. "How's it going?"

"How's it going? Did we just meet or something?" Murphy shrugged. Rex kept his hand at her neck. "I figured this was my rare chance to see my girlfriend up early."

Murphy swallowed. She waited for him to say more. He

didn't. The four of them stood there eyeballing one another, casting about for something to say until out of the corner of her eye, Murphy saw Leeda waving to her from the bathroom. "Royal duties," she said, walking backward.

Leeda was half dressed and agitated. "Can you just start on my hair until my mom gets here?"

Murphy pointed to the tangle on top of her own head. "Have you seen my hair?"

Leeda shoved a curling iron into the pointing hand. "Just curl it."

Murphy took the iron reluctantly and felt to see if it was hot enough. She gazed at Leeda, sizing up her head, then glanced back out through the bathroom door, which was propped open.

"What if your mom flakes out, Lee?" Murphy was just looking for a reason to have both of Lucretia's eyebrows waxed off at the Cawley-Smith Spa. She knew people who could do that. Aestheticians who owed her favors.

"She's coming." Leeda looked at her watch. "Nothing starts for another half hour."

Murphy started on the hair. When that was done, she started on the makeup. "Mom says put it on a little thick. You have to make sure it shows up from far away," Leeda said.

By the time Murphy was finished with her, Leeda looked like a cheap hooker from the seventies.

Murphy hesitated a moment before letting her look in the mirror. Already the confidence of an hour earlier—when she'd picked Murphy up at Anthill Acres, fresh as a violet—had seeped out of Leeda's face. When she stood up and looked at her reflection, any remaining self-assurance drained away. "I look like Elvira," she said.

For a long while, they stood in the doorway to the bathroom, Leeda's eyes scanning the crowd. At five till, she murmured quietly, "She's got the pecan goodies." The people at the beginning of the parade began moving. It would be a matter of minutes before the float at the back kicked into gear. "Maybe something happened. Maybe she's not feeling well."

Murphy's rib cage hurt. She tugged on her full bottom lip, shooting a sideways glance at Leeda. "Maybe she's on her way . . ." she found herself saying halfheartedly.

Leeda shook her head, crossing her arms tightly around herself.

The Pecan Princesses were waving to her expectantly. Dina Marie had a big, dramatically anxious look on her face.

Murphy didn't reach out to touch or hug Leeda. Wrapped up in her own arms and standing rod-straight, Leeda looked like she had an invisible wall around her, and Murphy didn't want to broach it. She was the picture of calm. Murphy knew that Leeda being calm was worse than being upset. It meant she was too upset to be upset.

"You better hurry. You can't let down the other nuts," Murphy said, trying to make light. But Leeda didn't acknowledge the comment.

She turned her gray eyes to Murphy. "Will you do this for me?"

Murphy looked at her, a small panic building in her gut. Leeda was gesturing down at her dress.

"Do what?"

Leeda waved her hands down at her dress again, then reached back to unzip it.

"Oh no." Murphy groaned.

"I don't want to be up there, Murphy." She started pulling at the neckline.

"Neither do I." Murphy looked at the float, at the princesses. Dressing up as one of them would be like Maribeth McMurtry dressing up like Satan. It was against everything Murphy stood for. "Just skip it," she said desperately. "They don't need a Pecan Queen."

"Please." Leeda clawed Murphy's wrist. "Please, please, please."

"Leeda." Murphy swallowed, looking at the float again. It disgusted her. "No way."

Leeda stopped unzipping. She looked Murphy hard in the eye. Her face settled into smooth, clean lines. And then she zipped herself back up and sailed out of the bathroom.

Birdie heard the booing before she caught a glimpse of the float. Now that the parade was almost at the last leg, some sort of small upheaval was rippling through the younger members of the crowd. Birdie stood on her tiptoes to try and see why. When she saw who they were booing at, she gasped, bewildered.

Leeda stood on the float in her long brown dress, her hair in straggly, puffy curls, her arms at her sides, shoulders drooped. Her eyes were made up in deep gray shadow and her cheeks were as rosy as a Kewpie doll's. A tight, quivering smile was plastered to her face. Then she looked down at her hands, which picked at each other nervously like cats in a fight. Birdie looked at her empty hands too and finally realized what the booing was about.

Where were the pecan goodies?

Leeda had never had so many people looking at her at once. Their faces were a mixture of confusion, disillusionment, and fear. She wondered if Murphy had put on the makeup a little too thickly.

In the crowd, she spotted Birdie and gave her a desperate look, as if Birdie could somehow rescue her. Birdie looked back at her and held up her hands helplessly. Leeda took a deep, shuddering breath. The worst thing she could do was let herself look like she felt. What she felt, more than anything at that moment, was angry at Murphy. She couldn't think what it would have cost Murphy to just step up, this one time, and rescue her. If the roles had been reversed, Leeda would have done it in a heartbeat. Leeda clenched her teeth, explosive inside.

From her spot on the platform, she had a bird's-eye view of a few interesting things. She could see her grandmother, intrepidly pushing to the front of the crowd, waving her little munchkin fists proudly. She could see Lucretia wasn't anywhere near her. And she could see the wrath that the absence of the pecan goodies appeared to cause. She had never let so many people down.

But she kept the smile plastered on her face. And then she felt the faint sting of something hitting her shoulder. And before she could make sense of it, there were more—hitting her on the head, the face, the back. Her smile faded. She shielded her face with her hands and peered around, finally taking it in. The little kids were rioting. They were pelting her with pecans.

Leeda wanted to sink into the bottom of the float. She wanted to cease to exist. Instinctively she looked around for Rex because for years that was what she'd always done. She made him out just at the back of the crowd, with Murphy, of course. The two of them—Leeda's ex-boyfriend and her best friend—were talking and laughing and sharing a fried Mars bar. Apparently they hadn't noticed the ruckus. Leeda's heart went steely, watching them. For a moment, she wavered between climbing off the float and disappearing into the giant pecan behind her.

Taking the humiliation up another notch, she could see Grandmom Eugenie running alongside the float now, wobbly and minuscule, as she grabbed one of the rioting kids by the ear. If Leeda hadn't been so close to crying, she would have laughed. It seemed entirely appropriate that only a geriatric munchkin had come to her defense.

Leeda felt the muscles in her body harden like they were rocks. The wave of anger she felt, at her mom, at Murphy, at herself, threatened to swallow her. It was sharp, but to her surprise, it wasn't new. It was like something that had been just behind her, waiting to catch up.

Leeda lifted her hands and began waving. She closed her eyes when another volley of pecans arrived. She adopted an old tried-and-true trick and pretended like she couldn't care less.

And of course, she kept smiling.

Fourteen

Thanksgiving evening, Birdie kept throwing glances at the stairs, looking for help that didn't come, like the *Titanic*.

Sitting at the table—at her old seat, next to Walter—was Birdie's mom. She looked great. She was like one of those hypothetical astronauts who go to space and come back young when everyone else is either old or dead. It seemed like since leaving her daughter and husband last spring, she had aged in reverse.

Walter seemed slightly tongue-tied to have Cynthia back in the house, but Cynthia made up for it by being so perfectly at ease.

"The garden is looking nice," she said to Walter. "I took a spin around the yard before I came in."

"That's Murphy," Birdie interjected, searching the cabinet. "Parsley, parsley . . ." she muttered to herself. Cynthia walked to the kitchen, looked over Birdie's shoulder, and pulled the parsley flakes from the cupboard, placing the bottle on the counter beside her. Her mom knowing where everything was just seemed to exaggerate the fact that she no longer lived in the house. She gave Birdie an affectionate pinch, then sat back down, telling Walter about her new job managing the Tea Room.

Birdie worked with a lump in her throat. She wiped the sweat off her face and glanced at her reflection in the window above the sink—her auburn hair was pasted to the sides of her forehead in sweaty squiggles, her eyes wet from the heat and steam. She'd had a vision of answering the door in the dress she'd picked out, with a clean kitchen behind her and candles on the table—the way her mom and Poopie had always put things together. Instead she'd answered the door with a hand covered in gizzard juice and sleepers in her eyes that her mom had swiped away, the dogs tangled between her ankles and yipping. When Majestic had seen the old family dog, Toonsis, she'd peed because she was so excited and Birdie had had to clean it up. The potatoes had boiled over and left sticky trails of potato water on the stove, onion skins piggybacked to bits of dough stuck to the counter. The turkey was still in the oven and looked suspiciously underdone.

As far as Birdie was concerned, it was all Poopie's fault. Poopie, who had spent the morning traipsing around the parade (Birdie had glimpsed her, munching happily on a fried Mars bar, and then later, waving an American flag at the Elks Club), had been weirdly absent all afternoon. Poopie—who had always been there to give Birdie advice even when she didn't want it, who if you asked her if your dough was too smushy not only said yes but took it out of your hands and did the rest herself—had gone AWOL.

Through the window, the orchard looked cool and inviting—the grass a muted green, the trees empty and serene in their rows, everything still and at peace except for the squirrels and the occasional cardinal flitting in the branches.

Birdie grabbed the gherkin jar out of the fridge and shook the tiny pickles into one of her mom's glass bowls. She laid it on the table with a thud. The bowl of gherkins was the only thing that looked like it was supposed to.

"Just a few more minutes and we eat." Birdie bent over the mashed potatoes, trying to relax, but the smoke alarm went off. She dove for the oven. She'd left the rolls in too long. She grabbed a dish towel and used it to grip the pan of rolls. She shoved open the window to let in the unseasonably warm November air. "I'm fine. Everything's fine . . ." she said, glancing toward the table.

Cynthia and Walter were staring toward the staircase, looking slightly aghast. Birdie took a few steps forward to see what they were looking at. The elusive Poopie was floating down the stairs. Floating. Wearing a long, straight, flowery dress and *lipstick*.

"How's it going, honey?" Poopie asked as she stepped into the room, glancing around the kitchen. *Thank God.*

"Perfect," Birdie said sarcastically, sending her an SOS with her eyes.

"Cynthia. How are you?" Poopie drawled. She sank into the chair opposite Cynthia, ignoring Birdie's distress call, just like the USS *Californian*.

"I'm good, Poopie. You look good," Cynthia said awkwardly.

Once Birdie had laid out the dinner, with help from neither her mom nor Poopie, she sat. There they were, everyone in their old places, Saint Anthony smiling down on their feast benevolently. The turkey skin crunched. The rolls were slightly blackened. Somewhere along the way, Birdie had added too much salt to the stuffing. Everyone smiled and congratulated Birdie and then drifted into silence, chewing with grim determination.

"Walter, I don't know why you haven't replaced that truck yet. I would have thought that'd be the first thing you'd get rid of once you got out of debt," Cynthia said. Birdie's mom had always hated her dad's truck.

Walter shrugged amiably. "It's okay."

Poopie was pushing her stuffing back and forth with her fork, staring at Cynthia from under her eyebrows. The oven had filled the kitchen with hot, stuffy air, so that it was only cool right near the window. Birdie turned on the ceiling fan and sank back into her seat cross-legged.

"It still runs great," Poopie muttered.

"Poopie, that truck is horrible." Cynthia waved her hands dramatically, but Poopie was unswayed. "It's probably going to explode at any moment."

"It may not be good enough for you, but it works for Walter."

Yowl!

Birdie spun around. Toonsis had grabbed Honey Babe by the scruff and the two were scratching and sliding around on the linoleum locked in a death grip. Majestic had squeezed into the tiny place behind the fridge and was trying to be invisible. Birdie darted forward and grabbed Toonsis by the hind legs.

"Birdie, don't grab him like that! The pet psychic says you just need to *ask* him not to do things. Otherwise he feels resentful. Toonsis, please don't play rough with Honey Buns."

"Honey *Babe*," Birdie corrected, with Toonsis struggling in her arms resentfully. Majestic leapt onto Walter's lap and let out a yip.

"You're right, Poopie," Cynthia said, turning cool. "Walter, does the truck still run *great*?" She knew, of course, that it didn't.

Walter looked at Birdie and cleared his throat.

Yip yip!

"Oh my God!" Birdie yelled, standing up and sweeping the two papillons under either arm. She yanked open the front door and deposited the two on the porch, taking a deep breath. The air smelled like dry leaves and fireplaces. She looked down at the dogs and took in their pitiful *Who, me?* faces. "I envy you," she said, before slamming the door shut.

The argument between Poopie and Birdie's mom about the truck had escalated. Poopie was digging into her stuffing relentlessly, twirling her fork around in it as they talked. The silver of her fork glinted and then, suddenly, a bit of stuffing was sailing across the table.

Everyone froze where they were. A piece of stuffing had landed in Cynthia's short blond hair and dangled there by her ear like an earring.

"Did you just throw food at me?"

Poopie leaned back and crossed her arms, looking both self-conscious and defiant. "Was an accident."

"That's fine." Cynthia reached toward the gherkin bowl and knocked it over so that the gherkins went tumbling onto Poopie's lap. "Ooh, sorry."

"Mom!" Birdie gasped. *The beautiful gherkins.* The only thing she hadn't ruined. But it was too late.

Poopie grasped a turkey leg and jerked it off the turkey, letting it fly out of her hands at Cynthia. "Ooh, sorry," Poopie mimicked.

Knock knock knock.

As if waking from a trance, everyone blinked in the direction of the foyer.

Birdie stood up from the table, trembling inside. "Um," she mumbled. "I'll . . . get it." Birdie walked to the door stiffly, glancing back over her shoulder. Everyone sat still, watching her, not looking at one another. She grasped the doorknob and pulled.

There, standing on the top step, a backpack slung over his shoulder, was Enrico.

"Surprise," he said, reaching his arms around her waist, pulling her into a hug. Birdie sank into him. He smelled like peach blossoms.

Fifteen

Leeda walked into the foyer of her house. The smell of turkey was drifting in the air, but the dining room table was pristine and empty.

That afternoon, she had wandered around Bridgewater until the temperature dropped with the sun. Now, standing face-to-face with the autographed photo of Lucretia as queen on the console, Leeda swiped at her dress, which was covered in big splotches of powder. Some kid had apparently run out of pecans and pelted her with his funnel cake. She felt her cell phone vibrating in her purse and pulled it out, hitting *Ignore* when she saw it was Birdie. Murphy hadn't even called at all. Birdie, of course, had called five times. Leeda turned off the phone and then brushed at herself as she followed the sound of the TV to the home theater.

Danay and Brighton were sitting on one of the recliners eating popcorn and watching a dog show. Leeda sank onto the armrest.

"Hey. Who did that to you?" No answer. "You missed Thanksgiving dinner. Mom's pissed."

Leeda opened and closed her mouth. She felt a fresh wave of venom rise up in her throat. "She missed my parade," she managed to squeak out.

Danay shrugged.

Leeda had the feeling you got in a dream, when you yell and yell and no voice comes out. She wanted to make Danay hear that it was a big deal. But Danay looked so impenetrable, chomping on her popcorn, devil-may-care. All Leeda could get out was a tight, "She said she wanted to see me on the float. With the hyperhalitosis and everything . . ." Her voice got infinitely smaller until it cut off completely. Because she felt infinitely small.

"It's hyper*hidrosis*. What does that have to do with anything?"

"Well, what if she dies?" Leeda spat out. Danay looked at her like she'd lost her mind. And Leeda couldn't make sense of the look. She couldn't even believe she'd said *dies* out loud. It seemed like some sort of curse.

Danay gave Brighton a sort of can-you-believe-this gesture. "Lee, all that happens with hyperhidrosis is you sweat a lot. The only thing that's in danger is Mom's ego."

Leeda felt like the oxygen had been sucked out of her. She leaned against the doorway. "I don't believe you."

Danay slapped her hand to her forehead. "Oh, don't be so dramatic. Brighton knows."

Brighton, who'd interned at Holy Cross the year before, nodded, his glasses glinting in the light of the giant TV. "It's true."

Danay turned her eyes back to the screen, but Leeda couldn't stop staring at her sister. She could have been knocked over with a feather.

Finally Danay looked over at her and did a double take. "God. You believed her?" She shook her head.

Leeda backed up slowly.

Danay turned to Brighton, rolling her eyes. "My mom is such a rat," she said to Brighton, amused. "I'm telling you, she can get her way with anyone. *Anyone.*"

Upstairs, Leeda packed her room piece by piece. She stripped her soft white comforter off her bed. She shoved as many clothes as she could into her big gray suitcase. She took her photos of Murphy and Birdie and her dad and stuffed them into the front pocket. She wanted to tear it all down. She wanted to tear down the walls.

She was hoping her mom would hear her and come to see what she was doing. But she didn't.

Finally she walked down the hall to her parents' bedroom. "Mom?" Her mom and dad were reading. Her mom was at the very side of the bed, while her dad was in the middle. They both looked up in surprise, taking in the funnel cake stains.

Leeda swallowed. "I don't understand," she said, her heart pounding.

"Where were you for dinner?" Lucretia asked, immediately going on the offensive, lowering her book onto the lap of her silky pink long-sleeved nightgown.

Leeda's words rushed out in a wave. "Why couldn't you just be there for me? Like a normal mom? Why is that such a problem?"

Lucretia stiffened. Her hands fluttered on her book. She looked trapped. "Leeda, I'm sorry, but Danay was here and . . ."

117

"Time slipped away from you, right?"

Lucretia shut her mouth, souring.

It was maddening to Leeda that pouring out her heart brought that kind of look in return. "Why don't you care if *I* slip away from you?"

"Oh, really." Lucretia rolled her eyes at Leeda's dad, who did what he usually did—he kept his face in his book, opting out of the controversy. It made Leeda want to scream. How could he not expect more? How could he live with her mom the way she was?

Leeda took a deep breath and tried to even herself out and capture some dignity. "I want it back."

"What back?" Lucretia asked, squinting at her.

"The Barbie."

"What?"

"I want the Barbie back."

Lucretia lifted her book again, as if to start reading. "Don't be ridiculous, Leeda."

Leeda scanned the room and saw it sitting on the bureau. She marched over and grabbed it. Lucretia leapt up out of bed. "You are out of line, Leeda."

"Why did you even have me?"

Lucretia didn't say anything. Apparently she didn't have anything to say.

Leeda felt punched down the middle with holes. She moved back to the doorway. "I just want you to know . . ." she sputtered, "that when you're old and sick and you need someone, I'm not taking care of you! I'm wheeling you off the dock!"

As Leeda sailed down the hallway, she passed Danay coming

to see what the commotion was and pushed right past her. She grabbed her suitcase from her room and hurried down the stairs.

When she backed out of the driveway, Lucretia was standing on the stoop in her nightgown, watching her go. Leeda couldn't tell if she looked pulled apart or just shocked. Leeda backed onto the road and slammed on the gas.

She knew where she was going before she really knew. At the intersection of Anjaco and Orchard, she threw the Barbie out the window and turned left.

As she reached the edge of orchard property, she stepped harder on the gas, feeling freedom, the closeness of redemption. She peered to her left to see if there were lights on up at the house and then glanced back at the road. At that moment, two tan blobs flashed out from the grass and she slammed on the brakes. She watched them disappear under the car with a *thump thump*.

She'd had just enough time to see that they were wearing sweaters.

Sixteen

*B*ecause she didn't want to wake Rex's dad, Murphy pulled up by Pearly Gates Cemetery and got out of the car, shivering in the breeze. Pearly Gates was actually gated only by a rubberized chain-link fence, tied together with a bit of rope. It looked especially morbid in the cold.

She walked along the white gravel that lined the side of the road and into Rex's yard—a one-level tan house with brown-lined windows and a bluebird painted on the black mailbox. Murphy's feet swished through the grass as she walked around back, where there was still an old swing set in the shadows. She knocked on the window, her heart in her throat.

When Murphy had looked for Leeda after the parade, she'd found her car missing. She'd figured Leeda wanted to be alone—or maybe she was giving it to her mom—so Murphy put her phone on vibrate and slid it into her pocket to make sure she felt it if she called. All day, every time it vibrated, it was Rex. Her thumb hovered over the Accept button but didn't get farther than that. Instead she'd ended up at the fifty-cent movie theater, watching *The Wizard of Oz,* which the Bridgewater Picture Show always showed on Thanksgiving. And then she'd headed home for Thanksgiving dinner with her mom. She'd put her cell phone under her pillow in her room. They had snuggled up on the couch and watched *Emmet Otter's Jug-Band Christmas*, which they'd recorded about twelve years ago on VHS. Finally Jodee had gone to bed, and Murphy—stuck with herself and out of distractions—had gotten in her car.

Now, after a few moments, there was the click of the latch and the window slid upward. Rex, shirtless, stood for a moment, trying to get oriented and squinting at her in the dark. Then he ducked and leaned out the window and put his arms around Murphy's waist and kissed her cheek. His skin was as warm as a chimney. Murphy felt her voice disappear.

"Come in."

"Um." Murphy looked over his shoulder into the warm air of his bedroom. "Can we go for a walk?" She needed to be in motion.

Rex was quiet for a moment, surprised, and then: "Sure. Hold on." He disappeared inside and then reappeared a few moments later wearing sweatpants, a long-sleeved shirt, and a jacket, pulling on his shoes.

They walked down the street and around a curve that rose to the right. Murphy felt like if she kept her feet moving she could stay ahead of whatever it was she was afraid of.

"I know what you're here for." The way he said it, so low, made her worry.

"I want to tell you something first before you say anything."

"Yeah." Rex stopped and gave her his complete attention, pulling her back toward him. Murphy's heart ached over the big, wide space of Rex. Murphy shifted on her feet, back and forth. She put her whole face against his arm and slurred into it, flatly, "I lurr you."

Rex laughed and pulled her curls back from her face. "What?"

"Don't make me say it again." Murphy felt naked, stretched out on a post.

Rex put his forehead against hers. "I know you do."

Murphy relaxed into his hands and rolled her eyes.

"I need to know if you're in or out, Rex."

Murphy waited for him to say more. When he didn't, she pulled away, stuck her hands in her pockets, looked up and around and at the side of him. "Here's the thing. I feel like I'm . . . that if we're going to do this. You know, if I'm going to show you all my yucky stuff . . . you know, all this stuff about me and everything that's really scary, I need to know you're with me."

"I'm *with* you, Shorts."

"The whole way." It was much more than Murphy wanted to say. She looked off and didn't make eye contact.

Rex reached out and pulled her close. She leaned into him, finally. *Thank God.*

He put his hand on her hair. "I just don't think New York is for me, Murphy."

Suddenly Murphy went stiff. She pulled back and looked him in the eye. He looked back at her solidly, focused, like he was being careful, like he was choosing his words carefully.

"My dad's here," he went on. "And . . . I don't feel that thing you do. I don't need to get away."

Murphy was reeling inside. She could feel him slipping and

sliding out of her fingers. She steeled her chin and went on. Maybe she wasn't saying it right or he wasn't quite hearing her right. "I can't stay here. I'll shrivel up and blow away if I stay here."

Rex stood back. "I know."

Murphy let her arms dangle at her sides. What could she say to that? She felt jealous suddenly of Rex's dad. She let the silence drift between them for a long time, hoping for Rex to cave or to give her something to go on. But he didn't.

"So if you stay here, Rex, what . . . what are you picturing for us?"

"I don't know. I guess . . ." Rex looked like he was aware he was stepping into a trap. "I guess I just thought we could enjoy each other while we can."

It hit her like a brick. Murphy composed her face carefully. The trust she'd felt in Rex a moment before vanished. She disappeared behind herself.

"That's very Zen of you."

"Murphy, I don't want to hold you back. You're going to have this amazing time, and I don't want you to spend it wishing you were somewhere else or with someone else. That would just kill me to know I caused that or took that away from you."

"You're right," Murphy said. "I don't want to be held back." She leaned against the chain-link fence behind her. She wondered how long forever was in Rex's world. She didn't want to love him anymore. It was like the flick of a switch. She wanted to backpedal and take back all the things she'd said. She wanted to be back on top of her heart instead of being buried somewhere underneath it.

Murphy was good at many things, but the thing she had always been best at was walking away. She shrugged casually. "Actually, I think it's better we start now. I don't think we should see each other anymore."

He shifted slightly, looking surprised. "Yeah," he said, as if he was trying to agree. "If that's how you feel, okay."

"You don't care about how I feel," Murphy croaked, looking away.

Rex didn't say anything back, which was worse than anything. He just stared at her calmly. Murphy fought the urge to kick him in the shins.

"Good night." He leaned forward and kissed her cheek. Then he turned and walked back toward his house.

Murphy didn't watch him go. That would be pathetic. She turned and walked, not to her car, but to the tiny bridge nearby. Rex would have to watch *her*. He would come after her.

The bridge was the lone place in Bridgewater where you had anything approaching a view of town. The water that went under it had slowed to a muddy trickle. The orange town lights made a patch in front of her that looked like a Lite Brite board. If you were passing it for the first time, it would have looked almost pretty. But for Murphy, the view held her disappointments, her letdowns, the times she'd been reined in, held back, judged. Just stuck, as if life were something you had to run in place.

Murphy waited for Rex to come back. She stood against the wall looking down at the trickle under the bridge and waited forever.

Seventeen

The smell of smoky leaves drifted into the cider house, and a few came skittering across the concrete floor. Enrico picked one up and tore it apart at the veins and Birdie watched, smiling. They'd brought out a candle, and the leaf in his hands made shadows on the wall.

They caught up fast. Enrico had been torn between telling her he was coming and surprising her. He'd taken the bus all night and then a cab from the bus stop.

"I go back tomorrow," he told her. It would take him over twenty-four hours to get back. He had gone through all that trouble just for *hours* with her. It made Birdie dizzy. "But I'll see you at New Year's. And I'll be back in April for spring break, for spraying." He played with her fingers shyly. "If you want me to."

"*If* I want you to," Birdie said, rolling her eyes.

Something about the way the orchard smelled in November, and especially the cider house, and especially when turkey smells were coming out of the main house, made her remember things vividly. She ran her hands through his hair. Now that he was in front of her, Enrico didn't feel unknown or fuzzy. He felt as familiar to her as any one of those things.

His hand held the remnants of the leaf he'd torn apart, and Birdie took the fingers and put them against her forehead, then against her shoulder. She felt like there was a hole in her heart a mile wide for saying good-bye again tomorrow. And Enrico seemed to sense this because he put his hand right there, over her heart.

For some reason, just that gesture made her feel perfectly intact again. She felt everything in rhythm—heartbeat, breath, legs, arms. All because Enrico had come when she needed him, like her guardian angel. And maybe because of more superficial reasons too. He was stunningly beautiful.

She took the bottom edges of his sweater and lifted it up over his head. His hair went into a spike and he looked at her, surprised. Birdie grinned back at him and kissed his neck, and he squirmed and laughed.

"I'm ticklish." He smiled, his low voice rumbling against Birdie's ear where she still rested on his neck. She sat up and looked at him and then, looking at the cider press, began to unbutton her mashed-potato-streaked shirt. When she looked back at Enrico, he'd stopped smiling and was frowning, seriously and thoughtfully.

"Please don't say no," Birdie said.

He leaned forward and gave her a deep, tight hug. And Birdie, mesmerized by the difference in their skin, the look of his head against her shoulder, the things she knew were in his head like books and peaches and Mexico and herself, was unafraid.

• • •

Birdie sat up, pulling Enrico's blue sweater over her bare torso, as if Enrico hadn't seen and touched every part of her. Running his fingers along the underside of her wrist, he looked at her like she was a cider house goddess. She pretended not to notice and stood up as gracefully as she could, tugging down the edges of the sweater.

"You okay, Birdie?"

"Yeah." She couldn't believe it. She couldn't believe what they had done. She felt like she might float through the roof. Or hide under the covers to hide herself from him and all that he knew about her now. "I gotta pee," she said finally.

Enrico laughed. Birdie burst into giddy laughter too, embarrassed and happy. She tossed her hair dramatically. "I'll be right back."

She could just duck out the cider house door and around the corner. Birdie squeaked the door open and hopped outside, doing a bit of a ballet move to make Enrico laugh again. She dipped around the corner and peed in the grass, then came back around, the sweater pulled down off one shoulder and up over one bare hip.

Poopie was standing at the door of the cider house, staring in and looking dumbfounded. Then she sensed Birdie and turned. The moment lasted forever.

"I was looking for the dogs," Poopie muttered, her eyes darting finally to the magnolia near the door.

Birdie blinked at her. She had gone mute. All sorts of words popped into her head that had somehow disappeared in the cider shed. Words like *don't*. And *we should wait*.

"Have you seen them?" Poopie asked. She still couldn't look

at her. They couldn't look at each other. Birdie shook her head at the magnolia too. As if it were their ambassador.

Poopie nodded stiffly, then turned on her heel and walked toward the house in tight, quick steps, like she couldn't get away fast enough.

Eighteen

The doorbell woke Birdie up. She pulled the pillow from her face and looked toward her bedroom window. It was just after dawn. She sat up, feeling a deep nagging weight that she quickly sorted into the events of the night before. And then it dawned on her that nobody ever rang their doorbell this early. She was instantly alert.

She sat and listened, afraid to go out into the hall, instinctively fearing that something bad had happened. Maybe Poopie had called the cops. Was it illegal for her and Enrico to have had sex? She didn't even know. She heard Poopie's feet creaking down the stairs and then the crack of the door opening. This was followed by a moment of whispered talking, and then Poopie let out a muffled cry. Birdie's stomach turned.

She tiptoed to her bedroom door and opened it, then doubled back in shock, a deep blush spreading up her cheeks. On the floor just outside her door stood a cadre of santos of every shape and size: short female saints, tall bearded male saints, patron saints of the sick and war, and God knew what else. They might as well have been twelve feet tall for how small they made Birdie feel. Poopie had already passed judgment on her.

Birdie tiptoed past them, carrying her guilt around her like a cloak that they could see, and moved slowly down the stairs.

Poopie was standing on the threshold of the kitchen. Tears streaked her cheeks. Her bottom lip was trembling. Birdie looked around the room, hot and cold flashes of confusion and guilt racing through her. "What . . . ?"

Poopie shook her head and nodded to the front porch. Birdie swallowed and walked up to the doorway, the sunrise hitting her right in the face. It took her a moment to put the image together. It was Leeda sitting on the porch with her back to Birdie, staring out at the lines of empty trees. A tiny tan lump was lying cradled in her arms, its two front legs in casts. The moment Majestic saw Birdie, she howled mournfully. Leeda's face was marked with tears.

"I didn't see them; I'm so sorry."

"Didn't see them?" Birdie didn't quite understand what *she* was seeing.

"I rushed them to the vet. The emergency clinic . . . ? In Laurens . . . ? But . . ."

Birdie looked around for Honey Babe. Her hand flew to the bottom of her rib cage. She felt a twirling sick sadness.

"I'm so sorry," Leeda cried, fat tears running all over her face. "My mom and I got in a fight. . . ."

"Oh, Lee."

Birdie melted down beside Leeda. Leeda buried her face in Birdie's shoulder, sobbing until she had calmed down to sniffling.

Her face flaming, Birdie couldn't think of anything else to

say. It sorted out quickly in her mind. The cause and effect. The *a* leading to *b* leading to *c*. She'd been the one to let the dogs out and forgot to bring them back in ... *because* ...

Birdie reached a loose arm around Leeda. She watched as Majestic hobbled her way onto her lap. Leeda sniffed against her shoulder. "Can I move in?"

It was more than logic. It was the same reason the saints stood outside Birdie's door. In Birdie's mind, Leeda's accident wasn't really *Leeda's* accident. It had happened because Birdie had gone the wrong way.

Poopie Pedraza had long been convinced the orchard was haunted. She swore if she stood on the porch at dusk, she could see the shades of people who'd come and gone on the property. One looked like Judge Miller Abbott at age seventeen. Another looked like Lucretia Cawley-Smith at age twelve. Others she recognized from old farm photographs. And although Poopie got the giggly-wigglies watching them, she was always looking for the ghost of herself. She feared that when she someday saw her own eyes looking back at her, she would know it was time to go.

Nineteen

Leeda was collecting pecans in a bucket because Poopie had asked her to. It was the first of December, cool and bright, and the Balmeade Country Club grass lay splayed out, Day-Glo green, on the other side of the fence. As she worked, Leeda kept pausing and staring at it, drifting off. She set her bucket down and leaned against the fence—which was rotting in places, the paint peeling so that some of it stuck to her pink cotton coat. From here, she could see that the clubhouse was almost finished. She could make out workers installing the windows. The country club was still rebuilding after the summer's big storm. But by the size of the new clubhouse, it looked like it was coming back bigger than ever.

Leeda looked behind her. She couldn't believe she was back living at the orchard. The grassy floor between the two rows of shaggy trees was carpeted in hard, round pecans that had fallen unharvested. Methuselah drooped on the far end, looking exhausted.

Occasionally a pecan ricocheted through branches somewhere far above and landed with a *crack* on the ground. Leeda heard each crack distinctly. Her ears were tuned to the sound of the winter birds, the rustle of squirrels, the vague crunching of bugs nibbling on leaves. That was what happened, she realized, when you'd been engulfed in quiet for days. Birdie had yet to come to the dorms, though she and Leeda had seen each other for meals before and after Leeda went off to school. Even at the table, Birdie curled over her food solemnly. Poopie wasn't eating with them these days. And Uncle Walter had never been much of a conversationalist.

Leeda understood. There were not enough words to tell Birdie how sorry she was, and she wanted to give her all the space she needed. But Murphy was something else entirely. Leeda kept waiting for Murphy's big apology. For abandoning her to the wolves at the Pecan Festival when she needed her most. But the apology hadn't come. In fact, Murphy had avoided her at school, disappearing at lunch, only nodding to her in the halls. It had knocked Leeda for a loop. Either Murphy was too nervous about being forgiven or she was angry at Leeda for some mysterious cause she couldn't imagine. Both options fueled the firestorm in Leeda's head.

She cast a glance toward the Balmeade property again, thinking about whether she should climb over the fence and lie on the well-groomed grass. It looked tempting—pristine, soft, smooth. At the moment she put one foot up on the lowest fence rung, she felt something thunk her on the back.

"Ow." She reached back and spun around. Birdie and Murphy stood behind her, Murphy laughing.

Murphy saw the look on her face and quickly suppressed the smile. "Sorry." Birdie stood beside her, the picture of grief, awash in black. She had fashioned a papoose out of black fabric and in it Majestic dangled like a seed pod, her little nose poking out and her accusing eyes drilling a hole in Leeda. Leeda couldn't maintain eye contact.

"You know some kids threw Snickers bars at me at Quick Trip yesterday," she muttered for Murphy's benefit.

"You're the pariah of the Bridgewater beauty queens," Murphy said. There was a harsh edge to her voice that set Leeda on edge.

"What're you doing here?" she asked coolly.

Birdie whipped something out of her pocket and held it up in the air like a finger. A red Sharpie. "Cast signing."

They sat with their backs against the fence, Leeda, then Birdie, then Murphy at the end. Birdie unsheathed one of Majestic's casted legs from the papoose. The dog sighed and settled its little chin against her breast mournfully.

"I'll go first," Birdie said, holding the back of the marker to her lips thoughtfully, then writing, very gingerly, *You are #1. Get well soon.* She held Majestic's face up to hers and repeated what she'd written, giving her a look to see if she understood.

She handed the marker to Murphy, who didn't need to think at all. She leaned over Birdie and wrote *Don't change.*

Birdie shot her a stricken look. When Murphy went to hand the marker back to her, her face went all innocent. "What?"

"Couldn't you have written something more heartfelt?"

Murphy sighed, then reached for the marker again. "Here, I'll cross it out."

"No, no, no, it's too late," Birdie said wistfully. She took the marker and handed it to Leeda. Leeda hated things like this. She hated writing anything permanent—even school papers. She knew that whatever she wrote, she would think of something better a few minutes later. She tapped the pen against her chin and then finally, unsurely, wrote the only thing heartfelt she knew: *Lo siento. I'm sorry.* She was pretty sure Majestic was bilingual.

Birdie lifted Majestic out of the papoose and placed her gently on the grass. "Go play." Majestic didn't go play. She didn't so much lie down in the spot as expire there and roll onto her side, staring at Leeda.

"I wish she'd stop looking at me like that."

"I guess *Lo siento*'s not good enough," Murphy offered. Birdie and Leeda both looked at her, surprised. How could she be so hard? Murphy's curls stuck against the little cracks of the fence. Leeda hadn't noticed till that moment the paleness of her face, the dark half-saucers under her eyes, how tired she looked. Like her whole face was working to show something she didn't feel. Maybe she felt terrible for what had happened at the festival after all. Leeda instantly wanted to forgive her.

They were quiet for a while.

"Do you believe in karma?" Birdie asked to no one in particular, unless she was talking to Majestic.

"I think so," Leeda said. Actually, Leeda really didn't know. She hadn't thought about it much.

Birdie let out a long breath and let her arms loll back behind her head. "What about retribution, like, from the universe?"

Leeda hadn't thought about that much either. She shrugged. "Nah. Look at all the bad guys that get off easy."

"The bad guys don't just get off easy," Murphy piped in.

"They win. Nine times out of ten. When the good guys win, it's an accident. That's how the universe works."

Birdie seemed to take this all in very seriously. Finally she said, "What do you think about that thing where if you're a sinner and Armageddon comes, you have to chop off your own head?"

"HA," Murphy laughed.

"Me too." Birdie rolled over on her side. "But what if you make a mistake—do you think God punishes you for it?"

She was asking Murphy, but Leeda felt like she needed to protect Birdie from Murphy's dark cynicism, so she said fast, "I don't think it works that way, Bird. I don't think God is like that."

"Rex and I are splits," Murphy announced out of nowhere, reaching around to pluck some paint off the fence. Birdie gasped and leaned in, grabbing Murphy's thigh. Murphy shook her head and put her finger to her lips. "Don't say sorry. Don't say anything." Murphy peeled the paint into fine little strings. "I'm fine."

Suddenly it made sense to Leeda. Murphy's recent behavior in the halls had nothing to do with her. She was sorry and hurt at the same time.

Birdie reached from the thigh to one of Murphy's hands, squishing their fingers together even though Murphy tried to pull hers away. Leeda marveled at how Birdie could do things like that so easily.

"He won't go to New York," Murphy said.

"So you guys decided to call it off now before it gets even harder to leave?" Birdie asked gently. Some people would have asked out of curiosity. With Birdie, it was always to get you to say what you needed to say. Leeda could only watch, frozen and unsure what to do. Murphy looked at Birdie and her eyes started to go watery.

"I decided," Murphy said flatly.

Leeda thought of Rex, of how he looked at Murphy, like all sorts of spotlights were dancing on her. He must be devastated.

"I'm sorry, Murphy." Birdie wrapped Murphy in a suffocating hug. Murphy folded her arms and tried to squirm away.

Leeda watched Birdie showering so much sympathy on Murphy, who had walked away from love. Leeda couldn't remember ever doing that. She could remember lots of times love had walked away from her, in the form of her mom, turning in another direction. In the form of Rex, when he'd kissed Murphy in the garden when he was supposed to belong to Leeda. When she had given Rex up to Murphy, no one had come over to hold her hand. She'd remembered distinctly that when she'd stood on the Pecan Festival float alone, Murphy had been eating a fried Mars bar.

"He would have stayed with you," Leeda said, almost to herself. "Until the last minute."

Murphy and Birdie both looked at her.

"But that's not the problem," Leeda went on. "It's not how much he's wrapped around your finger; it's whether he's wrapped all the way."

"Leeda, don't say that," Birdie said. Murphy looked too stunned to say anything.

Finally Murphy straightened herself up and said with a distant, sharp edge, "Rex is taking care of himself." As in, Leeda didn't know what she was talking about. As in, Leeda had no idea what the right thing was.

Leeda thought of the many little ways that Murphy had hurt her. She didn't know why she felt so deeply, hugely angry, but it was unstoppable. Still, she kept her voice even and calm. "Well, I'd think of anyone, you'd understand putting yourself first."

"Leeda!" Birdie said.

Once, when Leeda had been in fifth grade, she'd called another girl fat. It was something she'd heard her mom say a million times behind people's backs. But her teacher—Ms. Dubois, whom she adored—had heard her. She'd said Leeda's name, just like that: *Leeda*, and just stared at her. No punishment. No other words. And Leeda had felt like the smallest, unworthiest piece of dirt in the world. She felt that way now.

Leeda looked off toward the dorms. She needed someone to notice that she was here too, that she had been walked away from too. She didn't know how to say that out loud.

"Let's go inside and watch a movie." Birdie stood up and dragged Murphy by the elbow.

Leeda stood too, twisted up inside, wanting to hit, or tear, or claw. "I don't feel like it," she said, daring them to push her. She just needed to be pushed an inch. . . .

But Birdie just started walking. She turned to look over her shoulder with big, wholesome, disappointed Birdie eyes. "That's probably good," she told her. Leeda felt a stab at the words and stood frozen in place.

She watched their backs as they walked on down between the two rows of pecans, the trees' arms arching overhead so they looked like a couple in a military wedding. Leeda stood with her hands at her side. Her body felt out of place, like it had landed on the orchard from another planet. She had the strange, too-aware sense that the ground she stood on was all curves and she couldn't be anything but perpendicular.

Birdie and Murphy disappeared on the other side of the pecan grove. They didn't look back. And Leeda watched love walk away from her all over again.

Twenty

$\mathcal{B}$irdie lay on her stomach, her cheek mushed against her cool cotton bedspread. She'd pushed one pillow off to make more room, and her left arm dangled over the side of the bed. Her room was the safest place to hide from her dad and Poopie. Outside of meals, she hid up here pretending to do schoolwork whenever she was in the house. Every morning since Thanksgiving, for ten long days, she had woken up thinking it was the day her dad would give her some kind of horrible, uncomfortable speech. But so far, nothing. Ominous, scary silence. Of course, the speech would include her not being allowed to go to Mexico. She was sure of it. As sure as she was that Poopie had told him.

Birdie let out a groan. She did not want to think about Poopie at all. Poopie hadn't made eye contact *once* since the cider house. But Birdie didn't have to look in her eyes to know what she was thinking. She was thinking she was stuck in a house with an emotional mutant (Birdie's dad), a handicapped dog who couldn't go to the bathroom on her own (Majestic), and a Jezebel (Birdie, of course). If Poopie already had one figurative foot out the door, it was a wonder she hadn't taken off running yet. Maybe she was waiting for a good deal on flights.

On the other pillow next to Birdie, Saint Francis reposed, unblinkingly staring at the ceiling. Birdie wasn't sure who the patron saint of Jezebels was, so she'd dragged out Saint Francis, who'd always been her favorite.

Birdie knew it wasn't quite the way things were supposed to work, but she sometimes tried to communicate with her santos through mental telepathy. This time, she had tried to make him very comfortable first so he would be most amenable to hearing what she had to say.

Hi, she thought, looking over at the santo. Then a stream of thoughts about all her recent sins flowed out of her, beginning with the biggest. She sighed. She knew she was in no position to ask favors, but she needed to anyway.

If it was my fault that God took Honey Babe away, can you send me some kind of sign? she asked with her thoughts. Saint Francis stared up at the ceiling beneficently. Birdie lay very still for a long time, listening to the silence of the room, the winter air hissing around the tiny gaps in the windowpanes. She pushed up on her elbows, looked toward the window in case it was raining locusts or something, then plopped back down, cheek first.

Okay, well, if I promise not to do it again, can we forget the whole thing ever happened? She waited, and again, nothing. It wasn't like she was really expecting a sign. She wasn't *eight.* But just for reassurance, she leaned over Saint Francis and looked at his face carefully to see if the expression had changed at all. He still wore a blank stare and a peaceful smile. Or did it have a hint of disdain in it?

She sighed and shuffled across the cold wooden floor, placing him on her dresser next to a green urn that contained Honey Babe's ashes.

"Woof woof!"

Birdie jumped, thinking it was the urn barking. And then she remembered Majestic, who'd been lying on her dog pillow and was getting up to hobble over. Birdie scooped the dog into her arms. Majestic stared at the urn over her shoulder suspiciously, letting out a low growl. She growled at the urn a lot. Birdie didn't know if she just didn't know what it was or if she knew that it was a vase full of Honey Babe and was grumbling to object.

"I'm losing my mind," Birdie muttered. She was hungry. She peered out of her room to make sure the coast was clear and tiptoed down the stairs.

In the back of her mind, Birdie was constantly trying to figure out how she would break it to Enrico that she wouldn't be allowed to see him anymore. Part of her kept hoping to open up to Murphy or Leeda and ask for advice, but Birdie was too ashamed. She'd tried dropping hints to Leeda, letting out little sighs, sitting on the bed in her dorm room and swinging her legs, silence passing between them for minutes on end. But Leeda didn't seem to notice the lapses. At meals, she sat like a fine marble goddess. Between meals, she ducked to the dorms. Murphy too hadn't been over again since she and Leeda had argued.

At the bottom of the stairs, Birdie could smell a cloud of Poopie's perfume, as if she'd just been there. She walked into the kitchen and grabbed a box of wheat crackers from the pantry, then wandered into the office to flip through the bills.

After her mom had left, she and her dad had both been so shell-shocked. The office had fallen apart for a while, and now it was such a relief to see everything in order. The two of them—well, the three of them—had gotten their life harnessed together. Birdie marveled at how smoothly it ran now and how quickly it had happened.

She sorted through the bills and highlighted the due dates. She opened their insurance statements and tried to run down the numbers, but she couldn't focus. She kept thinking about things Enrico had done. Where he'd kissed her. The angle of her hand on his shoulder. A tiny bruise on his side. When she looked up, her dad was standing in the doorway. Half a wheat cracker lodged itself in her throat and she coughed, her pulse throbbing. Her dad returned her gaze solemnly.

"Your tickets came."

"Oh," Birdie managed to choke out, swallowing.

Walter stepped up to the other side of the desk and handed her the envelope. He watched quietly as she peered down at the address: *Barbara Darlington*. Birdie fiddled with the plastic window, running her finger along the edge, and looked up at him. When her mom had still been living with them, Birdie had gotten so used to the worry on his face that she'd come to think it was part of his features. Now, standing before her, his face creased in the way she'd remembered.

"How're the books looking?" he asked.

Birdie swallowed. She glanced down at the bills in front of her and the ledger, which she'd tallied up the night before. "Good." She had to say it again because it didn't really come out with a voice attached. "Good."

Walter nodded. "You'll have so much fun on vacation you won't want to come back," he said.

Birdie laughed. It was a tense laugh. What did he mean by *fun*? What did he mean by *vacation*?

Her pulse thrummed against her wrists as he stood there, looking at her. As if he had something more to say. And then he walked over and rubbed her head like he had when she was little. "You'd better come back from Mexico in one piece. I wouldn't know what to do without you."

He turned and walked out. Birdie slumped over, amazed, relieved, disbelieving. She folded the envelope in two and stuffed it into her pocket, as if at any minute someone might whip it out of her hands.

It took her a minute to put together that Poopie hadn't told her dad. And then to ask why. One answer immediately leapt to mind. It was that Poopie hadn't made it her business. It wasn't her concern.

Birdie's elation seeped out like helium, but she couldn't ignore the pricks of excitement running up and down the soles of her feet. She—Birdie Darlington—was going *somewhere*.

Twenty-one

Murphy and Jodee picked out a short, fluffy tree at the
tent set up in the parish parking lot of Divine Grace of the
Redeemer. Murphy stood and watched, her hands around a
Styrofoam cup of complimentary cider, as her mom flirted the
guy down to thirty-five bucks. Then together they loaded it
halfway into the trunk of the Pontiac, tying it down securely.

Murphy couldn't believe how good she felt. For two weeks,
she'd spent each night lying awake, sleepless with anger, her
fists balled, or thrown over her head, or wrapped strangle-like
around the pillow beside her. But today, and for the last few
days, she'd felt like she was at the top of her game, somewhere
she hadn't been in a long time. She'd turned all her energy to
thinking about May and New York. She'd spent countless hours
on the Internet looking at photos and maps, burning it all in her
brain, like a map to buried treasure. Now when she thought
about Rex, which was still often, she felt above him somehow,
like he'd let her down enough that she could give him up. She
felt powerful. Like if he appeared in front of her at that very
moment, she could have laid him flat with one swift punch.

She felt differently about Leeda. Part of the fist balling had been directed at her too and the things she'd said. The two had been avoiding each other, neither willing to make the first move to get back together. But Murphy didn't even know what, on *her* side, she'd actually done.

"You want me to drop you anywhere, baby?" her mom asked. "Maybe you should stop by and see Rex...." Jodee looked hopeful. It was unspoken between them that Jodee thought Murphy was crazy for letting such a good guy go. To Murphy, her mom's credo of *men first* was pitiful.

"I think I'll hang out here awhile," Murphy said, tossing the cider cup into a garbage can and sticking her hands in her pockets.

"You sure, baby?"

"Yeah. I can walk home."

Once her mom was gone, she shuffled around, directionless. Maybe it was because of TV or maybe that Murphy had been born for colder climates, but every year, she expected a layer of snow for her to stomp through downtown. But Main Street was clean and clear, with only the occasional snack wrapper blowing across the brick sidewalks. It was cold enough for a coat but not a hat. And as long as Murphy had been alive, snow had never fallen on Bridgewater at Christmas.

She stopped in Eckerds to flirt with a guy she knew there and get some free Blow Pops. She leaned over the counter and pursed her lips and moved up and down on her toes while he dug out all the watermelons, her favorite. There was a scale with a mirror next to the pharmacy counter, and she stared at herself sideways. With her low-slung jeans and junk store green army coat,

Murphy looked high-fidelity, full-color, and healthy. The counter boy's voice pitched high when he asked her, nervous and awed, if she wanted anything else. Murphy smiled and stuck a Blow Pop in her mouth as she turned and sauntered out the door.

Outside again, her feet took her toward Ace Hardware. She peeked through the glass door on her way past, casually, not really looking. She circled back and walked by again. She fiddled with a newspaper machine in front of the shop next door, pressing the coin release button over and over again.

"Hey, Murphy." She spun around. He was walking toward her, a length of steel cable in his hands.

"Hey, Mr. Taggart."

"I was just running an errand," he said, nodding toward the front of his store. The Ace. He looked genuinely happy to see her, but he was the kind of guy who was generally happy to see people. "You wanna come in?"

Murphy floated close to him. He held the door open for her, warm air and the smell of oil and metal drifting out. She peered through the doorway, unsure. "Okay."

The door closed behind her with a jingle, and Rex's dad led her down the crowded, narrow aisle. The store was a riot of tools and parts in yellows, greens, blacks, organized on floor-to-ceiling shelves. It smelled like men or maybe just masculine. It was the way Rex smelled. Murphy followed Mr. Taggart down the chaotic row toward the cash register. He laid the steel cable down beside it and rummaged behind the counter.

"Where has my son been hiding you?"

"Um." Murphy hesitated. Had Rex not told him? That wasn't a huge surprise. "Around."

"Uh-huh." Mr. Taggart nodded, making eye contact, giving her his undivided attention. When Murphy didn't say anything more, he smiled. "You wanna help me with this? We're sort of short-staffed today."

"Sure." Murphy held the cable taut while he cut it with a pair of pliers.

"Great," he said.

Murphy gave him a tremulous smile. She knew she should get going. But she couldn't move. "Can I help you with anything else?" she blurted.

He looked surprised. "Yeah, if you have the time. That'd be great."

They worked for over an hour, Murphy running down parts and stacking things on the shelves. Mr. Taggart tallied things up, gently focused on the computer at the front desk as he typed in orders, but he made sure to keep thanking her and looking her in the eye. There was a gentleness about him and also a sort of sadness. Murphy wondered if it was from when his wife had left. Some kinds of people never got over things like that. Murphy had always known she must be one of the people who did.

Finally, after about an hour and a half, Murphy ran out of things to do. She didn't want to admit it at first. She rearranged the boxes of nails three times pointlessly. Then she walked back to the counter and leaned against it.

"Well, Murphy, that's it, unless you want to apply for a job here."

Murphy smiled. "No, that's okay."

"You have bigger plans, I hear."

Murphy shrugged, a lump in her throat. "Maybe."

"We'll miss you when you head north."

Murphy didn't know what to say. She hadn't thought much about anything in Bridgewater she'd miss besides the people she loved. But she'd miss Rex's dad. Maybe she'd even miss Ace Hardware.

"Well, tell Rex to bring you home as much as possible before you run off."

"Okay," Murphy murmured. They walked up to the front and he opened the door for her. From the doorway, Murphy could see the gazebo where the judges sat for various parades. To the right, the redbrick courthouse with a stand of loblolly pines. Liddie's Tea Room, with two Red Hat ladies shuffling out the front door.

"Bye, Murphy." Mr. Taggart touched her arm gently. She felt the warmth of his hand on her wrist. When he pulled it away, it left a deep, wide void right in the middle of Murphy. She stepped outside, and the door slowly closed behind her.

By the time she reached the trailer park, Murphy's chest was heaving. She knew she needed to just crawl into bed and pull the covers over her head and find her way back to being angry. Inside, all the lights were on and Jodee was erecting the tree. She had it in the corner of their tiny living room/TV room/foyer.

Murphy hovered in the doorway. Now that she saw her, she wanted so badly to crumple up in her mom's arms. But she didn't know how to let her know.

Jodee stood facing the tree for several seconds, not noticing Murphy standing behind her. Finally Jodee turned to her, her face nervous, apologetic. Murphy's stomach tightened just slightly.

Jodee looked uncertain for a moment and then sidestepped to the kitchen counter, sliding a thin envelope off its yellow surface and handing it to Murphy. "I'm sorry. I opened it. I shouldn't have."

Murphy looked at the envelope with NYU's purple school insignia in the return address but didn't take it. Her throat went knotty. "What does it say?"

Jodee pulled the envelope back. "You've been deferred. For regular admission."

"Oh." Murphy just stood there, trying to compute. How was that possible?

Murphy reached for the letter. She took it to her room. After she'd read it three times, she lay back on her bed and stared at the ceiling, which was low, and her walls, which were close together. Her window too was the size of a postage stamp. She willed herself right through the roof.

Twenty-two

"Nonsense."

Leeda sat in the stuffy, doily-strewn parlor of Primrose Cottage, her grandmother's dollhouse-like Victorian home. She could feel the smell of dust and coffee sinking into her clothes. The couch she sat on was silk and straight-backed, and Leeda clutched the armrest rigidly, like she was sitting on the electric chair. If her grandmom said the word *nonsense* one more time, she thought she might faint.

Grandmom Eugenie was still in curlers, but otherwise, sitting in the throne-like settee chair to Leeda's right, she was elegantly dressed: a festive red wool sweater that reached up to her powdery white chin and black slacks. They were going to lunch at Liddie's Tea Room to celebrate her ninety-fifth birthday since Leeda had refused to join in on the family festivities that evening. But though she was escaping a run-in with her mother, she hadn't escaped a lecture from her grandmother. Her grandmother liked to give lectures on her birthday. It was like she'd marked it on her calendar, which was of course miniature-horse-themed and hung beside the fridge: *December 12, tell everyone what's what.*

"Families are supposed to put up with one another," she said, her mauve mouth steeled in righteous determination, her violet eyes taking Leeda in sharply. She had a mimosa in one hand and sipped it now and then. Grandmom Eugenie was always so sure she was right and always so blunt about telling her family what to do that it made Leeda feel like a paper doll. Like she wasn't quite three-dimensional. "Now, you go back to the orchard and pack your bags and move home. You'll never have time back with your family again once you're really gone."

It was the first good news Leeda had heard since she'd arrived. Eugenie stood up, set her mimosa down on the glass coffee table, and uncurled a curler out of her hair, then another. With Leeda sitting, they were nearly the same height. A curl hung in Eugenie's face comically. Leeda couldn't imagine being ninety-five and still spending so much time on her appearance. It was just one more testament to Grandmom Eugenie's steely resolve. "There's a box for you on the dining room table. I think that'll change your mind. I'm going to go do my makeup."

Leeda watched Grandmom Eugenie disappear up the stairs, uncurling as she went. Her makeup would take close to an hour; it always did. Leeda sighed, feeling like a caged animal. The whole house made her toes itch with claustrophobia.

She got up and walked to the dining room. The box was about a foot by a foot, a square hatbox. Some kind of fuzz ball had attached itself to the side of her palm and she rubbed it off on the floor, then went and washed her hands in the bathroom.

When she returned, she pulled off the note first.

Leeda, here are some things we thought you'd need. Love, Dad.

Oh.

She pulled off the lid and removed the items one by one. There were socks—lightweight spring ones. A white pair of sneakers she hadn't worn in two years. Contact solution. A toothbrush. If her mom had packed the box or even looked inside, it would have been filled with entirely different things. At the bottom of the box was a pink jacket and two envelopes. One thick one with *Columbia University* in the return address. In the bottom-right corner it said, *Welcome!* She didn't even have to open it. The other envelope was addressed to her in her mom's handwriting. Leeda's heart did a little dip, and she slit it open with her fingers. She peered in at what was enclosed, and her heart sank. She emptied out the hundred-dollar bill that had been folded inside. Nothing about the box was unpredictable. So she didn't know why it hurt. She'd felt so hurt lately, she didn't know how she hadn't run out of that particular feeling.

But then there was a surprise. There was one final item in the bottom of the box. She reached in and pulled it out. *Notes for a Truly Leeda Leeda.* She looked at Murphy's handwriting on the shiny red cover. The title was surrounded by stars. Leeda sank into the dining room chair beside her, leaning over the table without her elbows touching it, by habit, and opened the book with a throbbing, longing heart.

She flipped through the notebook. In most places, Murphy's large, crooked handwriting ate up the pages greedily, as if she couldn't write large enough to get her point across. Occasionally Birdie's more graceful handwriting appeared, adding asides or participating with Murphy in some kind of list she had thrown together, like favorite Leeda moments, or most unknown things about Leeda, or Leeda's top five best articles of clothing.

Mostly, though, it was all Murphy. Listing albums Leeda had to own before she died, like Janis Joplin's *Pearl*. Copied scraps of her favorite poetry: about nature and despair and cities and even one or two about love that Murphy had annotated with words like *Sickening, but she's good* and *Horrible but worth reading*. Dried leaves—pecan, magnolia, and, of course, the thin slivered shape of the peach leaf—taped in messy crisscrosses. A cider label Birdie had once kissed. A diagram of Leeda—outlined sloppily with colored-in blond hair, with words on the outside pointing to different parts of her: *brainy* pointing to her head, *good posture* pointing to her back, *hot gams* pointing to her legs, *impenetrable (ha ha)* pointing to her heart.

Leeda read the favorite Leeda moments again and again. It was eerie, but she felt like she was reading about somebody she didn't quite know. She didn't know how much of the Leeda they wrote about she really was and how much Murphy and Birdie were just filling in by conjecture.

Most striking, now that she hadn't looked at it in a while, was how filled with passion the pages were—Murphy's crazy, sprawling brain. You could almost hear her loud, unruly thoughts. The last time Leeda had read the book, she hadn't noticed all that much difference between her own ideas of herself and the ones that were on paper. But now she saw how Murphy saw the world in bold colors and tried to spin them around Leeda like the threads of a robe. As if Murphy could be the one to make Leeda visible.

Leeda touched one of the poems, running her fingers over the words. *I believe a leaf of grass is no less than the journey-work of the stars. —Walt Whitman.*

Leeda understood what the words meant, but she didn't feel like she had any claim to them. She wasn't full of bright colors. What she was full of was more like those bats she and her mom had seen—blind, dark, fluttery.

Leeda flipped through again, skimming for specific details. There was nothing in the book about Rex. There was nothing about the times that Murphy and Leeda hadn't liked each other, when they had still been mostly strangers. There was nothing about the times they had wounded each other or broken each other's hearts.

There was another huge difference between the last time Leeda had read through the book and now. Last time, it had flattered her, buoyed her up, made her giggle, and inflated her ego. But now, it just made her uneasy. She didn't want to lean on anybody else to tell her who she was. In fact, she wasn't sure she wanted to lean on anyone, period. Not when they could spin out from under you. She didn't want to be the person Murphy left standing in her pecan dress, or the person Birdie and Murphy left watching them walk away in the pecan grove, or the person her mom hadn't shown up for, for the millionth time.

There was a pair of scissors sitting on the end of the table, on top of one of Grandmom's sewing projects: an embroidered blanket for Mitsy, one of her miniature ponies. Leeda took the scissors and worked quickly and carefully. She needed to finish before her grandmom came down.

When she walked out the front door, it was with an equal amount of exhilaration and guilt. She felt right that she was actually doing something for herself—instead of going along with an afternoon that was going to make her miserable. She felt right that she was standing up to Grandmom Eugenie, in a way. She only felt guilty when she thought of Grandmom Eugenie coming down to the parlor and looking for her and finding the house empty.

On the dining room table, she'd left the cutout diagram of her paper self. She'd actually sat her up, propping her against a napkin holder, making sure her posture was perfect. Grandmom Eugenie could dress it up any way she wanted to.

On the way back to the orchard, Leeda stopped at Q.T. and bought a pack of cigarettes on a whim. And when she pulled up to the Darlington house, instead of walking to the dorms, she walked to the barn. She took the box her dad had sent, *Truly Leeda Leeda* book included, and dropped it in the trash.

Twenty-three

Murphy parked her bike in the driveway and crunched across the gravel to the dorms. She rubbed her hands together, feeling the cold through her cheap acrylic gloves, and looked around. The sky hung over the orchard like a fuzzy gray blanket and rained a fine drizzle. The air smelled like water and brown grass. Without their leaves to soften their crooked limbs, the peach trees looked like broken umbrellas stripped to their metal skeletons. One yellow light in the dorm house was on—the others were all dark and empty. Murphy picked some pebbles from the road and threw them at the window.

She waited. Nothing.

She walked up the steps to the dorm and pulled on the door handle. Locked. She looked up at Leeda's window. She knew she was in there. "Leeda, let's make up!" She expected a face to appear in the window, a reluctant smile. But it stayed blank. Murphy breathed on a downstairs window, then drew a frowny face. It was almost Christmas, for God's sake. How long was this going to last?

Finally she crossed the driveway and made her way up the spongy green lawn toward the house.

Before she was halfway there, Birdie appeared on the deck, wrapped up in scarves and a bunchy raincoat, and stood as still as a snowman. She was still in mourning—black raincoat, black jeans crusted with work dirt, black turtleneck peeking above her collar. Only her cheeks were bright from the misty cold air. Majestic's butterfly ears stuck out of her collar too.

"Is Lee inside with you?" Murphy asked.

Birdie shook her head. "She's in the dorms."

"She wouldn't even open the door for me."

Birdie shrugged.

The truth was, Murphy felt like the only way to get any of the heaviness off her soul was to tell Leeda and Birdie about it. Being deferred from NYU still didn't feel real. It had never even occurred to her she wouldn't get in.

Without deciding where they were going, Birdie and Murphy walked past the dorms again, stared up at the yellow window forlornly for a while, and then kept on walking to the edge of the property, climbing over the sagging wooden fence into Balmeade Country Club.

The short-hewn, wide expanse of grass was empty of golf balls and carts and people. Birdie turned her face to the sky occasionally and caught drizzle drops on her cheeks. Finally they came upon the shed where the carts were kept. Even though they hadn't talked about where they were going or what they were planning to do, they moved like one unit. Murphy picked the lock with her Swiss army knife and they both heaved the shed door open, heading for one of the green-and-gold carts.

Murphy felt around for the key while Birdie climbed in beside her. The cart lurched into motion, and they jostled over the green.

"I heard back from NYU," Murphy finally told her. "I got deferred. I'll find out in April."

Birdie looked concerned. "You better get some safety schools, Murphy."

"Yeah." It wasn't agreement, but an acknowledgment that Birdie thought so. Murphy had no intention of settling for anything other than exactly what she wanted.

When they pulled out onto Orchard Road, Murphy turned right, going the long way toward town, studiously avoiding the scene of the accident. Birdie cradled Majestic under her coat, as if the dog's body were a pregnant belly. Only the dog's head and casted front legs hung out from where she'd half unzipped her coat. She rocked slowly back and forth, as if she were riding a camel.

They craned their necks toward the pecan grove as they puttered past it. Methuselah stood a few feet from the road, looking tired.

Murphy was happy to motor away from the whole forlorn picture of the orchard. It was like the place was groggy on sleeping pills. But town was no better. All gray walls and gray sky and empty sidewalks and red lights and the occasional debris blowing out of a trash can and across the road. They drove to the Dunkin' Donuts drive-through and ordered two strawberry frosteds to take to Leeda as an offering, a wheat bagel for Birdie, and one large coffee for Murphy. Murphy had been hooked on their coffee ever since she had worked there, before she'd gotten fired for doing whip-its in the closet.

They parked in the side lot and sat, watching the cars go by and the trash blow around soggily. They ate and sipped and watched the people come through the drive-through while Murphy made fun of them. One woman had three kids in the back, all fighting, and Murphy pretended to strangle herself. Usually Birdie would have laughed while trying not to, but she was quiet and thoughtful, barely there.

"Are you excited about Mexico?" Murphy asked finally.

Birdie nodded. "Yeah."

It was the most underwhelming *yeah* possible. Murphy gazed at her, wondering what was going on in Birdie world. She remembered a book she had read about a dog named Fletcher. In the illustrations, Fletcher was so sad that he actually took the shape of the steps he was lying on. Murphy could picture his body perfectly—all accordioned along the stairs, his jowls hanging down. The whole world seemed like Fletcher today. They were both Fletchered out.

Pretty soon, Murphy ran out of people to make fun of. Her heart hadn't been in it anyway. There was no sound between them except for sipping and chewing. The scent of strawberry frosting hovered and stuck to their coats.

Finally Birdie seemed to rouse a little and straightened up. She turned to Murphy. "Murphy, are you ever going to talk about Rex?"

Murphy tapped her heels against the floor of the cart. "We already talked about it."

Birdie stared at her earnestly. Murphy hated when Birdie gave the earnest look. It made you feel like you had to be earnest too. "I mean really talk."

"Well," Murphy said, searching her mind for something she was willing to say. It had to be something that wouldn't knock open any holes. Suddenly she had an idea. The idea had been there all along, but she pretended it was the first time she'd thought of it. "Let's drive by his house."

Though Birdie and Majestic both looked uneasy, Murphy hit the gas. A few minutes later, she slowed down to a stealthy crawl. The golf cart crept slowly past Pearly Gates and past the house. Murphy pulled to a halt just beyond it, past the edge of the trees where they could be half hidden a few feet from the bluebird mailbox, and looked back over her shoulder. Rex's truck was in the driveway, and she could hear the radio coming from his room.

"He's just sitting home alone," Birdie said. "I bet he misses you."

Murphy was suddenly irritated. "You're supposed to hate him for me, Bird."

Birdie looked apologetic. "I do." It was like Birdie's *yeah* from earlier. It was only words.

"You wanna know something about Rex?" Murphy said, annoyed. "He was born bowlegged."

Birdie sank slightly.

"Yep," Murphy went on. "They had to do that thing where they straighten out your legs."

Birdie looked down at her bagel, sending the signal that she didn't want to know. They both knew how private Rex was.

"And let's see, what else can I tell you? He opens his mouth so wide when he kisses. It's disgusting." Murphy wanted to stop, but she couldn't. "And he wet the bed until he was nine."

Birdie stared, looking over Murphy's shoulder, and Murphy turned. Rex's dad was standing there. He had a hand on the mailbox.

"Hey, Mr. Taggart," Birdie said.

"Hey." He nodded to Birdie. "I . . . just came out to get the mail." He didn't look at Murphy. And Murphy knew with a fiery sinking in her gut that he had heard the whole thing. He reached into the mailbox and pulled something out. Then he waved the papers at them once, turned, and started back up the drive toward his house.

Murphy watched him, her heart pounding with shame. She felt like cold liquid metal had been poured down her throat.

She slammed on the gas, and the golf cart sped off into the dusk.

As December worked its way toward Christmas, the same old holiday stories began to make their way around Bridgewater. A favorite was an old English legend about Joseph of Arimathea—uncle to the Virgin Mary—who laid his walking stick down on a hill in Glastonbury, England. According to the legend, it blossomed into a tree known as the Glastonbury thorn.

But the people of Bridgewater had their own version, with this twist: Joseph had actually lent his stick to a cousin of his, who passed it on through his descendants, who moved to Georgia to farm pecans. And the theory was that upon being laid down on a lazy walk, the cane had sprouted into a holy tree somewhere in Kings County. But as to what kind of tree it was and where exactly it stood, no one dared to guess.

Twenty-four

The afternoon of Christmas Eve, Leeda sat on the couch in the Darlingtons' den, curled in an afghan Poopie had made, filling out college applications. She hadn't told a soul at the Darlington house about getting into Columbia. And she kept the papers in front of her now, tilted up like she was guarding her test answers, as if they all wouldn't find out eventually.

The cold, wet draft coming through the windows fought with the heat from the fireplace. The Darlingtons' decrepit old stereo played a quiet selection of Spanish and English music that Poopie had mixed together on a CD. The fire was roaring, and Poopie was stringing popcorn. Birdie sat in a rocking chair across the room, reading a book on Mexico and scratching Majestic's ears, her back turned to Poopie. Uncle Walter sat on the nubby, rust-colored carpet, looking through a box of old photos he'd pulled out from the built-in bookcase, where it had probably sat for five years.

The tree was strung—not with the familiar white lights of the Cawley-Smith house but with bulbs of every shape and size and color, some of them fat seventies Technicolor, others tiny blinkers. There was tinsel, popcorn balls, old ornaments, tiny mother-of-pearl angels, crosses made of shells and wire, glass balls, some of them with holy scenes of the manger. The tree was a true reflection of its surroundings—lopsided, pell-mell, messy.

Birdie came over and sat next to her. "Do you want to go for a walk?"

"No thanks."

Birdie moon-eyed her. She had been moon-eyeing her for weeks, ever since the day in the pecan grove. Leeda had been polite every time they ate together, every time Birdie appeared at the dorm door with cookies she'd baked or bags of extra toiletries she'd picked up on her errands. But Leeda had frozen Birdie out. It was more subtle than with Murphy, but Leeda knew what she was doing. At school, Leeda avoided Murphy in the halls and Murphy avoided her. At lunch, they sat at separate tables anyway—Leeda with her friends, of which she had several—and Murphy with hers. When Murphy arrived at the orchard through the front door, Leeda traipsed off out the back. They had always inhabited such separate worlds anyway. It was easy to separate them almost completely now.

"Do you want your present early?" Birdie asked.

Leeda looked over at the lopsided present Birdie had already placed under the tree, wrapped in red-white-and-green paper covered in little Santas. Clearly it was something she'd knitted, just by the lumpiness of it.

"I can wait," Leeda answered. It was slightly painful to watch Birdie stand up, crestfallen, and slink back over to the rocking chair. But it felt right for Leeda to stand in her place—proud and removed. She felt like, for the first time in a long time, she was holding her ground.

Leeda's mind drifted, from time to time, to what the scene would be like at her house. The family would be in the home theater, probably, lounging on the La-Z-Boys, watching some movie. They definitely wouldn't be sitting in the quiet with one another, doing nothing. The tree—which always stood in the sweeping foyer—would have been professionally decorated (Lucretia hated getting sap on her hands) with some kind of color scheme. It was sort of an empty vision, but a tiny part of Leeda missed it. She had never been away on Christmas.

Her grandmom had called three times, hoping to catch her, but Leeda had waved her hands to show Poopie she wasn't there, much to Poopie's obvious chagrin. Her dad had come by early that afternoon to deliver her presents: two suitcases for school, a thousand-dollar Simon gift card to the mall in Atlanta. Nothing that went in a wrapped box the way the presents under the Darlington tree did.

The sound of the rain coming down outside made her nestle deeper into the afghan. Through the room's twin windows, the empty peach trees were visible, drooping and bouncing under the raindrops and looking so thin and frail they seemed like they should break. Poopie hummed along with the music and shot occasional looks at Birdie's back that Leeda couldn't quite understand.

"Look at these, girls," Uncle Walter said. Leeda got up and lay on her stomach on the floor beside him. Birdie got off her rocking chair and sat on the other side. Majestic hobbled over and lay on her side next to Birdie, her butterfly ears flopping back.

Leeda looked at the top picture on her pile. In it, a much younger Uncle Walter had puffy brown hair. There were lots of photos of the house and the orchard.

"Look, Poopie, it's you." Leeda pointed to one that Uncle Walter had just uncovered, but Poopie just smiled vaguely, rethreading her needle. In the picture, Birdie and her mom were standing several yards in front of the barn, smiling, and behind them was Poopie, carrying a sack of peaches on her front. Her forehead was crinkled up from the sun and she was squinting—looking almost exactly the same as now—same hair, same type of clothes, though the hair was darker and shinier, less gray in it. It looked like she'd just been passing by when she'd noticed she'd wandered into the photo and grinned dutifully. Like she was part of the photo but not really. The sack of peaches slumped against her belly like a baby. Leeda wondered suddenly about Poopie and kids. Had she ever wanted them?

They flipped through more boring photos of people Leeda didn't recognize and a few she did. Birdie lit up when one of the workers from the summer appeared. "God, they've been working here forever."

Leeda squinted at one of a bunch of the kids in bathing suits and shorts standing by the lake, their feet and lower legs muddy. A little girl with white-blond hair sat on a lawn chair to the left like it was a throne, shielding her eyes from the sun.

"Your mom was always perfect, I guess," Birdie said.

Leeda studied the photo. The other kids together and her mom too precious to get dirty.

In all of the photos where her mom appeared, it was the same. Lucretia always looked better. Her hair was neater, her clothes were prettier, her smile was more majestic. She was always her own special and superior island.

"Her smile never reaches her eyes," Birdie said.

Leeda smiled sardonically. "That's because she's a robot."

When Leeda came back to the dorms, the dim winter light lay soft shadows on the springy old green couch and rust-colored easy chair. It felt empty, but the vague smells of summer life—cinnamon, chilies, sweat, grease, slow-baked peach tarts—floated off the wallpaper like ghosts. Through the nearest window, the peach rows waved in the breeze, as if they were trying to get her attention. Her eyes drifted to the water stains on the walls, the place where the floor was sinking in, the rust springing up around the faucet fixtures. She had never noticed the dorm was disintegrating.

Suddenly possessed, she walked over to the sink and opened up the cabinets underneath, pulling out a bottle of Windex, one of Mr. Clean, and a pair of yellow rubber gloves. She worked well into the night, scrubbing the sinks, wiping down all the windows, scrubbing at rust stains. When she finally put her hands on her hips at about ten o'clock and looked around for what else there was to do, the downstairs was pristine, but it didn't look any better. It was still falling apart.

Discouraged, Leeda peeled off the gloves and dropped them in the sink. She climbed upstairs, took a shower without washing her hair, and pulled on her silky pajamas, climbing into bed. She fell asleep so quickly that she was completely disoriented when she heard the door downstairs open a few minutes later. And then footsteps climbing the stairs.

Her door was opening a moment later. Murphy pulled off her shoes and padded across the floor, crawling under the covers at the foot of the bed, her knees pulled up to her chest. Cool air came with her under the blankets. Her cold feet butted against Leeda's toasty ones.

"What are you doing here?" Leeda didn't know why she whispered. There was no one else in the dorm.

Murphy was quiet for a while. "I don't know. I was just lying on top of the trailer today, thinking, I've never even been on a train. And I was thinking, isn't that weird? And I just wanted to tell you."

Leeda was quiet.

"I just . . . *needed* to tell you. It made me feel . . . worried or something. That I've never been on a train."

Leeda pulled the covers back against her chin.

"I miss you, Lee."

Leeda rolled over onto her side, facing the wall.

"And I want us to talk about New York and how great it's going to be. Because sometimes, I don't know . . ." She laid her hands on her knees. "Sometimes I almost forget."

Leeda looked at the wall in front of her. She felt a mixture of shame and triumph as she opened her mouth to speak.

"I called my aunt," Leeda began, still whispering. "I'm going to go out there in May, right after we graduate. And I'm gonna go to school in California. I'm applying now." Murphy was silent, taking it all in. Leeda could feel sharp heat running up her belly. "I'm not going to New York."

Murphy didn't say anything for a long time. And then she just slid out of the covers. In the dark, Leeda could hear her picking up her shoes and her coat. And then she slipped out the door.

Leeda felt a million explanations pop up that she didn't owe Murphy. She didn't plan on telling her any of them. She didn't need to explain herself to anyone anymore. But if she had, she would have said that California was the obvious—the only—choice for her. She didn't know why she hadn't thought of it, seriously, before.

It was as far away as she could go without falling into the ocean.

Twenty-five

It was sleeting when they pulled up to Hartsfield airport in Atlanta on Christmas afternoon. Poopie waited to the side while Birdie checked her luggage, and they got hot chocolates at Seattle's Best to kill time and have something to do with their mouths besides talk.

"You have your tickets?" Poopie asked, for the third time in a row.

Birdie nodded. She waited for Poopie to ask if she'd packed enough underwear too or her toothbrush. Then she would have felt like Poopie was really looking out for her and not asking just to feel like she was saying something. But Poopie only sipped her chocolate and finally grabbed someone's discarded newspaper on the table next to them.

When it was time for Birdie to head to her gate, Poopie walked her up to the long security line. They exchanged a stiff, awkward hug. Birdie didn't even try to look Poopie in the eyes. She made her long way to the X-ray machines, rolling her old, reliable teddy bear suitcase behind her, feeling juvenile, like the only thing missing was a T-shirt that said *Off to Grandma's House*.

In the air, Birdie thought about how she would broach the topic of sex with Enrico. That she didn't want it to happen again. But nothing she came up with quite fit the bill. Birdie had never heard of a precedent of doing it one time and then going backward. She had always thought that once it happened, it was smooth sailing.

She wondered if he'd be disappointed. But then she thought, he was a guy. He had to be. She wondered if she could *sign* it to him somehow. Like, make hand signals or something so she wouldn't have to say it.

Before she could figure anything out, she was already winding her way through baggage claim on the other end, through a sea of Mexican faces and voices. Among all the unknown faces staring at the passengers coming out of the gate was a kid— eight years old or so—pointing at her. Then she saw Enrico standing next to him, a steaming cup in one hand and a flower in the other, beaming. She'd only seen him a little over a month before, but now he looked incredibly grown—not so boyish. He moved forward to hug and kiss her, then took her hands. She realized her palms were sweaty and pulled them out of his, backing away quickly and looking at the kid. "My brother, Luis."

"In the photo, she looked like Kate Winslet," Luis said in Spanish, disappointed. Unfortunately, Birdie understood.

Enrico smiled at her apologetically. "She looks better in person." It seemed to Birdie that Luis wasn't convinced.

It was late and dark, and as they left the airport, they skirted downtown Mexico City altogether. The air was arid. Birdie avoided looking at Enrico as much as possible—his profile, his arms—and watched the landscape go by instead. She couldn't believe it all actually existed. It felt very real, of course. Not cartoonish at all. She could see the lights in the distance, with the remnants of the sunset lying just behind it, a soft pink stripe just below the skyline. Her pulse thrummed with the rhythm of the wheels. Her mind reeled at how far from home she was.

They drove for miles beyond the city limits, Enrico chatting happily about what they'd do while Birdie was there, and school, and the National Autonomous University of Mexico, which he said was probably the best university in the Spanish-speaking world. Luis had fallen asleep in the backseat, and Birdie stared out the window, letting Enrico rest his hand lightly in hers. Rolling nondescript brownish hills stretched along either side of them. The whole way, Birdie's nerves sang and vibrated.

About an hour and a half after they had started, they pulled through a brick entrance to a suburban development. A white statue of the Virgin Mary stood on a pedestal. Birdie eyed it curiously as they pulled past. Beyond that were one-level houses with large, dusty yards, situated in front of a rise to the mountains. She tried to picture Poopie here, but she could only picture her at home in Bridgewater, with a harness full of peaches, maybe, or gliding around the stove in the kitchen.

Enrico turned into the driveway of a small white brick house on the right, and they all climbed out. Birdie felt like she was on Mars. She stood looking at Enrico's back as he grabbed her bags. Somebody, a boy, was *carrying her bags*. There was already a thick layer of dust on her shoes, and even her skin felt slightly gritty. She shuffled behind him into the house.

All was dark. "They're asleep," Enrico whispered. "My parents wake up before six."

Luis frowned at her. "She's not sleeping in my room," he said in Spanish.

"She understands everything you're saying," Enrico said. He turned to Birdie and said in English, "He's always mean to the girls he thinks are cute."

Luis punched him and disappeared down a hallway. Enrico led Birdie into the kitchen and fed her out of the fridge—long slices of cheese he wrapped up in *flautas* and drenched in green chile sauce.

Afterward they sat on the couch in the dark and whispered about anything they could think of to talk about: Texas, the orchard, the weather. They talked about their plans. Enrico had already planned to join everyone on the orchard for spring trimming during his spring break. April seemed like a million years away.

As they touched on this and that, Birdie knew what they both must be thinking about underneath it all. When a lull slid into the conversation, she knew it was the moment to bring up what she needed to say. But she couldn't imagine talking about what had *already* happened between them. Making the embarrassing request for it to not happen again seemed far beyond her.

"Why do you want to go to school in Mexico?" she asked instead. It seemed obvious. But it was a good filler.

Enrico thought. "It is a great opportunity for me to go to this school. It is very old." He squinted in concentration, humble, thoughtful. "Many presidents, great writers, great scientists have come from there. It's a . . . political school, which I like. And it's an important school." He stroked her hand. "Birdie, I can feel myself getting more and more American," he explained. "I want to be Mexican."

Birdie couldn't imagine wanting so much from her future. Or thinking it was all there for her to take. Enrico's mind was always searching and moving forward. It reminded Birdie how much she didn't just like him, but admired him.

A few minutes later, when they heard Luis close his door and go to bed, Enrico snaked his hand down to her rib cage and snuggled into her neck. "I think about your neck."

Birdie sat up, swallowing. "I'm exhausted," she said, exaggerating a yawn. "Where's my stuff?"

Enrico sat up too. "You're in my room." Birdie must have looked horrified because he laughed and then said, "Don't look so worried, I'm on the couch."

At her door, after he'd put her suitcase on the bed, he stood in the doorway. Birdie stared mostly at his feet because looking at the rest of him did strange things to her. Had he gone through a growth spurt or something? He reached out for her waist to draw her in and kiss her good night and Birdie instinctively dodged it at the last minute, so that his nose collided with her forehead. They both jerked back, Birdie holding her forehead and Enrico, his nose.

"Sorry," she whispered, feeling herself going red in shades, like a sunset. Reflexively she raised her fingers to his shoulder and patted him. "Good night," she chirped. They both stared at her hand. She'd *patted* him. Birdie was mortified.

Enrico leaned against the doorjamb, abashed, a faint smile on his lips that tugged at her nerve endings. "Good night." He pulled her door closed, and Birdie stared at the wood, took a deep breath, and let it out.

After she'd listened to his footsteps retreating down the hall, she turned and surveyed the room, noticing a white cordless phone by the bed. She stared at it, biting her lip. She wanted to call Murphy or Leeda. But she decided to settle on imagining them in the room instead, like invisible cheerleaders.

But the minute she turned out the lights and crawled into bed, it wasn't her friends Birdie imagined in the room. She closed her eyes, and all she could see was Enrico.

$\mathcal{B}$irdie woke to a warm dry breeze streaming through the open window and the sun making shadows on her face. She sat up, looked out, and breathed deeply. It was impossible to reconcile that the cold, and Poopie, and Honey Babe's ashes occupied the same universe as the one lying outside her window.

She padded down the hallway into the empty family room, sunlight making rectangles on the rust-colored carpet. Outside the front door, she could hear voices.

Birdie opened the door and stepped into the bright sunlight on the patio. The air was dry and warm. She could hear birds chirping. Enrico was in the driveway, shirtless—which sent a tingle down Birdie's stomach—washing the car with his brother. Luis was crouched over the bucket, green hose in his hands, holding the nozzle under the water so it bubbled up. Enrico was rubbing at one of the rearview mirrors with a rag. He was so lost in what he was doing that he didn't notice Birdie.

A hand emerged from one of the white Adirondack chairs on the square of a lawn, waving Birdie forward. Mrs. Fiol had a neat, brown, boy haircut and salmon-pink capris. Her full lips were painted plum. She stood from her seat, kissed and hugged Birdie. "So finally we get to meet *the* Birdie," she said, gesturing for Birdie to sit.

As Birdie slid into the chair shyly, she threw a glance at Enrico. He looked over his shoulder and squinted, then smiled at her.

"What do you think of Mexico in the dark?"

"Good," Birdie said. "It's nice."

"Are you hungry?"

Birdie shook her head. She was too excited to be hungry. "Not really."

They sat for a while, Birdie trying to think of something to say, but Mrs. Fiol didn't seem bothered. "Has my son talked you into moving here yet?" she asked.

Birdie laughed.

"Don't laugh," Mrs. Fiol said. "If I know him, it's part of his plan. All he talks about is Birdie, Birdie, Birdie. All summer too, before you told each other how you felt." Birdie was shocked. It had never seemed, before they had gotten together, like Enrico was thinking of her all that much. Birdie glanced at Enrico again, sure he would be horrified to know what his mom was saying, but she was desperate and giddy to hear more. "He thinks you are a hero, Birdie."

The conversation rolled along easily. Mrs. Fiol switched from Spanish to English to Spanish, expecting Birdie to understand, and for the most part, Birdie did. There was the requisite bragging about her son, but then they talked about the different parts of Mexico Birdie should see someday—not on this trip, but on fictional ones in the future. Trips to temples and volcanoes and beaches. Villages and cities she had to see, each with some distinctive flavor Mrs. Fiol tried to capture with words. Whenever Birdie let her eyes drift toward the car, she found herself staring at the tiny movements of Enrico's finely muscled back and quickly looked away. They talked about school, and where Birdie planned to go, and the orchard. Mrs. Fiol wanted to know what growing up on a farm was like and whether Birdie had any other ambitions besides farming. Birdie didn't really know what to say. She had never thought about ambitions. It just wasn't something that was ever really in her head.

"Finished," Enrico finally said, appearing over her. His T-shirt had materialized back on his body. He scooped up the bottom edge and wiped his face with it, revealing his stomach, which made Birdie want to die. He reached his hand into hers, but she pretended to have an itch on her forehead and pulled it away. He seemed to notice because he frowned slightly as he swiped sweat off his neck. "You want to walk?" he asked.

They wove through the streets, Birdie gazing at the landscape. The rolling, dry hills. The small houses lined neatly along the street. It was all incredibly *open*. It was wide enough to make you feel like you were floating. Birdie fell instantly in love with it.

Twice Enrico took her hand, and she let her fingers lie there for a while like dead fish until she felt enough time had passed to pull them away. She was careful not to brush shoulders with his, but whenever she accidentally did, it zinged down her arm like fire. She wondered if her sign language was working.

He pointed to the houses, talking about various neighbors and exchanging hellos with a couple that walked by, his voice a low and soft rumble. Occasionally he laughed in the middle of some description of controversies between the neighbors or kids he had grown up with and what they had gotten into. He seemed to want Birdie to know about him, and it made Birdie feel treasured, like she was visiting royalty.

Even that made her physically tingly. What was she, some kind of fiend? Maybe she was one of those sex addicts like you saw on daytime talk shows, and she just didn't know it yet. She tried to think of Saint Francis, lying on the pillow beside her. She prayed to him to give her the strength to get her mind out of the gutter.

When she floated back out of her head, they had stopped walking and were standing in front of a little green house. A figure moved behind one of the windows. "That's Poopie's old house," Enrico said. Birdie came back to earth with a thud.

Birdie stared at it. It was an ugly house. Sixties green and dandelion yellow. Small and plain. "It's nice."

"That's her sister living there."

"Oh." Birdie waited to feel something. Maybe envy that this was more home to Poopie than Birdie's world was. But she just couldn't believe it. Her heart told her Poopie couldn't have lived here. Maybe a cartoon Poopie, but not the real one. That Poopie belonged at Darlington Peach Orchard. Birdie couldn't feel anything else.

"I think . . ." Enrico's forehead wrinkled. "A home is always beautiful when you've left it behind. Even if it's ugly."

Birdie shook her head. "I can't see her here."

He put his arm around her waist, but Birdie jerked and stiffened. Enrico immediately pulled his hand away. "Sorry."

The word *sorry* sank to the bottom of Birdie's heart. She turned to him. His brown eyes were cast at something on the grass ahead of them, confused and hurt. She opened her mouth to try to explain. But it was too much like jumping off a high dive. She was right there at the edge, but she just couldn't make herself take the step.

He tugged the bottom edge of her loose white cotton blouse gingerly. "Come with me."

They walked to the edge of the neighborhood, past people sitting in their yards soaking up what remained of their Christmas holiday or with their doors flung open so you could hear them eating, laughing, talking. Past cactus and jacarandas and other exotic plants Birdie didn't recognize. Finally the road curved away from the houses, back toward the entrance they'd driven through last night.

The white pavement, coated with a fine, uneven layer of white sandy dirt, reflected so brightly it reminded Birdie of the white dusty roads back home. The air smelled not like peaches, but like scrubby green bushes, low to the ground.

They came to the brick balustrade that stood on either side of the road. Enrico turned her toward the side with the Virgin Mary. Birdie studied the Virgin's serene face, her hands stretched out in welcome or maybe forgiveness, her stone skin smooth and faultless.

"The Virgin of Guadalupe," he said.

"It's very pretty." Birdie stood slightly awed, slightly spooked. Not the Virgin Mary.

"Here." Enrico gestured toward the concrete base. It was not as pristine as the statue it held. Apparently when the concrete had been poured, several kids had carved their names in with their fingers just before it had dried. Birdie smiled.

"Do you see it?" Enrico asked.

Birdie looked closer at a crooked, childish scrawl.

Poopie Pedraza. 1969.

Birdie's gut sank. She felt gut-wrenching, ugly jealousy flare up. Of the house, of the sister, of Mexico. Suddenly it made sense to her. The crooked words—made by Poopie—connected it for her more than any house could have. She'd left herself carved in concrete as evidence. Poopie didn't belong to Birdie at all.

"It's funny," Enrico said. "When I noticed this, it made me think of you as a little girl. I pictured you writing your name here instead of Poopie. Like you had been here."

Birdie looked at him. She didn't understand, but she also did. Enrico leaned toward her, and she lost her breath, longing for him, prickly all over. But she pulled back at the last moment.

He stopped mid-move and looked at her like he was taking something in or deciding something.

"Would you mind," Birdie asked, "letting me walk back by myself?" She knew it would only make him feel worse. But she desperately needed it. She hurried to add, "I just think I need to be alone for a couple of minutes."

He took this in too, then nodded. "Sure."

Birdie watched him go, his white T-shirt, his khaki pants, his gentle stride back the way they'd come. It seemed to her he was slipping through her fingers. That the trip was slipping through her fingers.

She sat by the Virgin statue and swirled her feet in the white dust. It was like the dust you saw in pictures of astronauts standing on the moon.

According to many a history textbook, Mexico City was founded in 1521, when Cortés and his men spotted an eagle eating a snake and interpreted it as a sign from the gods to build the Mexican capital upon the very spot. If anyone asked why an eagle eating a snake was considered a sign from the gods, it is not on record. The fact that the eagle had been driven south by a swarm of angry bats was never recorded either, or even guessed at. Mexico City, incidentally, went on to smell—on its best days—like cinnamon and cayenne pepper.

Twenty-seven

When Leeda opened the door, the first thing out of Murphy's mouth was that it was a New Year's miracle. In her puffy green hat with the earflaps, her faux-fur coat, and her big gray fleece mittens, Murphy looked like a jolly hipster elf standing in the snow, which was coming down in thick tufts. Murphy held out one hand and opened it, revealing a ball of tightly packed snow. "I brought you something."

Leeda leaned against the doorway, surprised. She looked down at the snowball, dubious. "Um, no thanks."

Murphy's smile faltered. She glanced at her offering, then bucked up, dropping it off the side of the porch, and walked past Leeda inside. "We're going out for New Year's," she said over her shoulder, heading up the stairs. Leeda followed along behind her, agitated.

Murphy skimmed through Leeda's closet, chatting about this and that, unsinkable. Her mom had apparently made girlfriends at Ganax because they were all going out tonight. A kitchen in one of the trailers at Anthill Acres had caught on fire and one of the firefighters had asked Murphy for her number. She swore she had seen a seal swimming in Mertie Creek. Tension sizzled in the air like electricity, but Murphy tried to override it, and Leeda let her try. Finally Murphy pulled out a red velvety top. "Can I borrow this?"

Leeda sank onto one hip and crossed her arms. "You never return anything you borrow."

Birdie, had she been there, would have been a buffer. She would have offered for Murphy to borrow something of hers. But Murphy wasn't like Birdie, and neither was Leeda.

"Well, then, I'm going in this," she said flatly, gesturing to her schlumpy outfit. "And you're stuck with me."

Leeda stared at her, flustered. She didn't want to take her up on the invite. Especially since it was more of a demand. But she was sick of being stuck inside. She had cabin fever. She stared at Murphy another minute. It didn't mean anything. It didn't have to mean anything.

Leeda pulled her coat on over her silky silver tank top and black jeans, and they tromped down the stairs. She glanced around the warm, toasty common room, considering bailing. She could picture staying in with a DVD and a glass of white wine. She could call Dina Marie, or her friend Alicia, or one of her other friends from school and see what they were doing. She didn't know why she followed Murphy out the door. It was one of those nights that you just knew, before it even started, that you were going to wish you'd never left the house.

Walter dropped them off outside the Cawley-Smiths' hotel. They hopped out with snowflakes landing in their hair and thanked him, and he made them promise to call when they needed a ride home, no matter what the time. Murphy wondered what he was eating for breakfast that was making him so cool these days.

Holiday music drifted out of the speakers attached to the lampposts on Main Street. Murphy did a little shimmy standing in the snow, looking at Leeda, who was distinctly unwilling to shimmy. But Murphy didn't care. She was determined to make the night great, even if Leeda had a stick up her butt a mile long. Murphy had never met a person she couldn't charm. She was mad at Leeda and hurt by Leeda, but more than any of it, she missed Leeda. And it was New Year's. If that wasn't a chance to get over your dumb crap, what was? As for her own dumb crap, it didn't even factor in.

The snowflake light arrangement over the door of the hotel was covered with ice. It dripped into Murphy's hair, finding its way down through the curls to her skin and making her shiver. They hurried inside.

The party at the Cawley-Smith Hotel was one of the only ones in town on New Year's. Last year, Murphy and her friends had opted to drive to Macon instead, and Murphy had spent much of the night dancing with the singer for the house band.

The club was downstairs, in a sort of basement. Inside, the ceiling was lined back and forth with tiny white sparkling lights that made everyone better looking. Murphy flashed her fake ID and got herself a Manhattan, because it seemed appropriate, and a stiff whiskey for Leeda. Murphy made it a double.

She shoved Leeda's drink into her hand and pulled her out onto the dance floor. They watched Janine—the old lady who worked at Dunkin' Donuts and always made Murphy her coffee—dancing alone, clearly toasted, spinning in slow little circles. Leeda sipped quickly and soon started moving more loosely.

It wasn't long before she was waving her arms and laughing at everything Murphy did. And there was nothing Murphy liked more than a plan that went off successfully, except for an appreciative audience. They danced for half an hour or more, shaking off their energy like fireworks and still building more, getting sweatier and happier. An American flag hung behind the bar and Murphy ran back and wrapped herself in it, making bug eyes at Leeda and pretending to be Rocky. Leeda laughed so hard she squeezed her knees together and doubled over.

"Adrian!" Murphy yelled.

Leeda laughed harder.

"Adrian!"

Murphy turned to get more leverage on the flag, and when she turned back, Leeda was looking at the door, the smile gone from her face. Murphy followed her gaze. At some point, Rex had come in. He was standing at the end of the bar, staring at Murphy in the flag. Dina Marie was beside him, her arm wrapped around his, twined all the way down to where they held hands.

Murphy froze, processing the hands and the fact that she not only saw them, but that they saw her, and that she was wrapped in an American flag, and that something was going off inside her like a land mine. Rex stared at her, and she stared back.

It was hard to tell whether he was staring with surprise or pity.

Twenty-eight

Enrico led Birdie through the electric-lit streets, moving like a swimmer through the colorful crowds. Birdie gaped at everything, the riot of voices and colors and shapes and art. The house where Diego Rivera and Frieda Kahlo had lived. The elaborate Zócalo—where crowds were gathering to ring in the new year, blowing on noisemakers, shouting, laughing. Birdie felt like a country mouse, bumping into people, getting nervous every time a part of the crowd separated her from Enrico. She felt utterly out of place, but she was enjoying herself too much to mind.

Every few minutes, she glimpsed something she would have never imagined seeing in her whole life—astonishingly beautiful buildings, people of every shape imaginable, foods drenched in green and pink and yellow, art everywhere. By three o'clock that afternoon, she felt she'd seen enough to think about for weeks. But now, hours later and well into the evening, she felt like the planet was a whole different thing than what she'd thought it was. Birdie had always seen the world from a safe seat in a still place, and part of her had only been able to see it—even when she knew it was in motion—as still. But everything in Mexico City *moved*.

As they walked, Birdie kept her hands at her sides. But the way Enrico walked through the city—the way he asked a million questions out loud, some about Birdie, some about the things they saw that he just hadn't figured out yet—intrigued her more and more. She felt an irresistible happiness to just be next to his restless, beautiful brain. The whole day had been like falling into something almost too big for her. And even though she could keep from touching him, there was no way to dig her heels in and stop herself from feeling it.

A little after nine, they ducked into a restaurant—old, with beautiful green floor tiles with a path worn down the middle—and ate. Birdie had chicken with mole poblano, a thick, dark sauce made with dried chilies, nuts, seeds, spices, and cocoa that made her want to keel over from how good it was. They walked to Enrico's university, and even *it* was unlike anything Birdie could have imagined. Finally they collapsed on the grass and just talked. From time to time, Enrico reached out to touch her knee or her arm, but then he'd seem to think better of it and pull back. For a while, a few stars were visible through the haze above the city. And then big rolling clouds began to drift overhead—tinged with pink and purple by the atmosphere.

"I hope it doesn't rain on the fireworks," Birdie offered.

Enrico shrugged. "We'll see."

When they started walking again, a fine drizzle had begun to fall. Enrico said he wanted to take her up into the hills for the best view of the festivities. They were walking through a hilly area known as Chapultepec when the sky opened up completely.

Birdie pulled up the hood of her sweatshirt and looked up, getting plonked in the eye by a big fat drop. Enrico reached out and grabbed her hand, tugging her forward so that they were both running hard, their feet sopping with loud slaps against the pavement. He led them into a gaping opening in a concrete wall. They found themselves in a dark, cool tunnel only slightly taller than they were. Enrico pulled her back from where the rain was spattering inward. They leaned side by side, their backs bending along the curved wall, out of breath.

It rained and rained. Minute after minute went by, and it didn't let up. How long did heavy rains like this last in Mexico? Birdie could hear Enrico breathing, and it made her nervous to be this alone.

"We may have to sleep here," Enrico said.

Birdie turned her face to him, horrified, but he laughed. "Kidding, Birdie."

"Oh." She swallowed, studying him. He looked even better all wet, the drops dripping from his dark bangs and snaking down the sides of his face. One was next to the corner of his eye, like a tear. Birdie did it as a reflex. She leaned forward and kissed the spot.

It was like a switch going off. And Enrico was suddenly two things at once. His arms floated down around her sides and his hands rested on her waist gently, but he kissed her fast and solid, pushing his soft lips against hers—like the rest of him wanted to move fast, and his hands were only there to steady him. A moment later she was curving her back into the wall again and he was moving in front of her, holding her so unsurely it was like she was a butterfly that might fly away. Birdie's throat went dry and she melted, and then, just as quickly, she went rigid. Reflexively she sidestepped her way out of the kiss, so that Enrico tripped forward.

"Um . . ." she said. She felt white-hot heat rushing up her neck, up her legs, her wrists. "I . . ." She didn't want to. She didn't want any of it.

She turned and walked out into the rain. Ran-walked.

"Birdie?"

She could hear Enrico emerging from the tunnel behind her. "Birdie, what did I do?" She hung a right and immediately regretted it because it was the direction that was straight uphill. But it was too late to turn around. She took big monster steps, as fast as she could. "Birdie?"

Suddenly she felt something hit her legs—something soft and warm. She took it all in at once. A chicken at her feet, a guy dressed in white restaurant duds running toward her. For a moment, Birdie felt she had finally landed in cartoon world after all, with the Swedish Chef.

The chicken was standing just behind Birdie, bobbing its head, as if it somehow believed she would be its savior. The guy in white met her eyes, then poised himself, walking slowly and gently. Deftly he leapt around behind her, and in a flurry, he emerged with the chicken held tight in both arms.

He and Birdie stared at each other. The guy smiled apologetically. "*Lo siento.*"

Birdie gazed at the chicken, still reeling. "He's getting cooked?" she asked. "*Comida?*"

The guy nodded.

And Birdie didn't know why, but she started to cry. The guy looked at her, stunned, the chicken now tucked under one arm.

Slop slop slop. Enrico's footsteps made their way toward her, and then she could see him in her peripheral vision, standing beside her. "*¿Puedo comprarlo?*" he asked.

The chef looked surprised, looked down at the chicken. "*¿Desea comprar este pollo?*" "You want to buy this chicken?"

Birdie too looked at Enrico like he had lost his mind. They went back and forth in Spanish, something about arroz con pollo. The chef said he had others and shrugged. A moment later, he was walking away with a handful of bills and Enrico was holding the chicken and looking at Birdie.

It was still raining, and he was standing in a puddle that was being rocked by heavy droplets. "Birdie, I'm sorry. Whatever it is, I'm sorry."

"Sorry for *what?*" she asked. He had nothing to be sorry for.

"I'm sorry if you're having a bad time. You don't have to feel about me like you used to."

"I'm having a great time," she choked out, sniffling. She shrugged up her shoulder and rubbed her face against it to wipe off the tears. "I just don't want to . . . do that again."

Enrico gazed at her for a minute, trying to understand what she was talking about. "Kiss?" he asked.

"No. *That*, that." She said this to the chicken, then darted her eyes up to his.

Enrico looked at her earnestly and deeply, recognition falling on his features. "Is it because you don't think I am the right person anymore?"

Birdie kicked at the ground. "No. I mean, yes. Oh, I mean, it's not that."

Enrico nodded, his brow wrinkled. "Birdie, I just want you to be happy. Whatever you want is fine with me."

Birdie softened. Enrico took a small step away. For the first time, it really sank in. "You're holding a chicken," she said.

Enrico looked down at the chicken. "I saw you crying, and . . ." He, too, seemed to suddenly get how funny it was because he grinned. "Yeah. And now I have a chicken."

Birdie burst into laughter, and then so did he. He tucked the chicken under his arm, and finally, all the tension gone from her body, she pushed her hand into his free one.

"Thanks," she muttered sideways at him.

"Of course, Birdie. Anything."

They both instinctively turned right and walked up the rest of the hill. The rain had washed off the haze that hung over the city. A stripe of clear black sky lay across the mountains beyond the skyline, creeping up on them. In the rainy glow, the buildings were only shadows surrounded by a low wet mist. There was a loud bang and the first firework went soaring into the sky, bright, white, and brilliant.

For just a moment, Birdie didn't feel like a country mouse at all. She felt like it wasn't the orchard she was rooted to, but the spot where she stood.

That night, long after they had gotten home, she lay awake, restless. Finally she pushed open the bedroom door and closed it behind her, her heart pounding. She found her way to the couch, felt her way to Enrico's shoulders. He stirred, and she could feel in the darkness he was looking up at her shadow. Without a word, he pushed himself against the back of the couch to make room for her. She crawled under the blankets and pressed against him, wanting to be understood in some way she didn't understand herself yet. Even if it was only by touch.

Twenty-nine

Leeda pulled Murphy out onto the sidewalk by the hand. When they were outside, she linked her arm through hers, not wanting to lose physical contact with Murphy, who was singing Christmas carols. Even angry, she found it hard not to want to steady Murphy.

The snow had stopped, but it had left a thick layer on the ground. They tromped along Main Street through the puffy, muted air and cut through the park to get to the road that would take them to the orchard.

It took them an hour to walk home. Though the rest of Bridgewater had turned gray immediately, the orchard, as they walked up the drive, looked pristine and white. Not a footstep had disturbed the snow covering the fields.

"Doesn't it seem warmer after it snows?" Murphy asked.

"I'm freezing." Leeda felt vaguely dizzy.

"Let's not go inside," Murphy said, staring up at the house. She held one of Leeda's hands with both of hers, and she looked, to Leeda, radiant. She looked radiant with hurt, radiantly alive.

Leeda wasn't sure if she'd ever been as alive as Murphy looked. But she felt for Murphy despite trying not to. If she hadn't had those drinks, she would have insisted on heading in. But she felt too loose and unguarded at that moment to say no. "What do you want to do?"

"Let's go check if the lake froze."

They didn't make it that far. Murphy and Leeda wove through the peach rows, watching their footprints in the snow. They ended up detouring into the pecan grove.

Murphy shook Leeda's arm loose and sat down. Then she let herself fall onto her back with a soft *thwuff.* "I need to make a snow angel in case the snow melts before Birdie gets back."

Leeda didn't have to ask why. It made perfect sense. "I've never made one."

"Watch the master." Murphy fanned her arms above her head and fanned out her legs, then stood up carefully. Leeda copied her.

"Now one for Birdie."

Murphy lay down in a new spot and made a new one while Leeda lay in the mold of the one she'd already made. Murphy fanned and fanned, and then she just went completely still, staring up.

Leeda went still too. They listened to nothing. It was the most quiet Leeda could ever remember hearing. When she turned her head, there were tears running down Murphy's cheeks. It shocked her how quiet Murphy could be about crying.

She didn't say anything. She didn't even take Murphy's hand. She pretended not to see and looked back up at the dark.

She felt the vibrations of someone walking toward them

before she heard them. She and Murphy popped up like gophers and looked around.

A figure was walking with a flashlight, swinging it around.

"Uncle Walter?"

The flashlight swung toward them and engulfed them in a blinding halo. It got closer and wider as Leeda shielded her eyes and stood up. Uncle Walter lowered the flashlight and put his hand on Leeda's shoulder. "Leeda, honey, your dad's on the phone."

In 1912, seventeen members of the Divine Grace of the Holy Redeemer were baptized in Smoaky Lake. Sixteen left town to find their fortunes—five as missionaries, seven as steelworkers, two as hobos, and one as an organ-grinder for the county fair. The night before each of them died, they swore they smelled peaches in the air.

The seventeenth stayed in Bridgewater. She married rich. She rescued her first miniature pony at the age of twenty-two. That was also the year she bought her first giant hat.

Thirty

Grandmom Eugenie—still ruling with her white-gloved fist from beyond the grave—had directed her funeral precisely. Her favorite song—"Blue Hawaii"—was played as her casket was lowered into the ground. The miniature ponies were brought in at the appropriate time and they stood, dutifully, to watch.

In the second row behind Leeda, Murphy, who exuded life in bucketfuls, even when she was trying to be discreet, felt conspicuous and loud—her curly hair insisted on sticking out exuberantly. She watched, once the ceremony had ended, as people drifted up to pay their condolences. She felt rebelliously young and alive. Cold bit at her ears.

Birdie—who had turned brown in Mexico—flanked Leeda's left. She and Murphy were like cold stone lions guarding Leeda from afar, but Murphy didn't know from what. All Murphy knew was that Leeda looked like she needed protecting as she accepted hugs and handshakes, her skin extra pale, so that tiny veins showed at her temples. She had picked a seat away from the rest of the Cawley-Smiths and away from Murphy and Birdie. She hadn't looked back at either of them once. For some reason, Murphy thought of flocks of geese and how sometimes you saw one flying far behind the V, alone. She waited for Leeda to send her some signal that she wanted them closer, but it never came.

Lucretia stood in the front row, not a hair out of place. Not a twitch in her glossy lips as she accepted condolences. People who seemed on the verge of hugging her as they approached hit some invisible force field at the crucial moment and reached out their hands instead.

Murphy tried not to notice Rex, seated diagonally across from her. She tried to be solemn and focused and not young and alive and wildly hurt. It didn't help that every time she glanced toward him, his eyes were on her. He looked nervous, fidgeting with his hands on the seat in front of him. Fidgeting was not Rex's style. Murphy wondered if it was Leeda's loss making him nervous or her.

When everyone migrated to the parking lot to leave, Leeda walked right past Murphy and Birdie, trailing behind her family like the lost goose she was. Birdie hopped up and trailed along behind her. Just as she caught up, Leeda made a small gesture of waving her off and ducked into her car. Murphy watched Birdie's shoulders slump as she walked back to where her dad and Poopie were waiting and got in the truck.

In only minutes, the parking lot was half empty. Murphy felt the cold and gray in her bones. It was hard to truly remember the heat that had allowed them to run around with almost nothing on all summer.

"Hey." Murphy turned around. Rex was standing behind her. "Can I give you my coat?"

Murphy looked at the jacket he held out in his hand. He looked freezing. "No thanks."

"You need a ride?"

"No." Murphy looked in the direction of her mother, who was across the parking lot talking to Judge Abbott and his wife.

"How are you?" he asked her, looking like he meant it.

"Great. I'm great."

"Yeah?"

She wanted to say *yeah* again, once more, with feeling. She didn't want to give him any more bits of herself than she already had. But her next words came out of her like air being let out of a tire. "Yeah, except I got deferred."

He frowned, seriously. "I'm sorry, Shorts."

Murphy balked at the nickname. She felt her anger rise up. "Maybe I'll be stuck here after all. Lucky you." She didn't mean it really. She didn't think she meant it, anyway.

"You know that's not what I want," he said quickly.

Murphy studied him. If it had been her on the other end, she wouldn't have been able to help wanting it. That was the difference between them. Whether Rex loved her or not, she wasn't sure. But she was sure that if he did, it was *less* love. "Yeah. I knew you wouldn't." She meant it to sting him, but he looked satisfied, like she had gotten it right.

Murphy couldn't think of anything to say after that. Except a slew of biting comments about Dina Marie. Thinking of Dina Marie and Rex made Murphy feel like she would evaporate. It was a physical ache.

They stared at the cars moving out of the parking lot. "I eavesdropped. You should hear all the things people said to

Leeda," she finally offered. "Like 'she lived a full life' and all that."

"It was her time ..." Rex added, smiling.

It struck Murphy that Rex would die one day. She wondered if she would hear when it happened. She wondered where they would each be. She couldn't imagine not missing him, ever.

Murphy's darkness, her aliveness, her anger bounced off the cars pulling past them. She felt like Rex could see it. He moved so close to her then that she leaned in slightly. They stood poised like that for a minute, floating. And then she backed away. He leaned back and blew into the air.

"Later," she said, backing up a few more steps and waving, trying to interpret the intent way he looked at her, if it was love or just sadness. Maybe it was the look of someone who'd become a stranger again.

Thirty-one

*T*ap *tap tap.*

Leeda woke to someone knocking at the window. It took her a moment to realize how eerie that was, considering she was on the second floor. Her heart thumping, she slid out of bed and moved to the glass.

Tap tap tap.

Leeda leapt back and held her hand to her rib cage. Then she breathed a sharp sigh of relief. She could see the long, thin branch snapping back and forth in the cold wind. She leaned closer to the window and peered out at the tree it belonged to. And as she did, she noticed something else—an orange glow by the barn.

Leeda slipped her coat over her nightgown and hooked her fingers into her fuzzy boots, tiptoeing down the stairs. It was probably Birdie, unable to sleep. She grabbed her coat from the hook by the door and wrapped up tight. The frigid air hit her in a gust as soon as she opened the door.

Making her way through the dark, Leeda's feet crunched on the fine patches of snow still remaining on the grass, and she caught her breath at the number of stars that were visible above. She thought, just for a moment, of how she used to stand outside for ages on a cold night to look at the stars. It had been a while since she'd done that.

The fire had been built in the dirt right outside the barn doors, which hung open to let in the heat. Leeda walked up beside it and held her hands out to it, welcoming the warmth as she peered inside, looking for Birdie. Instead she saw Rex.

When Rex worked on something, he lost himself in it. It was one of the first things Leeda had ever noticed about him. Normally his body moved carelessly, but when he focused on something, like he was now, you could see how intent and meticulous he became. He didn't hear her.

"Hey."

He looked embarrassed for a brief moment when he saw her, and then it vanished. "Hey," he said.

Leeda walked in beside him and looked down at what he was doing. A birdhouse.

"For Murphy's garden?" she asked.

"I couldn't sleep," he said, by way of explanation.

"Oh."

For the first time now, he really looked at her—taking in her boots, her pajama pants below her coat. "What are *you* doing up?"

Leeda didn't know how to answer the question. A tree knocked on her window?

She and Rex had known each other so well, and for so long, that the silence between them was comfortable. Leeda sat on a bench and watched him work, feeling the cold snake its way under her coat and across the silk of her pajamas. She knew Rex was too proud to ask if Murphy talked about him. But the question was written all over his face.

"Rex?" Leeda had wanted to tell someone. Rex seemed right. He seemed close enough to understand and far enough away that he wouldn't expect anything more from her. "I don't even miss my grandmom." She rubbed her hands together. Rex didn't say anything. Leeda thought of her grandmother running alongside the float at the parade, sticking up for her. She thought of all the times she'd avoided Eugenie's phone calls and the time she'd left the paper Leeda on the table. The horrible part was, she wasn't sure she would have done it differently if she could have. She ran a hand through her hair, neatening herself up. "I don't even feel anything."

Silence.

"Do you think . . ." She danced her fingers on her knees, flittering the tips, as if she were typing. Then she made herself stop. "Do you think if your mom doesn't love you, you don't get a soul?"

Rex stopped mid-tinker and gave her his sudden, undivided attention. "That's crazy, Lee."

"Sometimes I feel like she just didn't hand one down to me. You know, because she didn't care that much. Like I'm a shadow or something."

He came and squatted in front of her. "Lee, don't you know how much people love you? You're not invisible, trust me."

It almost felt like the old Rex. Old boyfriend Rex. When they'd been together, he had always managed to prop her up.

"How are things with you?" she asked, not wanting to go back there. "How are things with Dina?"

Rex stonewalled, giving a little nod. It was hard to tell what was going through Rex's head when he didn't want you to know. He could have been thinking things were good. He could have been thinking Dina was no Murphy. Leeda looked down at her hands. Her fingers began to dance restlessly over her knees again. "Rex, after we broke up, it never kept you up at night. I mean ... missing me. Did it?"

Rex looked at her. In his look was what she already knew.

"I love you, Lee. You know I do."

"Yes." She nodded.

Silence.

He squeezed her leg. "You okay?"

"I'm fine." She gave him her million-watt smile. The one she had inherited from her mother. "I don't know what I'm talking about." She stood up. She could tell Rex didn't want to let her go this way. But she smiled at him again. "I'm really tired. Good night."

She walked outside and started toward the women's dorm. The fire flickered a shadowy yellow path, pointing her back toward the warmth. But Leeda looked over her shoulder, in the direction of the peach rows disappearing into pitch winter darkness. Leeda pulled her coat tighter around herself and turned in that direction, feeling she shouldn't but crunching through the snow into the crisscrossing lines of trees.

On parent-teacher nights, as a kid, it had always felt odd to be in the school when the lights were off in most of the classrooms. She'd never seen the school closed down like that. The cold, dark peach rows felt the same way. Leeda could only smell ice and, occasionally, mud. There was no feeling that she was surrounded by anything alive.

She came out on the lake, a black absence in the patchy snow and grass, and climbed up the rock where the Barbie had been, sliding her feet carefully so she wouldn't slip. She dawdled at the top, looking up at the stars, looking down at the moon reflecting on the lake. She pictured Murphy in her bathing suit, executing daring maneuvers off the rock: dives, corkscrews, even somersaults. She wanted just a little of what Murphy had. That fullness that Rex had found. That had found Rex.

Instead she felt like a wisp floating over the rock. She wanted to be bold. Wild. True. She wanted to do something to be visible to herself.

Leeda slipped her coat off her shoulders and let it fall at her feet. She untied her boots and slid out of them, pulled off her long-sleeved top, and slithered out of her silky pants so she shivered in her undies. She scooted her feet right to the edge of the rock.

Her breath jangled her chest with nervous shudders. She took in a lungful of air and jumped.

She knew she had made a mistake before she landed. And then it was too late, and her body was racked by the cold. Leeda exploded above the surface, sharp aches shooting through her body. It was beyond cold. It was bare pain.

Sputtering and gasping, she splashed wildly for the edge of the lake. But she couldn't get her limbs to move the way she wanted them to. She flailed in the direction of the shore. And then it felt like her arms were being ripped out of her shoulder joints. She was being yanked hard upward, pulled out with arms around her like metal vises.

Leeda's arms lolled out to the side like a rag doll's and Rex pulled her close to him, wrapping himself around her.

Leeda curled herself in a ball.

"You okay, baby?" he asked, squeezing her tight. Leeda tried to gather her thoughts. She pulled away from Rex and rubbed her arms and her legs and blew warm air on her hands. It was over as soon as it had started. She could feel blood rushing back to her fingers and toes. She tried to compose herself into the right shape again.

Rex sank back, breathing hard, just staring at her wide-eyed.

"Can you get my clothes?" she asked.

Leeda pulled them on while he looked away.

"Don't tell anyone," she said. Rex hadn't yelled at her or asked her what she'd been thinking.

All he finally said was, "We should go to the hospital or something. Just to check you out."

Leeda shook her head. "No big deal. I was just being . . . stupid." She shot him a sharp glance. "If you tell anyone, I'll kill you."

He looked at her. Not intimidated. But not arguing.

"I'm fine."

That night in bed, Leeda shivered and shook. Weird thoughts circled her head. She couldn't stop thinking of tiny things she had messed up. Bs on papers. Things she'd said to Murphy or Birdie or Rex or her family that had come out wrong. Her mind kept picking at every single way she could remember she had ever slipped up. But when the sun started to rise, the thoughts vanished. By the morning, she just felt far away.

Thirty-two

*B*irdie knelt in the confessional at Divine Grace of the Redeemer. She was a firm believer that things happened in threes. The Father, the Son, the Holy Ghost. Chocolate, vanilla, strawberry. Honey Babe, Eugenie, and Z. If she was being punished, Birdie wondered if she could stop the cycle. And if it was too late, who the Z would be.

"Forgive me, Father, for I have sinned." She always spoke low at confession, not just because she didn't want anyone else to hear, but because Father Michael was always on the other side of the curtain, and she hoped if she disguised her voice, he wouldn't recognize her.

"How long has it been since your last confession?"

Birdie thought. What day was it today? January thirteenth, fourteenth? "Um, eight months?" It hadn't been since before the summer. She guessed it had slipped her mind.

"Go on."

"I . . ." Birdie cleared her throat. "I Googled a couple of answers on my history test."

"Yes?"

"And . . . I committed adultery and . . ." Birdie said it low and fast. "I . . ."

"Wait."

Birdie swallowed.

"Birdie, is this like the time you thought you committed adultery because you had mooned someone?"

Birdie's stomach flopped sickly. She tried to swallow again, but her throat had gone dry. "No, Father. I . . . I had *sex*," she whispered.

Father Michael was quiet. "I see."

Birdie had visions of him coming around the side of the confessional and throwing holy water on her like in *The Exorcist*.

"Have you shared this with anyone?"

"No." Well. Not intentionally.

"Birdie, I strongly urge you to talk to an adult about this. This kind of thing is a responsibility."

"Okay, Father."

"I want you to say twenty Our Fathers and meditate really hard about what God wants for you."

"Okay, Father."

Should she add that sex had turned her into the angel of death? Should she ask if God would kill a feisty old lady because *she* couldn't control herself?

She wrapped up with a few less-extreme sins instead.

In the house, Leeda was hunched over her laptop at the kitchen table. She looked almost as white as a marshmallow—her thin white arms curled around her textbook, her legs like toothpicks under her pink plush track pants.

Birdie slid out of her coat, then rubbed her hands together, then looked at the thermostat. "Lee, it's freezing in here." It was freezing outside too. The orchard slumped under the hazy sky, like somebody holding their breath.

Leeda shrugged. "There's mail for you." She gestured to a manila envelope on the counter by the phone.

Birdie picked it up. Enrico's familiar messy handwriting had addressed it, simply, to Birdie. She pulled out its contents: photos of her and Enrico's family. A miniature replica of the sun stone from the Zócalo. A pamphlet on the National Autonomous University of Mexico with a photo of Birdie's favorite building on the front. A letter written on a brown paper bag from a bakery where they'd had guava pastries in Mexico City. Birdie ran her fingers over the words on the paper, feeling so far away from Enrico's hands. She hadn't called him since she'd been back, and that had been a week and a half ago.

"Your dad was looking for you," Leeda said. Birdie looked at her. Her cheeks were almost as pink as her track pants. Birdie reached out to hold a hand against her skin to see if she was hot, but Leeda ducked her head. She pulled her hand back and folded her fingers together gently.

"You don't look so good, Lee," Birdie told her.

Leeda half laughed. "Thanks." When she felt Birdie moon-eyeing her, she looked up at her. "I'm fine. Really."

Birdie shuffled down the hall to the office. Her dad was behind the desk, his big thin-rimmed glasses on, concentrating on some papers in front of him.

"Birdie," he said, leaning over his desk. "I want to talk about something serious with you." Oh God. Birdie was blindsided.

She had thought the threat of this had passed. "Your mom doesn't think you're ready to hear it, but I do."

Birdie nodded. *Tap tap thump.* Birdie scooped Majestic from where she'd hobbled up beside her. Could Father Michael have called? Wasn't confessional supposed to be *private?* Oh God.

He looked uncomfortable, awkward. "It's about my will."

His *will?* "Your will?"

"Now that the . . . now that your mother and I have finalized the divorce, I need to amend my will."

"Are you sick?" Birdie gushed.

To her surprise, her dad smiled. "Birdie, I'm fine. It's just something I have to do. I just wanted to make sure of something before I do it."

Birdie waited with bated breath. She couldn't imagine what he was going to say.

"I know it probably goes without saying, but I want to leave the orchard to you. I need to know if that's what you want."

Birdie's stomach began to ache. It was the last question she'd ever expected to be asked. But hearing it like that made Birdie feel like a weight was wrapped around her ankles. "Yeah, Dad. That's fine."

"You sure?"

"Of course." Had there ever been any question? Except maybe a cartoon one? A momentary lapse of sanity.

Walter smiled again—which used to be a rare occurrence but seemed to come to him so easily these days. Birdie knew she had told him what he wanted, and needed, to hear.

"How's Enrico?" he asked generously.

Birdie gazed around the office, thinking how to answer that.

She knew every scuff in the wooden floor. Every crack and slope in every shelf. It was funny how you could go somewhere and your whole life could stretch out. And then you could come home and have it all shrink back again to the way it was before. It was funny that it didn't stay stretched.

"We broke up," she said, with a feeling of deep relief as the words left her mouth. Enrico didn't know it yet. But there wasn't a question in her mind, and that was what felt really good. It was how things had always been meant to be.

She stared around at the piles of papers, which she would inherit one day and in a way already had. For a second, Birdie almost wished she could be some other kind of teenager. Someone who could put rocks on a bus and hope to follow them.

Behind her, somewhere inside the house, there was a screech of wood sliding and a loud thud. Birdie ran into the kitchen, her dad hurrying behind her. The first thing she saw was one of the kitchen chairs lying on its side. Then Leeda, lying on the linoleum. Thin and perfectly white, she was spread across the floor like a ghost.

Thirty-three

$\mathcal{M}$urphy watched while almost every person in the senior class filtered in and out of the hospital room to see Leeda. But what really struck her was how little Leeda seemed to notice they were there to see *her*. How she managed to stay shrunk, even with all the attention. Lying propped on her white pillows, in red lipstick, she looked like Sleeping Beauty.

The room smelled like a mixture of antiseptic and exotic flowers. Everywhere bright bouquets and balloons stood out against the white walls, white plastic tables, gray plastic chairs. Only Leeda's skin—white as a cloud—seemed to blend.

Murphy and Birdie had taken up spots in the room like a royal court, sitting off to the side for hours while Leeda's fans came and went, letting themselves be hypnotized by the steady beep of the machines in the room. Birdie was knitting Majestic a new sweater, one that did not go with the *Amigo* that was no longer around. It said, simply, *Woof*. Murphy was trying to get through Franz Kafka's *Metamorphosis*, but she kept looking up to watch Leeda greet her visitors and watching the door for who might come through it. Rex would have to come at some point, and Murphy was torn between her loyalty to Leeda and making sure she wasn't here when he did.

Leeda didn't seem to want them there anyway. Whenever the room emptied out, she just looked out the window or flipped the channels with the remote. Birdie had tried asking her questions, like if having pneumonia hurt or if she wanted Birdie to bring her anything from home, but Leeda had muttered half-hearted replies, as if Birdie were a mosquito buzzing in her ear. Murphy wanted to reach out and shake her. She felt like shouting, *Don't you see us?*

The clock read 3:30. Murphy, legs restless, leaned forward, closed her book, and bit her thumbnail. "Lee, you want me to stay?"

Leeda shook her head, her eyes on a *Dawson's Creek* rerun. When Murphy said good-bye on her way out, she didn't even reply. Birdie shrugged and mimed a kiss to Murphy.

It had snowed again the day after Leeda had gone into the hospital. In the parking lot outside, the only snow left was caked around poles and street signs, but it was melting fast.

Murphy shivered under her wool hat and corduroy coat as she made her way across the lot, heavyhearted and mad. She didn't know what she was mad at. She was mad at the idea that had made its way into her head, that maybe they wouldn't have Leeda back ever. She wasn't mad at Leeda exactly, but something around Leeda. Whatever monster was surrounding her. And she was mad at not understanding.

As she walked, she scooped up handfuls of dirty snow from against the curbs, packed them hard, and aimed them at nearby trees, some of which already had the smallest hints of buds at their tips. Murphy wondered if the buds were optical illusions. In New York, buds would wait till the proper time to come out, she was sure. They'd wait till March, at least. Not the middle of January.

Murphy felt off-kilter and crooked inside. She'd read a poem once by Elizabeth Barrett Browning about how meeting Robert Browning had meant she could never even look at her own hand the same way again. Even though the poem was about this joyous love, it was really about mourning. Maybe she and Birdie and Leeda—what they were to one another—had changed the way Murphy looked at her own hand too. Maybe without them being like they were supposed to be, she'd always feel crooked.

Her attention was diverted by a high-pitched voice off to her left. "You're so sweet!"

Murphy turned around slowly. Dina Marie was standing on a curb, peering in through the window of Rex's idling orange truck. He was holding something out to her through the window from the driver's seat. Murphy squinted, and her blood went cold. It was a peach. Some damn imported out-of-season peach.

She watched as Dina Marie took a big bite out of it, grinning.

Something in Murphy snapped. She walked quickly in the direction of the truck. "Hey, Dina!"

Dina turned, and Murphy whaled her last snowball at her. It hit Dina right on her toothy mouth and bounced off, shattering on the concrete. Murphy put her hand up to her own mouth, shocked. Dina just stood staring at the ground, her fingers to her face, trying to make sense out of what had just hit her. A tiny trickle of blood appeared on her top lip.

Mortified, Murphy began backing away, then turned without looking at Rex. She made a beeline for the edge of the lot, turned left on the road, and hurried beyond the trees. She realized too late she was walking away from her bike. But there was no way she was doubling back.

Behind her, a few seconds later, she heard the rumble of Rex's truck. He pulled up beside her and rolled down his window. Murphy kept walking.

"I'm sorry," she said, but she picked up her pace.

"Get in the car."

Murphy shook her head and kept moving.

"Get in, Murphy."

She stopped and sighed. She got in. Rex put the truck into second gear and didn't say anything. He steered toward Anthill Acres.

"Where's Dina?" she asked the dashboard.

"She's pissed off." He tapped the steering wheel with his fingers for emphasis. "She left."

"I'm so sorry."

Rex looked at her. "Murphy, being sorry doesn't sit well on you. Tell her you're sorry, not me."

Murphy looked out the window.

"Dina's a nice girl."

"Yeah, I *know*. She's *so* nice. Nice, nice, nice." Murphy stole a glance at him to get his reaction to this. He was stone-faced, angry.

"She says you and I have things we need to work out," he said flatly. Like it was all her fault that his girlfriend had walked away from him. Which it was.

But Murphy couldn't find it in her to apologize for *that*. "You seem to be working out fine." She couldn't stop herself.

Rex slapped his hands against the steering wheel once, sharply, and then stretched his fingers, taking a deep breath. "Murphy, you dumped me, remember?"

Murphy huddled into herself. "It was a preemptive strike," she croaked, staring back at the dirty snow-covered road. Bridgewater at its best.

Rex sighed, pulled over, and let the truck idle. He put his thumbs up to his forehead. Murphy felt like he was working up to something and she didn't want to know what.

"I'm gonna walk." She got out of the car and walked through the clumps of icy snow. Rex got out too and came up behind her, then reached out for the back of her corduroy coat and tugged.

"I liked it better when you were sorry. Please stop."

Murphy ignored him. She felt like if she stopped walking, she wouldn't start again. A car sloshed past them and sent slush flying at her. Rex laughed, but she kept going.

"Murphy, I want to be with you. You know that."

Murphy didn't know. She felt like wild horses were running up and down her rib cage. She knew it would be more beautiful to keep going and not look back. She was wet and cold. She shivered and Rex caught up with her, put his arm around her.

"Come home with me. Let me keep you warm."

Murphy spun around in his arms and crossed her arms in front of her body, her elbows jabbing him. "I can keep myself warm."

"Well, then, come home and keep *me* warm."

Murphy wanted to. She slumped on her hip, stared around for an out, buying time. She didn't want to keep herself warm. She wanted to give in to the flow of what she felt. But like with everything, there was a catch. She knew that if she let herself, she wouldn't ever stop.

Thirty-four

The doctor had explained things to her in teenage girl language, as if Leeda wasn't capable of understanding compound sentences. They said her body had just shut down and restarted, like a computer. She was going to be fine. The doctor had said she just needed rest and quiet time. They were going to let her go home. But it might take weeks for her to feel like her old self.

Leeda stared out the window. Her dad stood there to the left, fiddling with the remote control. "What do you want to watch?"

"I don't care, Dad."

Lucretia sat monarch-like in the farthest chair, reading a copy of *W.* She'd only put on the minimum amount of makeup, which for her was groundbreaking. Her hair was slightly disheveled. The way her face sagged in places made it look like she hadn't slept. And she kept eyeing Leeda above her magazine, looking worried. But Leeda couldn't imagine her really wanting to be there.

Leeda tugged the light blue curtain to get a better view of the sky—overcast, flat—beyond the window.

"You leaning toward any of them?" Leeda's dad nodded toward the stack of acceptance letters that he'd brought to the hospital. UCLA, UC Davis, UC Santa Barbara, Pepperdine.

"Still waiting for Berkeley," Leeda mumbled, staring at the sky.

Her dad hovered for a few minutes. Mr. Cawley-Smith had always been good at navigating the murky waters between his wife and his daughter. He always gave them both the room they needed. It was like a bow to the fact that they inhabited a girly world he didn't understand. But sometimes Leeda wished he'd stick a toe in. "Well, I'm going to go get you a bagel. You look too thin. You want anything, Lucretia?" he asked her mother. It was amazing that over the years, he hadn't managed to shorten such a mouthful to Lu or something like that. It spoke volumes about how intimacy worked with Leeda's mother.

With her dad gone, Leeda flipped the channels, and Lucretia flipped her magazine pages faster and faster.

"I think you should move home," Lucretia finally said, laying the *W* on her lap decisively. "You're obviously not taking good care of yourself."

Leeda thought it was ironic that her mom thought she could take better care of her. But she didn't bother to say it. She was over fighting with her mother. Fighting was a way of trying to connect.

But Lucretia didn't let it go. She stood up and walked to the bed and perched on the corner, like she wanted to be close to Leeda but not too close. "You're going to Aunt Veda's this summer, and that's good. But next summer, we'll have to sort out something for you that's more structured."

"I'm not coming back next summer." Leeda yawned.

Lucretia looked surprised. "Oh?"

"I'll spend the holidays in San Francisco. I can stay with Aunt Veda or I can rent a place on my own." Leeda had all sorts of money coming to her when she turned eighteen. She had all sorts of options and none of them, in her mind, were coming back to Breezy Buds.

Several emotions crossed her mother's face: surprise, then anger, then recognition. Her mouth settled into a straight, practical line. "When will we see you?"

"Hopefully you won't."

"Oh, don't be so dramatic, Leeda." Lucretia opened the magazine again, flipping and flipping, as if she wasn't interested anymore.

In the past, this would have infuriated Leeda. But she didn't flinch.

She only leaned forward. She gently pulled the magazine away and looked her mother in the eye. She couldn't remember the last time she'd done that, fully, completely, fearlessly. "You think I'm just saying this because I'm seventeen and seventeen-year-olds say this kind of thing, but I am promising you, Mom, that when I go, I won't come back. I don't want you around me anymore."

Lucretia gasped so loudly that it seemed like a word. Her blue eyes were as wide and wounded as if she'd been slapped. She had been making Leeda feel that wounded for years, and now Leeda felt serene. She felt like she'd weathered some terrible storm. Like the last few months had been tumultuous and now she had arrived on the other side, somewhere far away, in calm waters, millions of miles from anything familiar. She felt like . . . what should you call a place far away from all the things that had messed you up before?

Leeda felt like she was her own *continent*.

There were always two ways to tell spring was coming in Bridgewater. One was the color of the sky—which made the gradual shift from a flat, lifeless gray to a smooth, hopeful blue. And then there were the people. They got a little excitable. They did things they normally wouldn't.

On February 3, three jumbo-size Sugar Daddys were shoplifted from the Bridgewater Drug and Dairy. On February 20, Maribeth McMurtry accidentally broke the Joseph in her life-size nativity set as she was packing it away for the year. And on March 20, Mayor Wise decided to take a detour along Orchard Road, completely out of his way.

With the windows down and spring air in his nostrils, he remembered sneaking onto the orchard once, at the age of thirteen, to pick the first peach of the season. He had heard that with the first bite of the first peach, you got to make a wish. Of course, being thirteen, he had wished a naked girl would show up in his front yard, like a free prize popping up in a box of Cracker Jacks.

He never realized it, but he had forgotten to specify when.

Thirty-five

Murphy woke up just as the sun was rising. Gently, gingerly, she rolled over and propped herself up to look at Rex. He lay flat on his back, one arm stretched out where it had been wrapped around her, the other flat against the back of the couch. They had fallen asleep watching *Late Night*. To her, he looked like some kind of Holy Grail that only she had been bold and brave and true enough to find.

Inevitably he sensed she was awake and stirred. She curled back into his warmth and pretended to be asleep.

"Faker," Rex whispered, grabbing her arms and kissing her sloppy style on the cheek. Murphy squirmed, her chin pressed against her neck, giggling. And then they both stopped giggling and looked at each other, and Murphy felt like she was hanging on what they had like a clothes hanger. Dangling, swaying, up high.

She had never wanted to hang.

But they'd been back together for almost two months now. Rex had landed back in her life with force, even more lodged in than he was before. And Murphy wasn't dancing away from him anymore like she used to. When she looked at him there on the couch, sitting up, all groggy and disheveled, she wasn't scared of him like she used to be. Or scared of wanting him as much as she did. She didn't feel like she needed to pin him down to make sure she had him. She felt like she knew.

Her mom was still asleep in her bedroom, her door open. Murphy could hear her gently snoring. She pecked him once more on the lips, then forced herself to climb up off the couch.

She shuffled to the kitchen, filled up the coffeepot, switched it on, and popped her hand out the front door. Outside, it had started to warm up just a tad. She could see the buds on the few straggly trees that hung over Anthill Acres. She reached into the little black metal mailbox at the side of the door.

When she saw the edge of the manila envelope, something in her just knew. She glanced immediately behind her, then stepped out onto the stoop, cold metal chilling the soles of her feet. She closed the door behind her, shimmying the fat packet out from the junk mail and the bills.

She ran her fingernail under the gummy lip of the envelope, her heart pounding. She squeezed the top open, not pulling the paper out, but instead peeking inside, reading the top sheet. When she saw the top few words, she crumbled inside. She felt the way she'd felt when her cat Perko had died. Like she had lost something she could never get back. She felt surprising, out-of-nowhere grief. She closed the envelope back up again.

The McGowens had a recycling bin that sat under the overhang of the stoop. Murphy had made her mom get one. Now she took the junk mail and the packet and stuffed them in. She put the coupon flyers on top, obscuring the envelope.

She walked back into the house past Rex and leaned over the kitchen counter, pouring out two bowls of Pops, even though she knew Rex thought they were nasty. Rex looked at her. "What's wrong?"

Murphy's mom was just emerging from her bedroom, her hair all sideways, her red Victoria's Secret robe all akimbo. She had a hand to the side of her face, like she was trying to pat herself awake, but she too looked at Murphy, perplexed.

Murphy rubbed her neck and stared up at her ceiling fan. "I didn't get in."

She didn't look at either of them to catch their expressions. She knew her mom would be relieved, but she didn't know if Rex would be crushed or happy or somewhere in between. She didn't want to know.

And anyway, she couldn't lie and look him in the eye at the same time.

Thirty-six

"The invoices go in the invoice files, which are alphabetical," Jodee explained, running a red nail along the red tabs in the metal filing cabinet. "The mail goes by person into this filing cabinet here." She flicked her fingers along another set of tabs, which encased tiny little names.

The radio was playing some insipid pop song, and Murphy kept glancing over at the dial, tempted to change it. But her mom was so serious about training her that Murphy thought looking distracted might let the wind out of her sails.

"The best part is you can look through magazines when you're done with the mail. And then you just have to answer the phones." Jodee had already explained the ins and outs of the phone system. Murphy had a headset, like the women on those adult education ads she'd seen on TV. It made her feel ten years older just having it on her head.

She must have looked as dismal as she felt because Jodee pinched her cheek. "It's not so bad, baby. The people are great. And it's only temporary."

"I know." It had taken all of two weeks to get Murphy

situated. She had applied at Ganax two days after she'd found out about NYU and now here she was working after school and sometimes on weekends. She was going to apply to schools close to home for the spring semester. And then, eventually, she said she'd try to transfer to NYU. In the meantime, she'd be at Laurens Community College with Birdie. Birdie had taken the news with tears in her eyes for Murphy, her hands over her mouth. And then she'd gotten ecstatic that they were going to spend at least the fall together. Murphy had tried to act less deflated by the idea of LCC than she was.

"You got it?"

"Yes."

"Oh, and don't change the radio station. Mr. Carter wants easy listening for when customers come in." Jodee kissed her, shimmying out the door in her knee-length maroon skirt. "See you tonight."

Murphy sat at the reception desk bathed in fluorescent light, feeling like an exhibit at the circus, and stared out the double glass doors at the outside. She couldn't believe the same town that harbored the Darlington Orchard could harbor Ganax Heating.

The four hours went by like five million years. She opened all the invoices and used her staple remover on the ones that were stapled. One particular company liked to staple their invoices—several sheets thick—in the very middle, and Murphy spent ten minutes digging under each staple with her fingernails before she realized there was a staple remover to do that. When she was done with the invoices, mail, and filing, she stared up at the fluorescent bulbs overhead, rocking back on her chair. She peered toward accounts payable, but everyone was facing their computers.

Murphy stared at the phone and at everyone's names. She made little paper clip animals to be in the circus with her and lined them up beside the nameplate that said *Receptionist*. She thought it was darkly funny that her name had become Receptionist. She thumbed through magazines, took her scissors, cut out the photos, and used them to make little collage scenes on the desk. When she got bored, she dug out a blank sheet of paper and addressed it to the company that stapled their invoices in the middle. *Dear Sir or Madam, I want to let you know that it makes no sense to staple your invoices like you do. It takes me ten times longer to open one of your invoices than anyone else's.*

She walked up to the double doors every half hour or so to look outside at the free world. The grassy parking lot medians were soggy. The whole world looked like it was finally in bloom.

When Rex came to pick her up at seven, Murphy had been staring at the minute hand of the clock for five minutes. She threw herself on him like he had untied her from railroad tracks.

"Let's go out to celebrate your first day."

They went to Applebee's, which was the only restaurant Murphy hadn't been kicked out of besides Kuntry Kitchen. She stared around at the lights, at the servers, as if she'd just landed in Bridgewater on a spaceship and was getting used to her new surroundings. Because staying was new. Not escaping was new. Every time she looked at Rex, she bravely gave him a smile.

"So have you looked at other schools in New York yet?" he asked.

Murphy shrugged.

"Murphy." He leaned forward on the table. "Can I ask you something?"

Murphy played with her napkin and then moved her fork to the other side of her knife. "Yeah."

"Why didn't you apply to any other schools?"

Murphy moved the fork back to where it had been originally. "Because NYU is the only..."

Rex shook his head and held up his hand. "I know what you told me. Now tell me something new. Why not?"

Murphy could feel her bottom lip start to tremble. She met Rex's gaze directly, but she didn't say anything back. She didn't know why not. She didn't want to say it was because of him. But she guessed maybe it had been. Maybe.

"Shorts." He moved to her side of the table and put his arm around her. He kissed the top of her head. And even though everything around them seemed superficial, and dull, and so much less than she wanted, he felt real and true.

Before they left, Murphy made her way to the bathroom. After she'd finished washing her hands, she stood in front of the sink and looked at herself. She looked smaller than she remembered.

Through April, Murphy, Leeda, and Birdie drifted in and out of the orchard like cosmic forces. Birdie and Murphy as twin stars, orbiting around each other. And Leeda, off at the edges of the galaxy, like a black hole.

On April 11, though nobody realized it, a pecan tree on the Darlington property crooked noticeably to the left. On April 19, a beaver took most of a Barbie that lay on the side of Orchard Road to use as dam fodder. And on April 19, as she stood on the porch unwrapping a stick of cinnamon gum, Murphy looked up and saw the strangest cloud floating by. It was in the vague shape of an arrow. It looked exactly like a one-way street sign. Murphy was so taken aback she swallowed her gum, the balled-up wrapper falling from her fingers.

Thirty-seven

*B*irdie watched the orchard wake up the way she had every spring of her life. Things began to grow so fast she could almost see them move. Like every year, the peach flowers began to blossom, draping the orchard like a filmy pink dress. Thousands of tiny pink petals fluttered in the breeze. And as quickly as they came, they disappeared. The blossoms withered to leave only shucks, and tiny, hard peaches broke through the shucks and began to grow.

For the first half of April, Birdie was so caught up in spraying, and getting things ready for the workers to arrive, and in the buzz and hum and color of the life waking up around her that she didn't think of Enrico for long stretches at a time. For weeks he'd called and sent letters, asking at first if she was avoiding him and then, later, when the answer was obvious, if he had done something wrong. But what could she tell him? That together they were bad luck? That they couldn't keep wreaking karmic havoc on the people around her? Eventually he'd stopped calling and writing. She still hadn't told Murphy and Leeda.

Birdie had expected cleaning out the cider house to be the hardest, but it was amazing how easy it was to put certain things out of her mind. She was back to being the old Birdie, doing the same things she did every year. She could see her life, her springs, stretching out in front of her like a book she'd already read. And it was nice to have such a long, clear view.

She wasn't nervous the day the workers were supposed to arrive. She was as calm as the breeze. If Enrico was on the bus, she could handle it. And if he wasn't on the bus, she could handle that too. That morning, she moved her stuff into the dorms, into the room next to Leeda's, with excitement. Now that spring was here, things would go back right. That was just how the universe worked. She neglected to remind herself that according to her definition of the universe, some third disaster—disaster Z— was waiting in the wings. It was easier to believe the good stuff.

Leeda stayed in bed when Birdie and Murphy went out to the head of the driveway to greet the bus. It lumbered up the white gravel like a slow black beetle, expiring just a few feet in front of them, its door whuffing open. As soon as the workers came climbing down the stairs, Birdie and Murphy were wrapped up in hugs and kisses. And when the last person had hugged her and the crowd cleared enough for her to see who was missing, Birdie felt only a small moment of hurt. Like the hurt of a memory.

That night, they sat around the fire, feasting on southern Mexican cooking—corn on the cob, fresh tortillas, chilies, white fish dipped in spices—and catching up on the year. Even Leeda came out and sat for a while, her skinny arms crossed loosely like ribbons, elbows on her knees, smiling softly. Everyone commented on how good Birdie's Spanish had gotten. Murphy used the little Spanish she knew. Emma, one of the workers who came every year, offered the girls beers, something she hadn't done last summer, and they squeezed lime wedges into them and sipped happily.

Poopie disappeared from the scene early. Birdie, who'd been sitting on the far side of the fire from her all night, watched her back as she walked toward the house.

Emma wrapped her arm around Birdie's waist absently as they all talked, and the whole evening felt like it had happened a thousand times before and that it was simply cycling back again.

Soon it was only Birdie and Emma and Murphy, staring at the fire and sipping their beers.

"What are you thinking, Avelita?" Emma asked her, leaning on her shoulder.

Birdie ran her fingers through her hair, smiling thoughtfully. "Just that everything's the same."

"Yes." Emma stared over her shoulder, back toward the peach rows they couldn't see in the dark, sipping her beer. "Nothing ever changes at this place." She studied Birdie's face. "The only thing changed around here is you."

"I haven't changed at all," Birdie said.

"Oh, Avelita, you need to take a look in the mirror sometime."

Birdie had forgotten to bring her warm flannely pajamas to the dorm, so after everyone had gone to bed and she'd kicked dirt on the fire, she walked across the dark lawn toward the house.

The smell of the night and the sound of the crickets reminded her of Enrico. Inside, Billie Holiday was drifting through the air from somewhere upstairs.

She looked in the laundry room for her pajamas, where she'd left them after folding them, but they were gone. She headed upstairs and looked in her room, but they weren't on her bed.

Birdie padded down the hall, standing in front of Poopie's door. She raised her hand to knock, but then she realized the music wasn't coming from there. It was coming from her dad's room. She heard a chair moving.

Birdie knew before she knew. The hairs tickled the back of her neck.

She turned to look at her dad's door, biting her lip hard, the blood rushing to her feet. She heard footsteps inside and moved to walk back down the hall, but the door opened too soon.

When Poopie came into the hall, they were a still life: Birdie, frozen. Surprised Poopie. And a hot pink nightgown.

Thirty-eight

It came back to Leeda quickly—the rhythmic motion of knocking the buds off the trees, the creak and swish of the branches, the *thud thud* of the buds falling past her ankles—as they cleared the excess buds to make room for the peaches that would grow. She remembered the rolling motion under her feet and the vague smell of peaches not nearly ripe. It wasn't a sweet smell, but a green one. Her arms moved like spaghetti as she swatted at the branches. It was the first day of clearing, and she'd come out to help not because she felt obligated, but because she was tired of staring at the dorm ceiling. She felt like she had spent the last few months watching the world as a movie going on outside her window. It got old.

She looked for Birdie and Murphy through the trees. She could see them, flashes of color among leaves and crooked branches. Murphy's blue jeans, Birdie's pink T-shirt, Majestic, appearing in patches of shade here and there, looking intently for fire ants and running away when she found them. Leeda wanted to keep track of Birdie and Murphy even if she wasn't really talking to them. It was a habit.

By noon, it felt like two days had gone by since eight a.m. Leeda dragged an arm across her forehead and slumped toward the nearest tree, still cradled in her picking harness. The tree was too small and thin to lean on, but she closed her eyes and let the tiny leaves enshroud her face. They tickled. She draped her arms gently along the branches, which bowed under the weight of her hands.

Leeda felt a pair of hands against the small of her back, propping her up. "Let's take a break," Birdie said.

"Um." Leeda stiffened. "No thanks. I'm . . ."

Whoosh. Birdie yanked her downward. Leeda looked at her in bewilderment, then followed her eyes. Poopie had just appeared a couple of rows beyond them, her powerful hands moving quickly over the branches.

"What?" Leeda whispered.

"Shhh."

Birdie took her arm with a vise-like grip and pulled her down the rows, looking down each one like she was looking down aisles at the supermarket, until she spotted Murphy in a navy blue baseball cap, knocking at the peach buds like a heavyweight champ. Murphy sensed them and looked over midpunch. Birdie made an exaggerated gesture to come over.

A few minutes later, they were bursting from the woods on the far edge of the rows onto the shores of the lake. Murphy lurched up to the water's edge like a mummy, discarding layers of clothes as she went, and simply collapsed in. Birdie crept to the edge to dip a toe in, and Murphy lunged forward and tugged on her ankle. Birdie let herself be pulled down into the water. Leeda stood with her arms crossed instinctively, several feet away. In another minute, they were running onto the grass, arms wrapped around themselves and shivering.

"Oh God, first dip." Murphy sighed, her chest heaving. Leeda didn't say anything. She felt a sort of pride that the first dip had really been hers. They sank onto the grass, so soft it felt like a bearskin rug. Leeda pulled her knees up to her chest. Birdie wrapped her goose-bumped arms around her legs and rocked, bowing her head and breathing into the space between her legs and her stomach to warm her face with her breath.

"So what's up, Birdie?" Murphy asked.

Birdie rocked once, twice. "I have something big," she said to her belly. Then her face popped up, looking at Murphy.

"You're eloping," Murphy said.

"No."

"Enrico bought you a house in Mexico and that's why he's not here bec—"

"Murphy . . ." Birdie looked so flustered—her brown eyes swimming—that Murphy clapped her mouth shut immediately. Leeda wasn't sure why Enrico hadn't come back to thin the trees this year. Birdie had mumbled something about school when Murphy asked.

"I . . . saw something . . . last night." Her face went cherry red in a wave, beginning with the apples of her cheeks, fanning outward to engulf even her temples.

"Poopie and my dad. Um. Poopie . . . in my dad's . . . They're . . . Oh." Birdie ducked her chin against her neck. "I caught them. Together." She looked up and nodded. "Together."

The words nearly knocked the wind out of Leeda. Murphy

became the face of what she felt inside, her mouth dropping open in slow motion. "You're not serious."

Birdie dropped her forehead back against her knees and shook her head.

"Bird, how do you feel about that? I mean, besides having the willies, because I do. I can't stand to think of your dad naked, and—" Murphy closed her lips tight because Birdie was looking at her like she wanted to die.

"Are you mad?" Leeda asked.

Birdie plucked some clover from the patch she was sitting on and threw it over her shoulder: left shoulder, right shoulder, left shoulder. She finally shrugged.

Leeda knew Birdie had never really gotten the hang of being mad at anyone. At least, on the surface. Usually she kept it deep inside until it blew like a volcano.

They just sat there for a while. Finally Birdie said very quietly, "Do you think Poopie wanted my mom to leave?" Her bottom lip trembled.

Murphy got on all fours and crawled over to Birdie, still drippy, and slung an arm over her shoulders.

"I thought she and I . . . I thought we had this thing." Birdie let out a long breath. "I just feel like a sucker. It's like they have this thing with each other and I'm just floating around over here, oblivious."

Murphy sank back on her palms on the grass, then scratched Birdie's back with one hand. "I guess Poopie is more of a wild woman than we thought."

Birdie shot a surprised, defensive look at Murphy.

"I'm not saying anything else," Murphy said, pretending to

zip her lips. But Birdie was back at picking the grass, thought-fully, maybe ruefully. "Except . . ." Murphy began, then stopped, eyeing Birdie warily. "Nothing."

A noise came from behind them and Emma, Raeka, and Isabel emerged from the trees. Emma had her hand in her hair, letting it down so it fell around her shoulders like black velvet. Bits were plastered to the sides of her face with sweat. She had a waterproof disposable camera dangling from her wrist. Raeka already had her shirt up over her head. They all froze, Raeka bumping into Emma and pulling down her shirt. The two groups stared at each other in shock. Finally Emma said, *"Hola."*

"Hola," the girls said back, low.

"¿Vienen aquí a nadar?" Emma said in Spanish. "Do you come here to swim?"

Leeda and the others nodded. "Yeah," Murphy said.

Raeka gestured to the other two women. *"Nosotros también."* "We do too." Leeda thought of all the times they'd come here, naked, secluded, thinking it was the only spot on earth that belonged just to them. But Raeka grinned, red-faced and sweaty, and pulled off her shirt. And just like that, the bubble surround-ing the lake for Leeda and Birdie and Murphy was broken. The three women went wading into the water, their teeth chattering. And after a minute, Murphy and Birdie drifted back in after them. The women gestured to Leeda, who shook her head and smiled politely.

They all swam around in circles, talking in Spanish and English, clutching themselves, shivering but unwilling to get out. They started splashing one another and laughing. To Leeda, they looked like Ponce de León's troupe, finally arrived at the fountain of youth.

When they crawled out, they sat on the grass, gathering around Leeda like flies. Emma stood up.

"This is nice photo." She ran and grabbed her camera where she'd left it on the grass and stood at the very edge of the lake, backing up with her heels almost touching the water. She motioned them closer together, palm straightened and perpendicular. Leeda wondered if she could tell where she and Murphy and Birdie had fractured. But then, maybe there were ways Emma, Raeka, and Isabel were fracturing too.

After the women had gone, yanking on their shirts again and linking arms, Murphy flopped back on the grass and Birdie leaned back on her elbows. "I liked Mexico," Birdie said out of the blue, softly.

She sounded wistful, but Leeda thought how lucky she was. She wondered what it must be like to know what you had.

The next morning, Leeda woke to the familiar sounds of last spring and summer—the workers moving in the kitchen, frying eggs and chatting. She lay there, very still on her side, as she heard them stomping out to trim the trees. She felt sick and stayed in bed. She didn't make it out to work in the peach rows again.

Thirty-nine

Murphy stopped, her arms aching sharply, and gazed off down the rows of peach trees, hoping to get a glimpse of Birdie. It was Easter Sunday, and the two were working alone in the rows while Poopie drove the workers to church. Murphy caught a glimpse of Birdie, several rows away, obscured by the thousands of tiny green leaves. The pink of her shirt peeked through now and then. Murphy stretched her arms high in the air and clasped her hands, arching back. She needed a break.

She made her way back to her garden and flopped onto her bench, looking around. She'd been checking in on it every couple of days since the weather had warmed up, and she was still amazed at how many weeds popped up in her short absences—their viney, spiky leaves poking out of the ground.

Still, the flowers were growing right along with them, miniature roses and hydrangea, lavender and peonies, magenta and red and pink and purple flowers. And not just in the garden, but all around, the orchard was bursting with green, and smells, and birds singing until long after dark. Maybe because of this, for the past few days, Murphy had been feeling less deflated by life in

Bridgewater. Ganax wasn't horrible. At least she had lots of free time to use her brain on other things. And Rex was, well, sublime.

Murphy, who'd always thought marriage was a farce perpetuated by society to keep people prisoner to each other, found herself fantasizing pretty often about someday, down the road, having some kind of funky, low-key wedding. They had spent many evenings on Rex's front porch, her head on his lap, just watching the world go by. There was something to be said for being able to do that. There was something to be said for being a spectator.

The birdhouse Rex had built her stood picturesquely at the end of the path. Murphy rubbed her hands together. She had the urge to see him. It was too gorgeous to ask Birdie for a ride home. She decided to walk.

She made her way toward the southwest edge of the orchard, where the grass at the edge of the property was crossed by a set of railroad tracks. The area was blocked off from the rest of the farm by a patch of tangled trees. Murphy ducked her head and moved branches aside as she cut through them, not hearing the radio until she'd come out on the grass again.

She stopped short.

There was a woman on the grass, stretched across a lilac-colored blanket. It only took Murphy a second to realize who it was, but still, she wasn't quite sure she could trust her eyes.

"Mom?"

Jodee McGowen rolled over and pulled down her sunglasses. She was listening to a battery-operated radio. A couple of sandwiches and a Diet Coke sat to her left. She held a book against her lap as she sat up.

"What are you doing here?" Murphy asked her.

Jodee shrugged. "It's Easter, baby."

"Oh." Murphy faltered. Jodee had said it as if it were obvious. But the last time Murphy and her mom had come back to the orchard for an Easter picnic had been years ago. "I didn't know you still came here."

"Yeah," Jodee said matter-of-factly, patting a spot beside her.

Murphy plopped down and took a swig of the Diet Coke.

"Sandwich?" Jodee asked, swiping a crumb out of the corner of her mouth with one long red fingernail.

Murphy took half the peanut butter sandwich and devoured it, then took another sip of Coke.

"You used to refuse to eat any sandwich but fluffernutters," Jodee said. "You've gone soft."

"You used to always say we'd get caught for trespassing," Murphy replied.

"And look what happened."

Murphy looked at the woods, trying to imagine a time the orchard hadn't felt like partly hers. Before Birdie and Leeda and Rex. It seemed like there had always been a hole there, waiting for them.

They ate companionably in silence for a while, taking turns with the soda.

"When you were little," Jodee said, swiping her brassy hair back from her face, "you were always impatient to get to the picnic and then you were impatient to leave." She smiled. "You were always ready for the next great thing. . . . It was always what's next? What's next? What's next?"

Murphy crossed her legs Indian style. "I bet that was annoying."

"No." Jodee shook her head. "No, not annoying." She paused. "Actually, it just made me worry."

"Why?"

"I don't know. I guess I always worried that maybe you'd *never* feel like you were standing in the right place."

Murphy felt a tiny lump form in her throat. It was true. She'd never felt that way.

Jodee sighed. "I always wanted to stay still. I always thought being happy with what I had was one of my strengths, you know. . . . But to always be looking for the right place and never finding it . . . that's kind of . . . sad."

Murphy picked the grass. She could feel some sort of words of wisdom coming. She peered toward the trees again, thinking of making a break for it. "Mom, if you're heading for some sage advice, I just . . . I'm not—"

"Murphy, I found it."

Murphy didn't ask what. She just grabbed more grass, like she was three.

"I was looking for coupons for Taco Cabana." Jodee took the last sip of the Diet Coke grimly and crumpled the can. "You always recycle those without asking me."

"Buy one, get one free?" Murphy asked glibly. Jodee shot her a straight, absolutely serious look. Murphy looked at the tiny green blades in her hand.

"You got in."

Murphy held her palms together, rolling the blades back and forth.

"Can I ask you something?"

Finally Murphy looked up. She hated how seriously her mom gazed back at her. She hated how it made her feel like she was five years old.

"Do you think I'm happy you're staying?" Jodee's voice took

on an angry edge, and her mouth gave a little tremble around her words. "Do you think I was happy when you told me you didn't get accepted?"

Yes, Murphy thought. Of course. Only now, it looked sideways to her. For the first time, it occurred to her that maybe she was wrong about that.

"How could you put me through that disappointment?" And then tiny tears began to gather at the corners of her mom's eyes, and Murphy wanted to melt into the grass like a drop of rain.

Jodee swiped at her eyes, leaving skinny trails of mascara. "I didn't work as hard as I have to give you a life that's not one hundred percent what you want it to be. Isn't that obvious? Or are you still more of a kid than I think you are?"

"I *want* to stay. . . ." Murphy protested, feeling anger boil up. "*You* always thought I should stay."

Jodee sniffled, looked around like someone needed to witness what she was hearing. "Do I look stupid?"

Murphy rolled her eyes and let out a deep sigh. She was on the verge of getting up. It wouldn't take much to push her.

"Murphy, if you give up the things you want most now, when do you go after the things you want? When does that happen if it doesn't happen now?"

"I love Rex."

"I know you do," Jodee breathed. "I really know you do. But you wanna know what I think?"

Murphy cast a glance at the trees. "What?"

"I think that's not why you're not going."

Murphy stared hard at her mom.

"I think..." Jodee went on. "You're using that boy as an excuse."

Murphy blinked at her for another second, then laughed. "That's so stupid."

Her mother's face had gone stony and superior. "I think you're scared, after all this time with the 'I'm too big for this town.'" Jodee waved her hands in the air in a mocking way. "You kept saying the minute you got the chance, *bam*!" Jodee slid one hand across the other. "We wouldn't see your curls flopping on the way out. But I think now that it comes down to it, you're scared that you're not too big at all. I think you're scared you're not big *enough*." Jodee shook her head. "And it just breaks my heart."

Murphy stood up quickly. She felt twisted up enough to hit something. "Whatever," she said, and turned to hightail it into the trees. She knew it was a horrible comeback. But nothing else came to her.

She half walked, half jogged home. A bunch of letters were poking out of the top of the mailbox, but Murphy let them be. She sank onto the stoop and looked around.

Almost everything she could see in the Anthill Acres parking lot was at least as old as she was, which was true even for some of the rusty soda cans still lying flattened and half buried in the gravel. The barbecue pit was flooded with murky water. Several people had had their Christmas lights up for as long as Murphy could remember.

Murphy was a soda can stuck in the mud. She was drowned under the puddle of water in the barbecue pit. She was Christmas lights left out too long.

And she couldn't leave.

Forty

When the car door slammed out in front of the house on May 2, Majestic made a beeline for the crevice behind the fridge. Birdie could see her little tail poking out, trembling, as she got on her hands and knees and scooped her up with one arm. She was amazed by the dog's stellar instincts.

"Let's do it in the living room," Poopie called, coming down the stairs.

They stretched Majestic out on the couch, Birdie with the back legs and Poopie with the front. Dr. Cawood slid the tip of his scissors in between the dog's leg and the tiny cast. There was a long drawn-out snip and then Majestic's one little leg was free. The vet did the same to the other.

Majestic leapt off the couch and barked at them, then ran into the kitchen. Birdie walked Dr. Cawood to the door. When she came back down the hall, Majestic was running joyous laps around the kitchen table, panting and growling. Poopie was doing the dishes.

"You want help with those?" Birdie asked.

"Okay."

The silence was punctuated only by sloshing suds and clinking glasses. Birdie looked out the window at the empty rows of peach trees. The workers had gone until June, but it felt like they were still here. Majestic slid up to their feet and yipped at them to play.

"Looks like she's over her grief." Poopie tried a tiny smile on Birdie.

"Looks like it," Birdie muttered, her eyes on the glass in her hands.

Poopie seemed to wilt. She too hung her head in the direction of the sink, but she went on. "She won't know what to do when you start school, though. Whole new reason to grieve."

Birdie scrubbed the glass spotless, way longer than she needed to. "I'll still be around," she said flatly, without a hint of warmth. "Majestic and I are stuck with each other."

Poopie looked up at her, tilting her head. "Why stuck?"

Birdie shrugged and scrubbed.

Poopie took a deep breath, laid her hand on the counter, and turned toward her. "Birdie, I know you're angry with me."

"I'm not angry," Birdie said.

Poopie slammed a hand on the counter. "Yes, you are. Just tell me you are. Yell at me. Do something."

"I don't own the orchard yet. I can't fire you."

Poopie looked like she'd been slapped. Then she raised herself up, straightening her back and lifting her chin.

"If you want me to leave, I will."

Birdie twisted the dish towel in her hands. "You left me already."

Poopie was very still for a moment. And then she nodded

thoughtfully and started for the stairs. Birdie looked back over her shoulder to watch her climb them with Majestic at her heels. *Traitor,* she thought to the dog. She listened to Poopie's feet padding down the hall upstairs to her room. Then she heard the sound of Poopie pulling something heavy out of the closet. It filled her heart with sudden dread.

Birdie laid down her towel and walked over to the stairs, taking two steps up, then stopped and listened, holding her breath. She could hear Poopie moving things around. She walked up two more steps and listened again. Then she walked up to the landing and hovered there, staring at her bedroom door, then down at Poopie's open one.

She crept down to the doorway. Inside, Poopie was stuffing clothes into a big black suitcase.

"What are you doing?"

Poopie sniffed. "Packing."

"Why?"

Poopie, kneeling, put her hands on the floor and hung her head. "Because I don't know what else to do."

Birdie was frozen. Tears trembled underneath her eyelids. She covered her face with her hands and sank against the door-jamb. "I thought you were retiring," she croaked. "I thought that's why you were acting so weird all this time." She knew she sounded like a little kid, the way her voice rose and fell jaggedly. She pulled down her hands and looked at Poopie. She couldn't stop crying. "I thought you were leaving for Mexico."

"No." Poopie shook her head violently. "Retiring? No. Birdie, I would tell you the minute I knew."

Birdie looked at her with the obviousness of her reply.

Poopie rubbed her hands together like she was praying. "Your dad and I didn't know how to tell you, Birdie." Birdie was shocked to see Poopie's hands trembling. "He wanted to tell you right away. But I thought it might . . . ruin how you saw me." She shook her head. "You already have a mom. But I never had a daughter. I only have you."

Birdie's body went slack. She felt a current of relief shoot through her. The anger was still there, but beside it was the knowledge that it wasn't one-sided. That she hadn't been wrong about them. She was in the middle of an anger, relief, anger sandwich. Poopie shot up and moved beside her.

"You judged me," Birdie said, all tear streaked and runny nosed now. "About Enrico. When you were doing the same thing."

Poopie tilted her head sideways, perplexed. "What judging? Judged you?"

"You put the santos outside my room. After . . ." Birdie perched on the edge of the bed.

Poopie looked lost for another minute. "Birdie . . ." She shook her head. "Those aren't about judging." Poopie grabbed Birdie's hand and pulled her back, sat her on the bed, and sat beside her. "Being with someone—like that—is always a risk. That's what those are. Just help." Poopie shrugged. "I don't even know if they work. I just want to believe that they do."

Birdie sat in silence for a while, taking it in.

"You don't think . . ." she began, then dropped to a whisper. "That God killed Honey Babe and Aunt Eugenie because of me, do you?"

Poopie put her hands to her mouth. And then she laughed. When Birdie looked at her, she turned serious. And then she laughed again. "I'm sorry. No, no, I don't. And Birdie, I love you. I have already judged you, a long time ago." She put her arm around Birdie. "You are perfect."

Birdie felt clouds lifting in her head. She didn't know why it took Poopie to lift them. But all of a sudden she realized that maybe the whole thing was crazy.

"What else do you want to know?" Poopie asked.

Birdie looked at her. "Are you in love with my dad?"

Poopie shrugged. Then nodded.

"How long?"

"I don't know. I didn't see it happening. I had different plans. Always to go back home. Always putting it off. There was one way I thought life would be and another way it was happening. But I couldn't see how far what was happening was taking me away from what I thought."

Birdie cleared her throat. "Did you want my mom to leave?"

Poopie hugged her. "No, honey. No, of course not."

Birdie studied her face. She believed her. It didn't change the hurt. It didn't make Poopie and her dad okay. But it made Birdie feel a little less betrayed.

"Dad wants me to take over the farm."

"He'd live if you didn't."

"I want to, though."

Poopie wrapped her arms around her and hugged her. "That's easy, then."

"I broke up with Enrico."

"I know. Why?"

Birdie found herself on the verge of crying again, but she smiled sheepishly. "I have no idea."

The front door cracked open and they heard Walter coming up the stairs. He walked into the room with his mouth open to say something to Poopie and then saw them both tear-streaked and leaning against each other. He cleared his throat, looked at the ceiling, and then turned around and walked into his room.

Poopie and Birdie looked at each other, and even though it was more pitiful than funny, they laughed.

That night, Birdie walked to the dorms and sank down with her back to the building, underneath what was once Enrico's window. She thought about the warmth of his body and wrapped her arms around herself, shivering from the soles of her cold, wet feet. She tried to make it enough to just be near where he used to be.

Heading back toward the house, Birdie made a wide arc left to circle through the pecan grove. She came to a dead stop a few feet away from the first tree. Around Methuselah's shaggy middle, about three feet up from the ground, was a red vinyl ribbon.

Red ribbons marked the trees slated to be chopped down. Over the years, her dad had placed them on a few trees that, for one reason or another, had needed to go. Birdie reached out to touch it, her chest aching.

She envisioned her heart buried under Methuselah, like Leeda had said. She pictured the tree standing above her grave. But the picture nagged at her. She was imagining the epitaph. Most people's had stuff like *loving mother, dear husband, giving spirit, beloved daughter*. Hers read: *Birdie Darlington, Held down the fort*.

When she trailed back to her room about an hour later, she stared at the phone.

She dialed his dorm and got his voice mail. "It's me. Birdie. Darlington. I'm ... sorry." That was it. She hung up.

Birdie was up before dawn. She'd left her window open all night, and the orchard had filled her room with the smells of swelling green peaches, shaggy pecan bark, and magnolia leaves. Birdie wasn't sure why, but it was all mixed up with the memory of jacarandas, dry sand, cactus, cayenne, cinnamon.

She crept down the hall, careful not to wake anyone, careful to position everything exactly right.

When Poopie woke and opened her door, it would be to a line of wooden saints in the hallway, all staring at her. They weren't a judgment, but a wish and a blessing.

They both needed all the help they could get.

The second week of May, several changes took place in Bridgewater that went unnoticed by a soul. At the Buck's Creek Nature Preserve, the bats began flapping inside their cave, their restless wings beating long into the night. Methuselah listed a bit more—so slightly that only the beetles crawling up and down her trunk noticed. The cinnamon smell that had settled over the orchard was replaced by the scent of roses drifting out of Murphy's garden. And in New York City, a pebble tumbled from the corner of a rubber stair and fell straight into an open sewer grate.

Forty-one

"I don't know," Birdie said, clutching the urn.

"C'mon, Birdie. She wants to be free."

Murphy sat in the golf cart, sweaty. Today had been her and Leeda's last day of high school—forever—and they'd come straight here to start getting things ready for the workers: cleaning the cider press, stacking the halters, picking the trees that were ripe early. She slumped in the seat, laying her head back in the sun impatiently.

Birdie was wearing a pair of Rollerblades, her hand cupped over the top of Honey Babe's urn. A long line of rope went from the back of the golf cart to the belt at her waist. Leeda sat shotgun, barely there, her wavy blond hair pulled back in a short and simple ponytail, her body listless in the seat like a string of licorice. Murphy suspected she'd only agreed to come because it was less trouble than saying no.

"Can't I just ride up there with you guys?" Birdie called.

Murphy looked back at her, tilting her chin chidingly. "Do you think Honey Babe would have wanted it that way?" Birdie bit her lip thoughtfully. Then she gave a conceding shrug.

To Murphy, it was key to have the ashes flying behind Birdie gloriously. She had come up with the idea, of course. She'd used her downtime at Ganax to write out morbid invitations with little skulls and crossbones. Even though Leeda was hardly talking to them these days, they'd all met at the barn, where they'd hidden the Balmeade's golf cart, at the specified time.

"Are you ready?" She glanced back at Birdie, who didn't look ready at all.

"Yeah. Okay." Birdie nodded, her knees pulled together unsurely.

Majestic, who'd been curled between the front seats, leapt onto Leeda's lap and started yipping. Murphy stepped on the gas, glancing back every second or two, and the cart picked up speed. Birdie held the urn tightly as she jostled forward. She smiled and Murphy stepped harder on the gas. Leeda put a hand against her forehead and shook her head.

Birdie held up the urn now, ready to let the contents flutter out. But her Rollerblade stuck in something, and she went flying forward. Murphy hit the brakes and swiveled in her seat in time to watch the urn toppling across the grass, finally landing upside down. Majestic leapt out of the passenger side and went dashing for Birdie. Birdie looked at the urn, its contents emptied in an unglamorous heap on the grass.

A second later, Murphy and Leeda were beside her.

"Are you okay?" Leeda gasped, sinking to her knees.

"It wasn't supposed to happen like that." Birdie pushed herself up on her elbows, her voice crackling, her hair hanging over her face.

They all stared at the pile. "It actually reminds me of Honey Babe's poo," Murphy said, trying to sound bright.

Birdie sniffled. Murphy kissed her on the cheek. "I'm sorry. It was a bad idea."

She grabbed Birdie's hands and hoisted her up. Deflated, they climbed into the cart and drove it back toward the Balmeade Country Club.

Climbing back over the fence onto the orchard property a few minutes later, Murphy was struck by the greenness of the grass, the peaches showing through the spaces in the trees up ahead of them like sun-colored polka dots.

"I don't feel it." Birdie sighed a deep sigh.

"What?" Leeda asked.

Birdie stuck her hands into her pockets. "Last summer. I thought it would feel like last summer."

They were silent for a few minutes. It didn't feel anything like last summer. They climbed over the fence back onto the orchard property, and Birdie looked around. "Sometimes I feel like I'm a small person for staying here. You know, forever."

Murphy looked at her. "Oh, Bird, at least you know what you want. And you're good at it. You're good at being here."

Birdie turned and peeled some paint off the fence. "Maybe there are other things I'm good at. And I just don't know it. Maybe I'm just being boring."

Murphy looked to Leeda, waiting for her to object, but Leeda's lips stayed closed, her face a blank slate. "You're not boring," Murphy said, leaning her elbows back over the fence and looking at Methuselah, droopy as ever, a red ribbon tied around her waist. "You're the farthest thing from boring. You're the kind of not boring that doesn't have to act all crazy to remind people she's not boring." She stuck her thumbnail in her mouth, like she was trying to think of the right way to say something. "Bird, you're a Mondrian."

•   •   •

Afterward Birdie and Murphy swam in the lake to wash off the ashes that had blown onto them. Leeda sat on the rock watching them like a siren—beautiful and far away. The crickets sang to them wherever they drifted, as if by swimming, they were directing an orchestra. Birdie hopped out first, shivering and squeezing the water out of her hair.

Murphy swam to the edge and let Majestic lick her wet arms, feeling like there was something to say as she watched Birdie clamber over beside Leeda. But she pushed off from the edge again back into the water. She floated on her back, looking up at the sky, some puffy clouds floating past. Then she swam forward again.

"I got into NYU," she said, slapping her palms gently on top of the water. She could hear Birdie gasp. "I lied before."

She could feel her friends' gazes on her, but she didn't look up. Instead of diving, she sank underwater.

When she came back up, Birdie was turning red, and for a minute, Murphy wondered why. "Enrico and I had sex," she whispered. Leeda and Murphy both looked at her, shocked. "And Poopie found us naked."

Leeda and Murphy looked at each other now, stunned.

They were quiet for several seconds, absorbing.

"And we broke up."

"Bird!" Murphy and Leeda both said at the same time.

Birdie scrunched her toes around some gravelly pebbles.

They were all silent for a second, and then Leeda said, "I'm going to Berkeley."

It was nothing like last summer at all.

Forty-two

Rex was sitting on his porch listening to the radio when Murphy pulled up on her bike that evening. She laid it against the mailbox and picked her way up the stone path like she was skipping her way across a stream. By the time she had made her long pilgrimage to the stairs, hands in pockets, head down, he seemed to know. She sank into the swing, and he pulled her across his lap. He put his fingers into her puffy curls. She stared up at the ceiling light of the porch. Moths were fluttering around it.

"Three days to graduation, huh, Shorts?" Rex said. His voice sounded flat and far away. Murphy nodded.

"I think we should drive to California for the summer," she said.

"Yeah, I was thinking that too."

"We can tool around for a while. Go to the beach. And then we can be there waiting for Leeda when she gets there."

"That's great, Murphy. That's a great idea." No Shorts. No Murphy Jane. No M.J.

Finally he pulled Murphy tight to him and curled over her,

putting his forehead against hers. "I was selfish," he said. "I never really believed you."

Murphy lost her voice. Deep down, she had known he knew.

His voice was rumbly when he went on. "When are you leaving?"

She cleared her throat. A tear dribbled out of the corner of her eye, down along the edge of her ear. "They offered me a work-study program for the summer. It starts Monday."

Rex just stared at her, into her, like he could see every part of Murphy. She wondered when someone would ever look at her like that again. If. "Can I drive you?" he finally asked.

Murphy shook her head. "I don't . . ." Murphy had known it would be hard, but she didn't know she would have so much trouble putting words together. She wiped the tear at her hairline. "I don't think I can see you again." This time, it was an honest request. Rex's forehead creased, as if he had a bad headache.

He pushed the swing back and forth, like a heartbeat. After a while, she said, "We should live in an Airstream trailer on a cliff. Looking down at the ocean."

"And grow nectarines," he added.

They went on and on about all the things they would do. They'd make their slow way along Route 66, staying in old theme motels shaped like wigwams or painted with neon lights. They'd see things along the road like the Blue Whale and Monument Valley. Being right for each other would be right enough.

"All the Bridgewater boys will cry to see me go off with you like that." Murphy grinned.

"The world is our oyster," Rex said.

"It really is, Rex."

He put his face gently against her cheek. They didn't look each other in the eye now.

Murphy listened to him breathing and the sound of his blood rushing wherever it was going beneath her ear. She thought about when she was with him, when she touched him, she wasn't just touching skin, but all the things Rex was, and all the things he'd seen and the things he knew how to do, and all the ways he had shown her he was hers. She thought of the blood rushing its way through his heart.

Murphy woke sometime late. The house was dark, and Rex was leaned back on the seat, asleep. She sat up slowly so she wouldn't wake him and tiptoed across the porch. She was a shadow walking to her bike, pushing it down the driveway and turning to walk it past the cemetery. She'd wait before she got on and pedaled. If she woke him, they'd have to do some kind of good-bye.

Walking across the bridge, the view looked different to her now that she knew—*really* knew—she was leaving.

There had been bonuses to being stuck in the mud that Murphy had never noticed. Over seventeen years, she'd managed to get a lot of firsts tucked under her belt. But she had never once had to say a real good-bye.

Forty-three

It looked like Murphy wasn't going to show for her own going-
away party. They waited, called, waited. Birdie kept swallowing
the lump in her throat, and Leeda just stared at her, looking like
it was the last place she wanted to be anyway. Finally she said
she was tired and slunk off to the dorms. Birdie watched her go,
something breaking inside for Murphy.

Around eleven, Birdie rubbed the sweat from her neck and
drifted toward the back porch. She closed the door behind her,
sat down on the top step, and fanned her face with her hand.
She noticed the tiniest movement in the dark and realized there
was somebody lying on the dewy grass in front of her.

"Murphy?"

"Yeah."

Birdie got up and then lay down beside her. The wet grass
sent cool chills down her back as it seeped through her shirt.
The sky was low and thick and dark. Birdie stared up at it,
relaxed but sad. The cicadas were achingly loud. "Why are you
in the back?"

Murphy didn't answer for a while. Then she raised herself on an elbow and looked over at Birdie. Birdie couldn't make out her face, just the flop of her curls and the shadows hanging over her eyes. "I don't want to look at the peach trees."

Birdie didn't really need to ask why. She imagined it was like looking away from something that made you too sad to watch.

"Will you stay up with me? I don't want to lie in bed and wait to fall asleep."

"Sure." Birdie thought. "You wanna go do something? Something away from here?"

Murphy seemed to be thinking. "Yeah."

"We can do anything you want."

Murphy seemed to think some more. And then she sat up all the way, and Birdie could finally see something of her in the dark. She could see the white of her smile. Birdie knew to be immediately afraid.

Mayor Wise's house was set up with alarms, sprinkler systems, double bolts. It was indicative of the fantasy world he lived in that he thought the mayor of a place like Bridgewater would even need to lock the door at night.

Birdie and Murphy stood poised on the edge of the lawn. Murphy was leaning slightly forward and breathing excitedly, like a bull being enticed by a red flag. The house—large and white with giant pillars—gleamed in the moonlight. One light was on, on the second floor. Birdie could just make out a lamp and the top of a head. *Oh God.* She looked at where they'd piled their clothes a safe distance away, and at her own naked body gleaming like a white bike reflector in the moonlight.

Murphy took her arm to position Birdie like she was, like a

runner at the beginning of a marathon. "They're going to know as soon as we do it. So just keep running, okay? If we get separated, I'll meet you back home."

Birdie didn't have to ask what she meant by home.

"Ready?"

Birdie nodded. She wasn't. But then, she was as ready as she'd ever be.

When Mayor Wise looked out his window on the night of May 14 to see not one, but two naked girls on his front lawn, running through the sprinklers, his reaction was quite different than it would have been forty-one years before. Then he would have fallen on his knees to thank his lucky stars. But as he peered out the window, pushing his glasses up on his nose to make sure he was seeing what he thought he was seeing, he didn't even smile. He frowned seriously, thoughtfully, and said to no one in particular, "Somebody should get those girls some clothes." And then he went downstairs to call the police.

By the time the cops arrived, however, the girls had vanished into thin air, and the only thing to indicate they had ever been there at all were disappearing footprints under the water jets still soaking the grass.

Forty-four

The night seemed shorter when you were awake.

After streaking across the mayor's lawn, Birdie had lit a fire by the lake. They had managed to get mostly dry, sitting through the night, hardly talking, just watching the sky and listening to the leaves. Murphy didn't want Birdie coming to the bus station with her, so just before dawn, she walked her to the dorm.

Big fat tears ran down Birdie's cheeks. But Murphy felt like she was glowing. She could run a marathon. She bounced on her feet, smiling bigger than ever. She could feel her freckles like stars. She was, in a word, defiant.

Standing in the familiar dorm hall, Birdie finally released her from her grip. Murphy watched her, sniffling, disappear into her room and close the door. And then Murphy stood, watching the doorknob, the threat of something not-defiant nibbling at her. Finally she moved down the hall.

But she stopped at Leeda's door. She stood there for a moment, her heart beating in every part of her, and then she knocked softly. "Leeda?"

Nothing.

She steeled herself and knocked again gently. "Leeda?"

Nothing.

Murphy sank against the door, her head against the wood. Her curls hung down like curtains on either side of her face. "Bye, Lee," she said, tears creeping out. She stood up and held her head back until they'd crept back in. And then she walked away.

Leeda was lying awake when she heard Murphy knock. She had been awake all night, staring at the blinds on the window, running her fingers along the ridges in the wall, turning from her stomach to her back to her side. When she'd seen the sun start to rise, she was sure she'd missed her chance to say good-bye. And then there had been the knock. And Leeda had held her breath, as if Murphy would hear her breathing and decide to barge in.

Now she could hear her making her way downstairs and then the sound of the door opening and closing. For a few minutes afterward, she didn't feel anything. Only that her heart had just sort of flown away, hovered somewhere, and hid.

It wasn't until the sun reached over the trees into the sky, the gray turning soft yellow, that Leeda's heart made it back inside her, and then it nearly knocked her over with how much she missed Murphy. She missed a million things about her. Her freckles and her jokes and her bouncy feet and her sarcasm and her sharpness. She remembered the first time she'd seen Murphy swim—the crazy fearlessness when she'd jumped off a tree into Smoaky Lake under the moon.

Leeda knew it would take a while to figure out all the things that she'd miss.

Forty-five

$\mathcal{B}$irdie got up about an hour after she'd gone to bed, slogging into the house to make eggs. She kept glancing at the clock, counting the minutes until Murphy's bus would leave.

After breakfast, she and Poopie played War, staring at each other as if they were both thinking the same thing. Finally Birdie couldn't take it anymore. She laid down her cards and stepped outside. She walked to the barn and stared at the defunct items she'd put around the bat cave. She let out a sigh and busied herself picking up the bowls and the faux bat. She kicked the rotten fruit aside. Sometimes you had to call a spade a spade. Sometimes you just had to let it go.

She dumped it all in the trash can in the barn and then walked the rest of the way down the long gravel driveway.

She dawdled like that by the road for twenty minutes, kicking pebbles around, back and forth, back and forth. When she saw one that was pure white, like marble, she put it in her pocket. No reason why. No reason why she felt she needed to stand by the road. No reason why the pebble.

She heard an engine roaring off to her left. Rex's orange

truck turned the corner and then, inexplicably, sped past and disappeared. A moment later, Birdie heard a horrible screech of wheels. In another split second, she was off running.

She could smell the burning rubber before she could see the truck. It had ended up parked completely perpendicular to the road. When Birdie saw Rex climb out of the driver's side a moment later, she nearly fell over with relief. She ran to catch up with him where he stood, his hands on his waist, looking down. Birdie threw her hands to her mouth when she saw what he was looking at.

Birdie walked up beside Rex and they both stared down at it together. Methuselah, dead at last. With the roots on one end and the limbs on the other, the tree looked like the world's largest baby rattle. Birdie looked at Rex, then at the tree again, then at Rex. He reached out for her wrist and lifted it so he could see her watch, then laid her hand back at her side.

Suddenly something dawned on her. "Were you going after Murphy?"

Rex looked like he didn't quite know.

Birdie stared at the tree. "It would have been the wrong thing," she finally said.

"Yeah," Rex agreed. "I knew that."

Birdie didn't know what else to say. She squatted beside Methuselah and laid a hand on top of her as if she might feel a pulse.

Forty-six

"Y̶ou sure I can't stay and wait for the bus with you, sweetie?"

"Yeah, Mom." Murphy was curled up against the car door, peeping at her mom sideways.

The Pontiac pulled into the parking lot behind the bus stop. Jodee popped the trunk, and they both got out. Murphy hoisted her backpack over one shoulder. Her mom dragged her suitcase onto the pavement by the handle and then held it out to Murphy. Her hands were trembling. "I want to get on that bus with you."

"I know. I want you to too." Murphy had never thought she would want that. But she did. She felt like she needed her mom like she never had. Which was ironic. For obvious reasons. Don't know what you've got till it's gone and all that. She wished that at some time, they had tried harder to find a way for her mom to save up so that she could come with her and help her make her dorm room feel like home.

Jodee reached out and squeezed Murphy tight, engulfing her in the smell of powdery perfume. She pulled back and smiled. "I know you can do this."

Murphy tried to look sure and nodded. "I know." She didn't know, really. She only hoped she knew.

"You call me if you need anything."

"Yeah."

"I'll be up to visit as soon as I can save up."

"Okay."

"I love you, baby."

"I love you too."

Jodee hurriedly got into the car and pulled away, her hand resting on her chin agitatedly. Before Murphy knew it, the Pontiac had disappeared around the corner, and she had officially said good-bye to the last person she knew.

Murphy wheeled her suitcase to the bus stop and dumped her backpack on the bench. She stared at the entrance to the parking lot. Waiting for something. Not for the bus. Something else.

The minutes ticked by, and Murphy listened to the sound of the cars, the buses, the trucks along the highway. She rubbed her sleepy eyes even though she felt wide awake. She stared at where the road turned in from town.

A familiar sound made her turn again in the other direction. She could hear the bus as it lurched from the exit beyond the trees. Amazingly, she finally knew what the New York bus, specifically, sounded like. And then it materialized slowly from around the corner. It lurched to a stop and the doors hissed open. Two people climbed off, but Murphy was too preoccupied to judge them.

A hatch opened on the bottom. Murphy hauled her luggage into her arms and tucked it underneath, the way she'd seen others do. Then she walked up toward the front.

Murphy's heart had begun to pound so hard it felt like it would pop. Just as she arrived at the doors, she heard the sound of a car pulling in. She turned, elated, sure it was him, coming to beg her to stay. Right then, she couldn't say for sure, but it felt like she would have. But the car, she saw immediately, wasn't Rex's. It came to a slow stop, and the two people who'd just climbed out made their way over.

Murphy gave one more look to the empty road behind her. She turned back and stared at the black rubbery stairs.

Something wild and liberated took over her. A smile took over her lips.

She stepped on.

That morning, Judge Miller Abbott passed Jodee McGowen driving into town. Thinking of his recurring dream, he turned around at the Big Boy drive-through and drove straight to Smoaky Lake for the first time in seventeen years. There he touched the tree where he had carved her initials, marking the one night they had spent together down by the lake.

As he fingered the creases in the wood, he felt the hole in his heart as wide and as deep as the morning she had bounced away from him, on to the next adventure and the next boy. The hole throbbed for a moment and then it quickly moved into the shadows—somewhere deep, and hidden, and almost forgotten.

That night, the dreams stopped coming for good.

Forty-seven

Leeda pulled her graduation gown out of her closet and held it up to the light. She had been awake since Murphy had left, and now she felt groggy and dizzy. She hadn't decided whether she'd actually go to the ceremony that evening or not. She had thought that maybe staring at her gown long enough would give her the answer. But it only gave her the urge to clean her closet.

Birdie lay on her bed, watching her mournfully. As Leeda pulled a shoe box off the top shelf, a bunch of papers fluttered out, swishing through the air and landing all over the floor. There had to be at least twenty slips of paper.

Slowly, tiredly, Leeda crouched down and picked one up. They were all IOUs from Murphy. *IOU your green sweater. IOU your suede coat.* Leeda frowned, irritated. She hadn't even noticed so much was missing.

"What's wrong?" Birdie sat up. Leeda held up one of the IOUs.

"Murphy."

Leeda flipped through the IOUs and sighed. Her favorite sweater. Her favorite jeans. They didn't even fit Murphy right.

"What?" Birdie asked.

"Just all this stuff she borrowed that she didn't bother to return." Leeda could feel her blood boiling. The more she thought, the more she was so mad at Murphy for so many things.

"I'm sure she just forgot," Birdie offered.

Leeda shot her a look, then pointedly counted up all her IOUs. "You don't just forget eighteen times."

Birdie was quiet for a long time, but Leeda didn't notice. She pulled everything from the closet, folding. Dressy in one pile, casual in another, underwear in a third.

"You sound so bitter."

Leeda didn't look at Birdie; she just kept folding.

"You know who you sound like?" Birdie went on.

"Who?" Leeda asked.

"You sound like your mom."

Leeda looked at Birdie. Then she shoved her piles into her suitcase. "Screw you, Birdie."

She got her purse and walked out of the room, dropping her keys three times before she got them into the door of her car.

It occurred to her once she was driving that she had nowhere to drive to.

Leeda let herself into Breezy Buds and stood in the white tile foyer. "Hello?" When nobody answered, she went into the kitchen, opened the fridge, and pulled out a plastic container of food, digging into it with a fork. When she was finished eating, she went upstairs to her room and read her mail, then sorted through her drawers, pulling out some spring clothes and laying them on the bed.

"Leeda."

Leeda whipped around. Her mom stood in the doorway.

"Hey. I'm just . . . getting some things." Leeda hadn't seen her mom since the hospital. Lucretia wasn't wearing any makeup. She looked a lot older without it.

"Graduation's tonight."

"Yup." Leeda went back to packing, pretending her mom wasn't there. Finally she couldn't ignore her anymore. "I wish you would stop looking at me like that."

Lucretia continued to hover. At last she floated in and sat on the far corner of Leeda's bed, holding herself erect.

Lucretia glanced down at her hands. "I always had the best hands. Now look at them." She held them up, but Leeda didn't look. "I never believed I'd have hands like this."

"I really don't care." Leeda truly didn't. She and her mother didn't need each other or even want to be near each other. They didn't have to pretend.

Lucretia studied her and then looked toward Leeda's shelf.

"What did you do with the Barbie?"

"I threw it into a ditch."

Lucretia's mouth tilted at one corner in an ironic smile. "That's appropriate, I guess," she said. When Leeda didn't bite, she went on. "It wasn't really mine, you know. It actually belonged to a friend of mine." Lucretia had a tone in her voice that was undone. She *looked* undone.

"You should Google her," Leeda said.

"Carolina. Everybody liked her everywhere we went. It didn't matter—post office, store, whatever—she was a *pet*." Lucretia laughed. "I don't know why she was friends with me.

"We used to meet at the orchard. We'd both show up with these plastic cases full of Barbies. I had tons more than she did, but I always made her let me use her favorite one." Lucretia shook her head. "I loved it best because she did, I guess. She never wanted to give it to me, but she always did."

"Sounds about right." Leeda zipped her suitcase and put it on the floor.

"Leeda. I'm trying . . . I want to tell you . . ." Lucretia shook her head. "I was this . . ." She paused. "Monster, I guess. I thought that if it wasn't done my way, I'd be invisible. Or maybe it was that I didn't want people to get too close to me. Maybe I *wanted* to scare them off; I don't know. I had all these *rough* edges that Carolina didn't have. I always felt . . . I don't know . . . like a jar of tacks." She went on, "When I got older, I tried to be better. But I didn't even think I wanted to be a mom. I didn't think I'd be any good at it."

Leeda stood impassive, watching the confusion cross her mother's face. She cleared her throat. "Carolina and I were playing one day on the rocks and I dropped the Barbie down the crevice. It was an accident. And it just disappeared. We got the longest sticks we could find, but we couldn't dig it out. Couldn't even see it. And she never yelled at me or anything. She just sort of drifted away afterward. Not that it was just the Barbie. I think it was the final straw. I mean, how long can you be friends with someone like that? I'd call her and she wouldn't call back, that kind of thing.

"Do you know I must have gone back to that spot about a million times looking for that stupid doll? I brought a flashlight, clothes hangers twisted into long hooks. I was caught up with the idea that if I could dig the Barbie out of the muck, it would be this big, dramatic apology. The look on her face when I could hand it to her. Here it is. I'm sorry for being this . . . person."

"But you never found it."

Lucretia shook her head.

"Mom, what are you saying?"

She stood up. "Well, I guess I'm talking about your parade."

"*Your* parade," Leeda shot back.

"It was just how much it seemed to mean to you. The kind of mom you needed to be there. It's not me." Leeda squinted at her, and Lucretia rubbed her fingers over her fingernails just like Leeda always did. "You're not the only person who thinks I'm horrible. That's my point, I guess. Some people just . . . put up with it. You never have. You've always looked so . . . crushed. Like you expected something else. That's the big difference between you and Danay. I think she figured out a long time ago the way I am. She never needed me the way you do."

Lucretia took in a deep breath and then let it out slowly. "The truth is, Leeda, I'm not the best mom. Not nearly. Maybe I'm somewhere near the bottom rung." She shrugged, almost casually. Her face kept that open, undone, slack look for a moment longer and then settled into one more controlled. "I'm sorry. I really am." She looked like she wanted to say something more. But she made a helpless gesture with her hands instead and then turned and walked off down the hall.

Leeda stood, unsure what to do. She wanted to throw something. More than anything, she felt like she'd come up against a brick wall.

When Leeda moved past the living room a few minutes later,

her mom was on the phone, sounding like she always did. Like nothing ever changed or ever would. Leeda stepped out onto the sunlit patio and closed the door behind her, then stepped back against it, startled. Birdie was sitting on the stairs.

Leeda sank on the step beside her. They both dangled their hair toward their feet and felt the sun on their necks. "I got this from Mexico." Birdie handed her an envelope, slightly crumpled.

Leeda thought it would be something from Enrico, but when she pulled open the flap and looked inside, all that was there was a photo. "Raeka sent a copy for you." Leeda studied it. The scene had been smudged in a place where the sun was blotting the subjects, but still you could tell who was who—Isabel and Raeka, dark dripping arms around each other. Murphy, with one of Raeka's hands resting on her wild hair that hung like wet oodles of noodles. Birdie with Murphy's hand on her knee, smiling in a pained but hopeful kind of way. And Leeda, sitting next to them, with her arms around herself, straight and aloof. Like her own special, superior island.

Leeda hung the photo between her knees, defeated.

Finally she asked, "Why do you keep loving me, Birdie?"

Birdie looked at her like she was really thinking about it. "I love you because you're Leeda. I just . . . I don't know, I guess it's too late to not love you. So I just accept you."

Leeda tried to harness what she wanted to say. It was hard to put it into words. "I can't even imagine what kind of person you see when you look at me. I mean, I can't think of who it is you think you're accepting."

Birdie put her hand on Leeda's and crushed her fingers in her brave Birdie way. "Just you, Leeda. I just love you whoever you are."

Forty-eight

When Leeda got back to the dorm, she flopped onto her bed, unable to move another inch. Her clock stared the time at her accusingly, but she lay still, gazing at the ceiling. She kept thinking she should get up and get moving if she was going to make the ceremony, but she couldn't even move her fingers.

Then she realized what she really needed to do. It was the perfect moment for it. She sat up and opened the window wide. And then she rolled over toward her purse, grabbed the pack of cigarettes she'd bought so long ago and hadn't opened yet. She unwrapped the cellophane and pulled one out, lighting it from a pack of matches on the dresser she used to light candles. Lying there, she took a puff and winced. It was disgusting. She didn't hear the flapping until she'd taken her second puff.

And then a black bulge came hurtling through the window, squeaking loudly, its wings brushing her face.

Leeda was up and screaming, tumbling onto the floor and running into the hall, beating at her face, at her clothes, sure it was still on her. She burst out onto the grass still screaming and flapping madly at her hair. Finally she came to a stop and spun around. No sign of the bat. She inspected herself again and again. And finally breathed a sigh of relief.

She walked out farther into the grass, stood with her hands on her hips, and took a deep breath of fresh air. Now that she was standing, she realized she actually felt strong. Healthy. As if the last vestiges of pneumonia had died off while she sat on the bed. She decided to take a walk.

She wouldn't have remembered the cigarette at all if she hadn't seen the plume of smoke rising above the trees about ten minutes later. Leeda came to a standstill then. She rocked back and forth on her feet, once, twice, looked around as if, if it really was what it might be, she could figure out a way to pretend it hadn't been her. But she got over that quickly. She launched into a run, yelling toward the house.

After the fire department had been called, all Walter, Poopie, Birdie, and Leeda could do was watch the building burn.

Because it was breezy, the fire had spread, almost gently, like it had just reached out and embraced the men's dorm in a thoughtful hug. The two now stood next to each other very much ablaze. Nobody said anything for a long while.

"Well," Walter said. "They had to come down sooner or later." He put his hands in his pockets.

The four of them looked at each other. Leeda wondered if they were all thinking what she was: that it was the end of an era. Or at least, the era as they knew it. And Walter didn't seem all that concerned.

"Leeda, you want a ride to your graduation?" Poopie asked.

Leeda looked back at the fires. "Yeah."

•   •   •

As Becca Wise, the mayor's daughter, cracked her way along the peaks and valleys of the national anthem, Leeda looked over her shoulder at where her family—Danay, her dad, her mom, Birdie, Uncle Walter, Aunt Cynthia, and Poopie—sat. Birdie sat not far behind them, looking proud. Leeda looked back at Murphy's empty seat, thinking she had been right. Graduations were worth missing.

After Becca, there were the speeches, then names were called. As each graduate rose to accept his or her diploma, there were loud cheers and wolf whistles from families in the back.

Leeda fidgeted until she heard her name, followed by a low round of clapping and cheers, but there were no wolf whistles. Her wolf whistler was missing. Murphy would have made a fool out of herself to yell for her.

When everyone threw their caps in the air, Leeda tucked hers into her robe and walked out onto the lawn. In the gaggle of hugging students that poured onto the grass, she was grabbed and squeezed and congratulated. She smiled and laughed, but she quickly made her way back behind a pillar of the tent.

As Leeda watched from her secret spot, her family materialized in the crowd—her dad carrying the camera and shaking hands with one of the teachers, Danay and Brighton hand in hand, Birdie and Poopie whispering about something. And her mom. Her mom stood apart, watching. Playing her role. Careful not to give anything away. Just like her.

When they all left for the graduation dinner at Liddie's a few minutes later, Leeda detoured by the orchard. She dug around the side of Orchard Road, searching the dried leaves and debris. All that was left of the Barbie was a head without a body. She stuck it in her pocket, thinking what Murphy would have thought—that if anyone saw her walking around with dismembered doll heads, she'd look like a psychopath.

When she arrived, Lucretia was sitting at a white-draped table with a group of women from the Magnolia Garden Guild. Leeda walked up beside her and put the Barbie facedown on the table.

Lucretia squinted at it, then looked at Leeda, bewildered.

"I don't think this was ever mine." Leeda crouched down by her mom's chair, feeling her nerves along her skin, like she was fully there in every part of her body. She felt solid and Leeda-shaped, whatever that shape might turn out to be. And she felt a little bit Lucretia-shaped too, for better or worse. She was both.

Leeda wrapped her fingers around her mom's wrist with a kind of intimacy they didn't use with each other. She could feel Lucretia's pulse through her skin. The skin felt as fragile and soft as a butterfly's wing. She made a promise to herself to do this more. To be more fearless. To stop loving her mom by her mom's rules and to stop expecting her mom to love her by Leeda's own. Lucretia stared down at her hand, her lips tight, her jaw straight and stiff.

"Mom, I . . . need . . . something." Leeda lingered on the word *need*. She didn't want to use it lightly. There were things she had thought she needed that maybe she didn't, and there were things she needed much more than she had thought.

Maybe it wasn't too late for her to dig them both out of the muck.

On the afternoon of May 16, Poopie Pedraza was standing on the front porch of the Darlington farmhouse when a swarm of bats surrounded her. They circled her head like a halo for a few moments, her arms outstretched to swat them away, and then they swarmed down the gravel drive and off toward the barn. There they disappeared down a hole, its entrance no longer littered with junk, and into the caves that ran beneath the Darlington Orchard. Some things were better when you just let them run their course naturally.

Forty-nine

Murphy got lost three times on the trip from the Port Authority to campus. After thirty hours on the bus, though, the delay seemed like a drop in the bucket. In Bridgewater, she had always felt like she moved so fast compared to everyone else, but it took five minutes on the streets of New York for her to feel thoroughly, achingly slow. In New York, apparently, Murphy was inept, clumsy, lopsided. She took wrong turns. She stared with big bumpkin eyes. Murphy had always sneered at people who had big bumpkin eyes. The only thing she'd recognized so far was the Empire State Building, far in the distance.

It took her an hour and a half to find the campus and another half hour to find the student life building. She walked to the desk expecting some kind of welcome, but all she got was brusque directions to Hayden Hall, room 412. The number seemed ambitious. She felt more like a one or a two. Maybe a negative two. Without a bunch of people around who knew more about her than she wanted them to, she could feel her idea of herself shaking apart, and she'd only just arrived. What would a week do?

At her building, she squeezed in the door behind the person in front of her and made her way to the elevator, feeling as wobbly and lopsided as ever. She rode it to the fourth floor, stepped into the hall, and peered around. The hall was lit by long fluorescent lights, not sterile, but clean and bare.

A couple of girls were standing by one of the doors, talking. "Hey," she said. She tried to paste a look of indifference on her face as she wobbled past them. She disliked them immediately.

They *hey*'d her back and she kept going. She was surprised to find how close she was to turning around and heading back to Port Authority. She actually slowed, hovered, and looked over her shoulder.

When she turned back around, she saw a pair of legs poking out from one of the doorways at the end of the hall. Murphy decided to dislike whoever owned them. They were long, perfect, expensive legs—the least likable kind. And her heart sank as it became clear—by counting the door numbers ahead of her—that they were sticking out of her dorm room. Finally she had wobbled along far enough to see who they belonged to. When she did, she came to an abrupt halt.

"You left me all these IOUs," Leeda said, holding out a fistful of paper scraps. "I need to cash in on them." She smiled. "See, I don't have a thing to wear," she said in an exaggerated Southern drawl.

Murphy tried to pull herself together again. She blinked at Leeda, then leaned against the dorm room door opposite hers like someone had pushed her into it. She let go of her suitcase and it wobbled between them.

Leeda stood, leaning back too. There was a bit of Lucretia in her; Murphy could see it. "Mom bought me the ticket. I think it cost, like, eight hundred dollars with two hours' notice."

"She owes you," Murphy said.

"Yeah."

Leeda peered about and Murphy followed her eyes down the hall. It was like they didn't know each other even though they did. And then Leeda leaned forward and just sank into her, squeezing her tight, and all that disappeared. "I just needed you, Murphy."

Suddenly she was all Leeda. The fear in the air evaporated— Murphy's and Leeda's. It flew up to the clouds. Something about the two of them holding on to each other sent it drifting south.

And Murphy, who'd wobbled her way all the way from Bridgewater, caught her balance again.

Fifty

Walter left Birdie in charge the day the workers were supposed to arrive. It was a big measure of trust. It was also the first vacation Birdie could ever remember her dad taking without her. He and Poopie were driving to a bed-and-breakfast in Savannah. Birdie tried not to think about how weird it all was.

Without anyone but Birdie there, the orchard seemed bigger than usual. Birdie caught up on the last of the preparations for the workers. Several times that day, like every day, she wondered what Leeda and Murphy were doing at that moment. She walked the perimeter, watching her footsteps. She wanted to think about anything but the bus. In the back of her mind was the idea that despite everything, Enrico would be on it. Or rather, at the topmost part of her mind there was the back-most possibility that he might show up in a few short hours and set everything right again.

She wound up and down the rows of peach trees. The peaches dangled from the branches in clusters, like cells, ready to be picked. Birdie felt around a few, her fingers squeezing gently on the flesh, testing, pulling lightly until she found the right one and pulled it off. She bit into it deeply and immediately knew she'd been too hasty. It was sweet, but it wasn't perfect. She ate the rest anyway, relishing the fuzz on her tongue and the way it felt when her teeth met the pit, and because it was a superstition of hers with first fruits, she made a wish.

She couldn't believe how slow the time went. When she checked the clock in the kitchen, there was still an hour to go. An hour might make her fall over and die. She decided to trek to Murphy's garden.

Already in the three weeks since Murphy had left, lots of weeds had crept back in. Birdie wasn't sure she'd find the time to dig them all out again. But she could stave them off for a while. She knelt and began grasping and yanking. She worked there for a long time until the sound she'd been waiting for yanked her out of her thoughts. She wove through the garden, across the lawn, and situated herself in front of the porch.

They trailed off one by one, waving and moving toward her. Emma, Raeka, Fonda, Alita, Isabel . . . She hugged them and watched over their shoulders, so intently that when he climbed off the bus, she thought she was going crazy and seeing things. He had a look of concentration on his face, and then he looked straight at her. Or more like through her. He didn't smile. He just tucked his hands in his pockets and stared around as the others pulled their bags out of the luggage hatch.

Birdie swallowed. She didn't move as she watched him make his way to the hastily built new dorms, which were clean and white as marshmallow cream. She couldn't react. It was like she had dropped deep down inside herself, like a rock dropping into a well. The ripples went on somewhere below the surface. She answered the others' friendly questions, watching him from the corner of her eye, already picturing turning around, walking into the house, closing off her heart, covering the well. It would be easier.

Finally the rest of the workers migrated off toward the dorms with their bags. Birdie turned and moved up the porch. She walked through the front door and down the hall, then right out the back door. She circled the house, staring at the dorms. Then she walked onto the stairs again, and again into the hall. Majestic looked at her like she'd lost her mind.

She crouched down and rubbed Majestic's ears intently. She thought of Honey Babe. Standing still had never kept things from changing. She walked back out the front door and, her ears already going red from embarrassment, set a path for the dorms.

The men were standing in the hallway talking when Birdie walked in. They all looked at her, curious. She didn't say anything and moved through them, walking down the hall, peering in all the open doorways.

He was facing the window. He must have sensed her standing there in the hall because he turned around. "Hi, Birdie," he said, resigned, as if he hadn't wanted her to come. Again he didn't look at her as much as past her. She felt her hope flag.

Birdie shoved her hands in her pockets. She was wearing the same overalls from days ago. She could feel the round white pebble she'd picked up from the road. She squeezed it hard, like she was trying to crush it.

"I just wanted to see if . . . we were okay," she said, feeling relief. "Just to make sure we can be friends. I don't want it to be weird, you know?" *Friends?* Different bits of Birdie died as she said it. It was like stars exploding and burning out one by one. She wondered if this was part of getting older. Parts of your heart exploded and died.

"We are friends." Enrico looked her very straight in the eye. It was how much he seemed to mean it that made her die most of all.

"Good."

"Good," he said.

They stood in silence. Birdie swallowed so loudly she was sure he could hear it. She squeezed the pebble. She could feel the moment tumbling out of her fingers. She had to say something more. She just didn't know what.

"I . . ." she started, and stopped. She held out her hand, her palm flat, to show the pebble. She stared at it because she didn't want to look at him. "I picked up this pebble the other day. And I didn't really know why I did it. . . ." She cleared her throat, glancing around the room. "But I think it's because Murphy puts rocks on the bus."

Put. Past tense, she reminded herself. Murphy had gone. Birdie was getting flustered. She didn't know how to make it make sense to someone else. Birdie sighed. "You know, rocks are really old. It's probably been here for a million years. I mean, what are the chances it would ever end up anywhere else?" she said finally, as if that said everything.

She thrust the pebble into his hand and held his fist closed. "I don't want to be friends."

Enrico didn't pull his hand away, so Birdie reached her arms around his neck gingerly. She pressed her head against his shoulder and held him, tighter and tighter. She leaned her head against his ear. She moved the bridge of her nose up the side of his cheek. He kept his face very still.

She touched the top of her cheekbone to the top of his. She put her fingers on the bones of his shoulder, deliberately, like they were buttons she wanted to press. Like she wanted to know how to operate him. She felt the terror of not knowing if he wanted her there. Birdie was dangling in space.

And then he moved just slightly, and she felt his breath on her cheek, and then his lips, softly, right near her ear. One tiny kiss. And then he sank into her.

Of course, Birdie thought. Of course he did.

Over his shoulder, she looked out at the peach trees beyond the glass. The branches reached for one another across the rows.

At times on the orchard, the leaves fluttered like locusts. At times they turned upside down and showed their white undersides in an almost embarrassing way. At times they turned orange and brown. And at times they came spinning off the trees like whirligigs. Now they were perfectly, sublimely still, like an audience.

Birdie moved her lips to Enrico's and sighed into them, touching her forehead to his.

From the trees, they looked like full-grown lovers.

Epilogue

There were traces left behind.

At the Darlington Orchard, a garden began its slow decline back into wilderness. Weeds sidled up to the flowers, cautiously at first. The kudzu began, slowly but not that slowly, to climb the trellis, intending to cover it completely.

In the Darlington house, a little crayon Poopie drawing hid behind the pasta jar in the pantry, looking for all the world like the Virgin Mary. A silver gum wrapper dropped on the porch sat balled up and wedged indefinitely in a corner of the doorjamb. A red notebook covered in exuberant handwriting and messy black stars sat at the bottom of a trash bin. It would stay there for twenty-three years.

In the pecan grove, Methuselah's offspring grew taller. At the Balmeade Country Club next door, a peach tree began to grow on the ninth green. In the house next to the Pearly Gates Cemetery, Rex Taggart went to bed with a hole in his heart. Over the years, it wouldn't heal, or shrink, or weaken. That night, it would only begin a slow journey to a place where it could hide.

In a dorm room in New York City, Murphy and Leeda lay on Murphy's bed, studying. The room screamed Murphy. She'd flung CDs and notebooks on every surface that was hers. Her dirty clothes hung from the corners. And a postcard sat stuck in the frame of the mirror above her desk. Occasionally Murphy or Leeda looked up at it, like it needed to be included. On the front was a photo of the campus of the National Autonomous University of Mexico. On the back were the words: *School here is amazing. Mexico is amazing. You are amazing.* It was the only postcard they ever got from Birdie. She preferred to send letters.

For a while, Poopie Pedraza swore she could see the ghost of a little girl walking around the orchard property, age seven or eight, with an auburn ponytail and chicken legs. It was the way Poopie would always see Birdie even though she saw the grown Birdie too.

And as fall turned to winter, the Darlington peach trees started dropping their leaves again, gently, like they were letting them go. It wasn't the same as giving them up.

It wasn't the same as losing them.

Acknowledgments

I would like to thank Sara Shandler for her dedication, insight, and all-around loveliness. I would also like to gratefully acknowledge Kristin Marang, Elise Howard, Josh Bank, and Les Morgenstein, as well as my wonderful agent, Sarah Burnes. I wish to thank my friends Lexy James, Erika Loftmann, Jennifer Bailey, Liesa Abrams, Nancy Giarraputo, and Bud Paytas for their kindness and generosity. Finally, I would like to thank my family, who make me feel constantly blessed.